Mr. Right-Swipe

Mr. Right-Swipe

RICKI SCHULTZ

GC

GRAND CENTRAL
PUBLISHING

NEW YORK   BOSTON

Copyright © 2017 by Ricki Schultz
Cover design by Connie Gabbert
Cover copyright © 2017 by Hachette Book Group, Inc.

Grand Central Publishing
Hachette Book Group
1290 Avenue of the Americas, New York, NY 10104
grandcentralpublishing.com
twitter.com/grandcentralpub

First Trade Paperback Edition: June 2017

Grand Central Publishing is a division of Hachette Book Group, Inc. The Grand Central Publishing name and logo is a trademark of Hachette Book Group, Inc.

The publisher is not responsible for websites (or their content) that are not owned by the publisher.

The Hachette Speakers Bureau provides a wide range of authors for speaking events. To find out more, go to www.hachettespeakersbureau.com or call (866) 376-6591.

Library of Congress Control Number: 2017934403

ISBNs: 978-1-4555-9722-2 (trade paperback), 978-1-4555-9721-5 (e-book), 978-1-4789-1562-1 (audiobook, downloadable)

Printed in the United States of America

LSC-C

10 9 8 7 6 5 4 3 2 1

To Mom and Dad,
(Sorry about all the penis jokes.)

Mr. Right-Swipe

CHAPTER 1

I shoot back the tequila, and it's smooth. No cheap stuff this time. Patrón. No retching, no face to make. Just pure, unadulterated DGAF juice to parasail me off to my happy place before this idiot gets here.

If he even shows up.

Track lights hang in funky zigzags, amber pendants misting down a warm glow on all the sad stories strewn across the barstools: The lady in the leopard-print miniskirt, who crosses and uncrosses her legs with such fervor while she flirts with the Jack Palance–looking hombre across the way that she's either DTF or she's already got some kind of lady infection. The couple nestled in the corner, who won't shut up about how it's "date night" and they can't believe they trusted Dude's kid sister to babysit. The squirrely fifty-something whose khakis look like they haven't lost their pleat in the better part of a decade, who's been spinning his wedding ring out in front of him like it's a frickin' dreidel.

And then there's me.

"Another?" the bartender asks before I've even wiped my lips, my sinuses suddenly clear.

"I shouldn't." I touch my fingers to my sternum—*My, what a lady*—and I'm the epitome of demure as I dab my mouth with a cocktail napkin. "This gloss cost more than the damn drink," I tell him.

"So yes, then?" His mouth quirks at the corners, and either the shot has just hit me or his pheromones have. My legs ignite from the ground up, and part of me wonders what that mouth would feel like on my neck. My chest.

My phone buzzes, and I jump.

Valerie: GOOD LUCK!!!!!

Again.

Quinn: Is he there yet???

It's our group text. And, by their timing, I know they're together, sucking down a bottle of red in Valerie's living room and watching *The Real Housewives of Atlanta* or some shit.

"You know what?" I slap both palms on the bar. Decisive. "Why not? I'm a goddamn adult," I say to the bartender, which widens that succulent grin.

I take to my phone as he goes for the bottle.

Me: You two are ridonk. This is just drinks. Relax.
And stop using so much punctuation!!!!!!!!!!!!!!!!!!!!!!!!!!!!!!

I smile at my textual punishment, and my gaze drifts to the

curve of the bartender's back. The way his black button-down stretches across those shoulders.

He slides the shot glass toward me like we're in a salary negotiation and meets my gaze with the darkest of eyes. "Your date is a very lucky man."

That accent of his. Portuguese? It might even be put on, but I don't care.

I give a snort. "Oh yeah. I'm sure he'll feel like he's won the Powerball."

I down my next, and I feel it in an instant. A tingle in my toes like a sticky summer night with Jesse. The two of us tucked away in that hole-in-the-wall hookah café.

A hand grazes the small of my back, and I leap from the stool. "Rachel Wallace?"

I give the barkeep a look like he's my gay best friend— *Girrrrl!*—and spin back toward him. Readjust.

"The one and only," I say and stick out my hand. "And it's Rae."

I take him all in. A moment's assessment as he performs his as well, eyes roving over me with what looks like relief.

Polo shirt, fine.

Dark jeans that aren't tighter than mine, check.

High-tops. *What the balls?*

And a faux hawk.

He's a dude.

But at least he's shaven and he doesn't seem to exude anything worse than the hair and shoes.

Workable.

"Rae. I like that. I'm Ty, by the way."

He sets his blue eyes on me, and I stifle a laugh. That's just— not the name of a real person.

"Of course you are."

"I'm sorry?"

"No need to be yet." I spin back around and indicate the stool next to me. He emanates Armani Code and I'm okay with that, so we shall proceed.

He gives the bartender a look like he's about to be swallowed whole into the abyss, and then I feel a pang of something beneath my clavicle that I decide to rub away. I can't wait to tell the girls I have feelings.

Progress!

The bartender comes back with two more shots.

"Be still, my beating heart," I say, hand to chest once again. And I check for a ring on his third finger. None.

Focus.

On Ty, not the bartender.

"Nice to meet you, Ty. Please excuse my—"

"You're absolutely terrifying."

He says it with a wink, though, so I'm not sure how to take it.

I melt into a smile and offer a quick nod. "Terrifying. I like it." *Probably a little too much.*

This crack seems to put him more at ease. He exhales for the first time, and my hand is already on my glass.

"Shall we?"

He reaches for his. "Definitely. To us?"

"To us."

Clink.

*   *   *

While the others at the bar have shifted or filtered out—Ants-in-Her-Pants left with her rugged ol' cowboy and the pleated pity party probably went home to shoot himself—Ty and I have tackled all the important questions. Like which of Valerie and Mike's kids is the smartest or how many pairs of cargo shorts we think Mike actually has. (I Price-Is-Righted it: sixty-one to Ty's sixty.)

Once we hit that lull where there's only so much more you can analyze about your mutual friends, the beautiful buzz I've got going is the only thing keeping me here—a warm flush that curls up in my cheeks like a lazy old dog in an afghan on a rainy afternoon.

Alex, the bartender—we're on a first-name basis now—is feeding me stuffed green olives like he's my cabana boy and I'm the queen of Sheba. I don't even know if that makes sense, but I don't care. My palm digs into my cheek, and I'm listening to Ty tell some oppressive story about how he and Mike went golfing last week…and that's when Valerie got the idea to set us up…and he somehow comes off as the richest, most successful friend Mike has (read: small penis).

He seems to get the hint, though—after, like, six hours of story—and he tosses some nuts into his mouth.

Ha-ha. Ha-ha-ha-ha. Okay. I should really stop drinking. I've regressed to fifth-grade boy humor.

"So Valerie tells me you write books?"

Ugh.

My face gets even warmer. And I hope my chest isn't all splotchy.

I stick out my tongue in a fake gag—I'm sure it's super attractive. "Thanks, Val," I say to my phone screen. "I mean, kind of? I don't know." I take a life-affirming swig from my dirty martini and allow a breathy *ahh* of an exhale before I continue.

He furrows his eyebrows—probably too sculpted for my taste—and I realize he doesn't know what I mean.

"I mean, I dabble."

I squirm in my seat, and he cracks a smile.

"Dabble?" He seesaws his head like he's trying to make it dirty, but really I think it's that he doesn't know the word. "I like to dabble as well." He loops an arrogant finger under my spaghetti strap, and—*clap*—my hand shoots over it.

"I'm not published or anything," I say, guiding his hand back into his personal space, where it belongs. "I'm working on a manuscript. But I don't have an agent or anything."

He gives me a squinchy face again, and I try not to judge him.

Regular people don't know what the hell you're talking about, I tell myself. *Why would he know about the industry?*

I shove another olive in and talk with my mouth full. Fuck it. "Well, you need one if you want to publish traditionally. As in, have your book in a bookstore, etcetera."

I see the familiar glaze in his stare. The one regular people get when I start talking publishing. That's what was so great about Jesse. The one thing. He got it. And he listened.

Probably because his wife didn't get it.

Something clamps around my heart—or am I choking on a stupid olive? I can't breathe all of a sudden. Why did Valerie do this to me?

I bang on my sternum to loosen whatever is causing the tightness, and Ty's gaze drops to my chest. Halle-frickin-lujah—he's back.

Guess my tits woke him up.

"What do you write, then?"

God. Dammit.

"Erotica?" I say, still rubbing at the sore spot, and I chew my bottom lip. Watching any chance I had of him not eye-fucking me the rest of the evening fly away like the olive particle I just accidentally launched across the bar.

He scoots in. "Really? But I thought you were a teacher."

I'm definitely red now. I give an awkward shrug. "I am . . . but I work under a pen name—and, no, I'm not going to tell you. Anyway, the market for erotica is really more e-book based, but I'm trying to break in traditionally. It's stupid, I know." I wave it off, even though I most definitely do not find it stupid; I just find it easier to shrug it away on a first date.

In fact, I like to avoid the subject of writing entirely because, inevitably:

"You know, my aunt is writing a book. A memoir about our family. You should read it sometime."

I stare at the stirrer in my drink and my eyes bug to the size of the last two olives Alex has left. "Um, yeah. That'd be—"

He scoots way in, his breath hot in my ear. It sends tickles all down my side.

"I'm hot for teacher. You know that?" He gives me an elbow like he's the Alexander Graham Bell of that joke, and I just nod.

But I'm glad he interrupted because there's no way on God's green earth I'm looking at someone's shitty-ass memoir or listening to him blather on about how he's always wanted to write a comic book series about some polo player who turns into a flying Clydesdale or whatever.

"Good one." I point at him, then swipe at the goose bumps.

He licks the salt from his lips. "You know, I have to say . . ."

Alex has some smooth jazz sashaying on the air, and this crowd of what seems to be regulars loves it. The table of leather-faced singles swinging near the back has gotten up and they've all begun a clumsy, slow sway—all stuck together like snails mating. It's making me uncomfortable, of course, but I can't quite bring myself to look away.

"You have to say what?" I'm entranced by their movements. And amused that I'm the youngest one here. By eons. This might be my new place!

"This may sound like it's out of nowhere..."

His voice is low, and I meet his gaze now.

Maybe Ty and I will be here, grossing out thirty-somethings, in forty years. Maybe he'd consider non-faux-hawking it and maybe he's not married to that chain wallet.

I fake a real smile—let it crinkle the corners of my eyes and everything—and chew the end of the stirrer.

"Well, I'm an out-of-nowhere kind of girl." I lift a brow. #killingit

"The way you talk doesn't match your look."

I frown. Hmm?

He fidgets a sec, sloshes the bourbon around in his glass, and then turns back to me, full-on. "I mean—you're smart. Girls who look like you don't tend to be smart."

And as quickly as the alcohol and sultry music—and the promise of a lifetime of gross dancing—bamboozled me, his comment snaps me out of it.

I press an *Oh-hellllll-naw* hand out in front of me.

He grasps at it like it's the string on the end of a balloon that's floating away. "No," he says. "It's a compliment." He pulls my fingertips to his chest, his heartbeat increasing.

"Which part?" I squint, and this poor douche isn't even ready for the inner she-beast clawing its way out of my body. "The part where I look stupid, but—yay!" I applaud. "I'm actually not a total dumbass!"

He flinches and glances around the place.

"Or the part where I rubbed some sparkly lotion on my legs and sucked myself into a low-cut dress, so that means I look attractive to you, I guess? And therefore—"

People are looking.

"Therefore"—my tone takes on a touch of the Foghorn Leghorn—"if I'm hot that means I'm dumb?" I cross my legs the opposite way and rest my elbows on the bar. Chin in palms. Expectant. Twirl a strand of brown hair. "Do you think you could explain it to me, because I got a wax this morning and so I don't understand your big words so good."

I think he's gonna cry. He clears his throat a couple of times, and the rest of the place picks up with its background hum of conversation. Retirees, body to geriatric body once again.

"I just haven't met many girls who"—he's talking to his nut bowl now; cashews curl up at him like little shrugs who can't get him out of this one—"are as good-looking as you are, that I can have a conversation with. When I walked in here and saw you, no. I didn't think you'd be very smart. Is that bad?" He kinda…winces.

I snort. "I don't know, pal," I say, and I grab a handful of nuts from right out in front of him. Gnash on them. "I'm sorry if that was bitchy. But—"

"No, I like it," he lies. I can tell he's really trying to keep his tone bright. "You speak your mind. That's good."

That's funny; his stare is about ten inches south of my mind.

I hitch a thumb at Ty and talk to Alex. "He's a real progressive, this one."

We sit in silence for what feels like twenty songs. But they're all so smooth and flowy, like the ladies' long dresses, it's really hard to tell when one ends and the next begins. Saxophones all sexing up the place and keeping Viagra in business as the number-one import in Plantation this side of Boca Raton.

After a while, Ty scoots his stool a bit closer. Lowers his voice a tick. "Look, Valerie told me. I get it."

"Told you what?" I narrow my gaze.

"That you're tired of dating. So I get that you might be a little sensitive—"

"This is not my first rodeo, no," I say, and I drain my glass.

As the vodka hits the back of my throat, there's also a rawness I'd rather not feel.

I see my ex Daniel when he proposed. All shiny. Besuited. Eyes so full of babies and minivans and trips to Connecticut to see his folks. All the things we had talked about and dreamed about. All the things I have always wanted and still want—just, as it turned out, not with him.

I can't stay here another second, free drinks (and olives) or not.

"Excuse me one minute." I hop off the barstool and smooth my silk dress. "Little girls' room," I explain.

"Another?" Ty indicates toward my drink, and I toss him a quick thumbs-up before I go off to the bathroom. (Okay, fine.)

I stumble into the stall and whip out my phone.

Who to get me out of this?

After a hazy moment, I decide it can't be Quinn or Valerie; they'd look down their noses at my request. Hell, Val might even cry, being the matchmaker for the evening.

No, this calls for the big guns. Well, the twenty-something guns, anyway.

This job has Sarah written all over it.

Me: Can you call me in ten with an "emergency"?

Sarah: That bad, huh?

Me: I gotta get out of here.

Sarah: We just got to Posh. Come have some fun!

Me: Will do—you just have to "get mugged" or something.

Sarah: I'm your girl. :)

*   *   *

After her call, I guzzle the drink that was waiting for me when I returned from the bathroom—maybe he's not all bad—and Ty walks me to my Uber.

Once we get outside, the humidity sits on my skin and the gentle breeze does little to cool me. A stipple of sweat beads at the base of my neck, my hairline.

"Sorry I had to cut it short. Rain check?" I lie.

He gives me a quirk of a smile, and just as I realize it but before I can elude it, he launches at me. Full-on. Out of flipping nowhere, his too-big lips sucking the fifty-dollar gloss off mine. All dick and tongue pressing into me—squishing me against the Honda Civic and then sliding his hand up the front of my dress and cupping my now-straight-up-sweaty breast.

Wha?

He's one of those dudes who licks your lips for some reason. Is that supposed to be sexy?

And then this facial assault ends as quickly as it started. *Mental note, Rae: The sex probably would too.*

"I had a nice time tonight," he says, hands still on me.

"Ah—yeah." I pull away and push him back up on the curb.

"I can't wait to thank Valerie." I smooth my dress once again and give him the double thumbs-up.

And then I slide into the car and slam the door shut.

*　　　*　　　*

Sarah's all screeches and hugs when I duck inside Posh twenty minutes later. She hands me something cold in a highball glass, like she's Alfred to my Batman, and gives my shoulders a little rub.

"You poor thing," she says with a hint of a pout to her full red lip.

"I owe you." I nod and take in all the non-thirty-year-olds writhing around to the beat.

I'm the *oldest* one in *this* joint by eons, and I don't even care. The AC is cranked, and it's blowing my dress all kinds of every-where, but I pretend I'm in a Beyoncé video. Totally likely that's exactly how I look too.

Just when I find my rhythm, arms flailing to the music like I'm drowning in the high seas, the tallest bro in the joint makes his way over.

A smirk from Sarah, the bangles on her wrists glinting off the purple neons as she moves. She shimmies a few feet farther away and offers me an exaggerated wink, like *You're welcome for the privacy.*

I chuckle and shake my head at her in return.

I let the guy press me anywhere he wants because it's magic when we're dancing. The smoke billows at our feet. It smells like Abercrombie and sex on the dance floor. The alcohol is strong enough and the lights are low enough that everyone is the best-looking person I've ever seen.

I'm not thirty-four and he's (probably?) legal.

"I'm Harrison," he purrs deep in my ear, and I press a finger to his gorgeous mouth. Two pillows of perfection.

"Let's not ruin this with talking," I shout over the thrum of the music.

And he lets out a laugh. Twirls me. I'm dizzy with desire. Dizzy with Harrison.

I close my eyes and feel his solid body move behind me, sliding down and slithering back up.

Smile.

Just another Sunday night.

*   *   *

Billie is beside herself with wiggles when I finally roll in. I don't want to, but I know she needs to walk, so I pull on some basketball shorts and a tee and I stumble around my apartment complex like the wonderful dog mother I am.

The moon is big and bright and it spills in pools onto the blacktop. I almost have to shield my eyes—but that's probably more my liquid dinner than real brightness from the moon.

I rub my arms as we walk. The late-night breeze finally adds a hint of cool to the September air.

I wish Jesse and I had gotten to dance.

We never did.

Not that we were together all that much, and not that he, yanno, followed through with his divorce, but it still would have been nice to have the memory of dancing with him.

This stupid thought starts the insta-tears, and I feel like the most subhuman creature on the face of the planet.

What's worse than the walk of shame? Snotting all over your

apartment complex at three a.m. with a beagle who won't shit—that's what.

"Shit, Billie. Shit!" I stage-whisper and wipe my face on my arms—and immediately start cackling like a crazy person at how ridiculous the scene has to be.

At least my mom isn't alive to see this. And Dad's too distracted by his new plastic surgery princess to come back to Florida.

That makes me laugh even more.

"Who wouldn't want to get with this?" I think. Or maybe I say it aloud? I don't really know.

All I know is Billie finally does her thing and I'm carrying a plastic bag of dog poop and my teeth are chattering and I'm glad Jesse's fat now, but I still wish we'd have gotten to dance.

After I dump the dump, I'm back to just staggering around the rest of the loop and then we finally reach home.

I dig my phone out of my purse. Glad I remembered to bring it home this time, I tap an index finger to my temple and nod at my brilliance.

Two missed calls—one from Valerie, one from Quinn—and one text.

The Tongue: Tonight was fun. Next time, we'll have to do dinner.

I snort, and Billie looks up at me.

"I wish I could just lick myself like you, girl. You're my hero," I say. And I snuggle her tight.

*   *   *

CHAPTER 2

I squeal into my primo spot—the one by the Dumpster. More accurately, the first spot I can access when I get stuck in the carpool line, like I do almost every morning.

The throb of this headache slowed me down some getting ready, but I rallied. Nothing a handful of Tylenol can't quell.

I climb out of my Camry and straighten my blazer. The air is as thick as the Spanish teacher's accent. I heave my bags from the backseat over my shoulder—what in baby Jesus' name do I have in my purse?—and only *maybe* flash Dr. Something or Other in the Cadillac SUV as I do so.

I wave at him—*You're welcome*—and *click, click, click* my way through the Benzes. The BMWs. The Land Rovers and the Porsches. Maybe I'm just imagining it, but I swear I feel parent stares scorch me like the morning sun behind their D&G sunglasses. Through tinted windows, so I can't quite make out which students are theirs.

"Morning, Rae!" The lady with the mullet beams.

What's her name? Quinn and I have called her Mullet Lady

for so long I don't remember her real name, but it will come to me. I know she does something with the arts program and she has a propensity for white polyester pants. Labor Day rule be damned!

She's helping direct traffic, opening car doors for the kids like we're not only their teachers but their valets as well—and I'm pretty sure she's just here to make my walk to the building extra annoying.

I answer with a sarcastic wave, because—balls—no one should be allowed to speak before nine a.m. (eleven a.m.?)

Regardless, I'm pretty sure she's only saying it so sweetly because she knows I'm late. I catch the cursory glance at her rhinestone-encrusted watch.

But then I feel bad.

Like, maybe she is just being nice and I'm The Actual Worst.

Or maybe she doesn't know or care about my tardiness because she has a life and my insecurity is working overtime this morning.

I suck it up and play the game. "Haven't had my coffee yet!"

"Oh, you don't need it! You're always a Rae of sunshine!" She lights the whole parking lot with her veneers and I fight the urge to gag.

"Did you have a nice weekend, Carol?" *Carol!* #nailedit

"Oh yes," she trills. "Not long enough!"

My stomach curls as I realize I've stopped and now I'm helping some little ginger out of her daddy's Lexus.

"Watch your step," I say.

My God. What's happening?

I wiggle some fingers at the dad through the open back window and pat the adorable little tootie on the head. I've always had a soft spot for redheads.

I have to Adult for a few more minutes—just until I can get away from Carol and to the sanctuary of my classroom to do my thing with the kids and be left alone.

Away from the judging eyes of others. (Whether they're really doing it or I'm just perceiving it that way because I'm insane.)

That's one of the great things about working with kids. They laugh at my dumb jokes and appreciate my goofy antics in earnest. I don't have to pretend to be what someone else thinks I should be, nor do I have to work to impress them; they're already happy and loving and impressed.

"Ugh—Monday. Am I right?" I toss a hand at another lululemoned mom before shutting her SUV door—and then I sprint up the stairs, leaving Carol in my wake before she recruits me to be a member of the party planning committee.

I'm just chucking my stuff into my classroom when I hear Deborah's voice echo from down the hall.

Giving her spiel at Monday Morning Meeting already. Great.

"Hey, girl!" Sarah appears in the doorway and I nearly fly out of my heels. She's got her hair in a ponytail, she's holding a venti-sized something or other, and I can tell she did what I like to call the Slovenian Shower this morning. (Half Slovenian— I'm allowed.)

"Glad to see you recovered!" She hip-checks me and snaps her fingers above her head, doing the same white-girl dance we did at that club.

I wince. "Today's gonna be a 'Miss Wallace has a migraine' kind of day. 'No lights, no talking. Just draw pictures of your favorite woodland creatures while I try not to puke in my desk drawers.'"

I wish. But I like my job.

That, and six-year-olds can keep their mouths closed about as well as blow-up dolls, so although my stomach's already gurgling, it'll be reading, writing, 'rithmetic, and...hopefully not retching for me.

"Wasn't it worth it? That guy was seriously hot."

Her golden hair and twenty-six-year-old outlook on life are too bright for me, but alas, I must take off my *Breakfast at Tiffany's* shades and face it all.

We pass the third-grade hall, the water fountain, and the entire length of the library before I can bring myself to speak again.

"I mean, not really," I say as we make our way to the conference room. "I could do without being a party trick. 'How old do you think she is?' What is with that? Stop it."

She bonks me on the shoulder. "Oh, come on. No one thinks you're actually thirty-four. You can hang, girl!"

She stresses *actually* too much for my liking, and I stifle a snarl. Or maybe that's just because the entire place smells like Expo markers and glass cleaner.

"They may not think it, but it doesn't make it *not* true. Just—I can't do this shit anymore," I say a little too loudly as we cross the threshold, and now the entire faculty's staring, mouths agape.

Please. Like they never heard the word *shit* before.

I offer an awkward laugh at our principal. "Just your run-of-the-mill *Lethal Weapon* paraphrasing to start out the week—right, Deborah?" Sarcastic arm swing. "No?" I clear my throat.

"Good morning, ladies. We're just wrapping up," Deborah

says, cutting her stare over her glasses like a disapproving father.

And, if we're keeping score, she's kinda dressed like one too.

Clusters of women, all shapes and sizes, sit like lumps of Play-Doh around child-sized tables. Marj Raynor's ass all but engulfs a miniature plastic chair, and I'm mesmerized by this sheer feat of craftsmanship that prevents the whole thing from pancaking to the industrial carpeting.

There are only two males among us—Hot Sub Guy, who started showing up last week, and Cliff Jones, Wesson Academy's own computer teacher and tech dude extraordinaire. He's slumped behind a newspaper and looking super chipper for a fifty-six-year-old who still lives with his mother.

"How are things going with the first-grade play?" Deborah points to me.

"Still looking for some volunteers to help with the set, since the parents I e-mailed backed out, but I'm not worried. I'm so on it."

Psh. Of course I'm on it. I wrote the damn thing.

I salute, which not only seems appropriate but also elicits some halfhearted chuckles from the room. Hot Sub Guy even offers a grin.

Valerie and Quinn crack smiles and shake their heads from the table by the Keurig. Even if I did forget about Thursday's rehearsal, I know the two of them didn't. They've been bailing me out of jams since high school.

When Deborah lets us go and the rest of the embittered old wives club file out, perfume clouds lingering in their memory, I clomp over to my friends like that big brown ogre Muppet and give them sorority-girl air smooches. Sarah's beat me to the Keurig and already is making a second cup, so I'm huffing at the available pods and trying to decide which roast will be the most potent and get me closest to resembling a human.

"So…how'd it go?" Quinn's voice is all singsong, her cascades of dark hair swept back in a long braid like she's Katniss fricking Everdeen.

I bang on the coffeemaker as if that'll speed Sarah along.

"Looks like she was out pretty late. I knew you'd like Ty!" Valerie's beside herself with excitement and she gives a bunch of annoying little claps like I'm a child taking her first steps.

Sarah's done, so I nudge her out of the way. Hearing The Tongue's name reminds me these two have a lot of nerve, and I round on them.

"We're not friends anymore." I rebuke them over the sound of my delicious cup a-brewing.

Valerie gives a rapid blink, her doe eyes glassy, and I lean on the counter. Pop my hip.

"Well, I—I mean, he's Mike's golfing buddy. Thirty-nine, single. Perfect. I don't understand what you—"

I swear, she's about to burst a blood vessel somewhere underneath those side bangs.

I pinch the bridge of my nose and close my eyes. "Love, just because someone's a certain age and single…does not a perfect boyfriend make."

With one scoff, her tone goes from walking on eggshells to launching missiles at me. "What was wrong with him?" She crosses her arms.

"Where do you want me to start?" I tick things off on my fingers. "He walks in there and spots me." I slip some husk into my delivery. "'I'm Ty, by the way.' *By the way?* That's how you start an interaction? And he was wearing high-tops' like a ten-year-old."

"So?" Quinn curls her perfect Kylie Jenner upper lip at me, but her bitch glare is full-on Kim K.

"He has a cat. A cat, Valerie." I shudder.

A laugh bursts out of Sarah, now over by the mini muffins. "A guy who has a pussy—well, need I say more?" She tosses me a muffin and we high-five, and my very dear, very thirty-four-year-old high school best friends just scowl at her.

"Ew—I hate that word." Quinn grimaces, her half-Dominican features so silken she almost doesn't look offended.

"Me too," Sarah concurs, "but what do you want me to call it?"

"Nothing. I want you to call it nothing. I don't want you—or anyone—to talk about that ever." Valerie can't even bring herself to open her eyes when she's answering the question. She's all hair and shakes. A walking Garnier Fructis commercial.

"And he's a terrible kisser. Just awful." I grimace back into my mug.

"You kissed him?"

I might as well have told Valerie I'd set his gross cat on fire.

"Okay, now you sound like you're in seventh grade." I chuckle. "Let me rephrase. When he attacked my face, I wanted to throw up. He licked my lips. Who does that?"

"A weirdo." Sarah gives a soulful *mmm-hmmm* that she can't quite pull off, being whiter than the Coffee-Mate she hands me.

"Yes—thank you!" I punctuate the point, a conductor's wave of a red stirrer.

"But he's what you told me you're looking for." Valerie's long fingers are outstretched like even they are at their wits' end with me and my Expectations. "He's never been married—"

"Thirty-nine and never married? There's a reason, Val. There's always a reason. And I'm okay with the divorced thing. Hi—remember that time I was married? Just as long as I can see his papers, if I so choose."

"What are you, the gestapo?" She laughs in Quinn's direction, but Q knows better than to return the merriment.

I threaten her with an eyebrow. She lets the moment pass.

"What did you do, then?" Quinn gets us back on track, her copper stare twinkling up at me. "Get all wasted and screw him?"

"Um. Hello—no." I blow air from the side of my mouth. Clap a palm to my chest. "What do you think this is, a month ago? Geez." I hitch a thumb at her like *Get a load of this* and glance at the other two. "I did what any mature woman would do. I texted Sarah, and she called with a 'lady emergency.'"

"What the hell is a 'lady emergency'?" Quinn spits fire.

I wave it off. "Whatever he needs it to be to feel good about himself. Look, I was very polite. I left him forty bucks—"

"—and then she met me out dancing and spent the rest of the night pinned against the wall by some insanely hot British dude."

"Love of my life," I deadpan. "Look, I'm sorry. But no more fix-ups. Your idea of the ideal man for me is not *my* idea of the ideal man for me."

"Your idea of the ideal man for you is Jason Segel."

I yank back. "Your point is…?"

Quinn gestures skyward and shakes her head. *"Ay dios mio."*

"It's not so crazy. We're both writers…" I talk with my hands.

"He's a movie star and he writes children's books. You don't even have an agent yet."

"*Et tu*, Q-te?" I rub at the invisible stab wound. Curl a lip. "I'm almost there with this latest manuscript. It's not so far-fetched that we'd bump into each other at a conference or something…"

They all just blink at me. Sarah's the only one with a smile in her blue eyes.

Valerie sinks her head into her hands and Quinn's one-and-a-half-carat rock winks in the overhead lights as she gives Val's back a light scratch.

"We need to talk," Val says, finally looking up and shrugging off Quinn.

"Are you guys breaking up with me?" I pour the hell out of some sugar and stir it into my coffee.

Valerie stands and she starts to pace. Her ombré waves nestle perfectly at each shoulder. "How long have we all known each other?"

I offer another eye roll. I'm not a child. "Since ninth grade."

"And, in all that time, how many guys have you dated?"

I chew a corner of my ChapSticked lips and feign counting on my hands. "Nine-hundred…seventy-four?"

"Be real," she demands.

"Too many. I know." I shrug.

Quinn interrupts my coffee-perfecting ritual and takes my hands. Leads me to the table donated to the lounge by some periodontist.

"Is this an intervention?" I snort as my ass hits the wooden chair.

"I know it's been hard since the divorce. Daniel was—" She glances away. Her voice is soft like when you're trying to calm down a crazy person. Or settle a wild beast. "Mine was hard for me too. That summer you and I spent in Europe right after was just what I needed. And what you went through afterward with Jesse…" She purses her lips and stops a minute. He's become the real Voldemort of our friendship circle; his name is not one we allow ourselves to utter often. "We know. We know you haven't recovered yet—"

A tickle at the back of my eyes.

If she makes me cry before class and my students pick up on it—like they pick up on everything because that's just their job—I'm going to rip those pearls right off that pretty little neck of hers.

"But enough. You've got to stop this," she continues. "Valerie and I just want what's best for you. We want you to be happy. Like we are."

I pull my hands away and examine my ever-chipped nail polish. "Then don't mess with a woman's morning coffee," I say with a grin, working hard to keep my voice even.

Wondering how happy they really are.

"We are the luckiest." Her tone brightens. "Are you kidding me? We stayed friends after all these years? We all got hired to teach the same grade, at the same school? We're a team. And that's why—"

"Oh no, no, no." I rise and put up both my palms.

"Oh yes, yes, *yes*." Valerie gets in my face. "Sit your ass down."

"I want you in the wedding," Quinn says. "I'm not taking no for an answer this time."

There it is.

I avert my gaze over to the pencil sharpener screwed to the wall. Kinda how I feel.

"I had a panic attack at the last wedding I went to, and

I wasn't even in it. I love you, Q, you know I love you, but—"

"Then you'll suck it up and do this for me."

There's a hopefulness in her stare that pricks at my chest, and the tickle behind my eyes starts all over again.

"And that's not all." Valerie wags her index finger like she's reprimanding one of the nose pickers in her class.

I groan. "We have first graders waiting—"

"You're going to bring someone to the wedding. Someone real. Not Jason Segel. Not some twenty-year-old from Barbie's band of friends—" She indicates Sarah with a languid hand.

"Hey!" Sarah laughs and double flips them off as she makes her way toward the door. "You're on your own, fabulous," she says to me as she exits. Blows me a kiss.

"You have five weeks to find him, and we're gonna help you."

"Like you helped with that dude from last night?"

"No. No more setups," Quinn says.

My ears perk. "I'm listening."

"You're gonna find love the twenty-first-century way."

My chest tightens, and I direct my attention upward like I'm thinking. Bite at my bottom lip. "At Whole Foods?"

"Online."

"The Spark app, to be exact." Valerie practically bursts with pride like she's Spark's mother or something.

"Oh, gross." I lean back in the chair, and it squeaks. "And I've already tried it. It was all gay dudes."

"That was Glitter, you idiot."

"You have to let us help you with the profile—"

"And you have to let us help you pick which guys you talk to."

"Oh Lord." I'm shaking my head. "If I say yes, can I drink my coffee in peace?"

"Yes," they both say, like we're back in the eleventh grade and I've agreed to let them do the makeover this time.

"All right—I'll do it," I say. "Now get the hell out of my way. I've got young minds to mold."

*   *   *

CHAPTER 3

I look out over my kids and smile. Most quietly chattering away, Ollie Oswald humming to himself for some weird reason...all happily doodling and thinking it's like a national holiday because I gave them some extra art time this morning.

Adorbs.

"Miss Wallace, look what I made you!" Dylan struts over and hands me his masterpiece.

"It's—an elephant?" I bug my eyes at what pretty much looks like a big gray phallus.

"Like the one we read about last week!" he chirps, aglow at my recognition, the poor little thing!

I want to hang it up—I really do—but I also don't want to get fired.

"Looks awesome, pal. Thank you so much!" I squeeze his arm. "Why don't you draw me a different animal from that lesson. Maybe a lion—"

"Or a giraffe?" He beams.

I can't stop a conceding grin at the picture of a yellow,

orange-spotted penis-looking thing he'll inevitably be showing me a few minutes from now, and I give his hands a pat.

"That sounds awesome, sweetie. Math time in fifteen," I say to the class as he scampers back to his desk.

The kids groan, and I giggle. Been there.

And then I grab my phone.

Me: I know "Coffee Fairy" isn't in your job description as Deborah's administrative assistant, but we've been friends for a few years, I was good to your boys when I had them in class, and I look like this today:

I take a puppy-dog face selfie and send it to the mom of the school, Ida.

My phone buzzes not three seconds later.

Ida: I may be able to send you over a little something in a few. Sit tight. ;)

Me: God. Bless. America.

Ida: Good thing I like you.

For the next ten minutes, my computer screen hypnotizes me. I'm trying to plot out the end of this magnum opus, but all the words run together except the ones I could get fired for having visible, of course. Like *ORGASM* and *NIPPLES*. Those seem to be in 60-point font and highlighted in flashing neon.

Or maybe I'm imagining it.

"Knock, knock," comes a male voice, and I start at the sight of Hot Sub Guy leaning half in the doorway, a boyish charm gleaming from his wide smile. "On second thought, maybe I should take this coffee back?" He laughs and makes like he's leaving.

"Mr. Greene!" the class cheers.

He was in for the PE teacher last week, so I guess that's why they know his name?

"For me, uh—Mr. Greene?" I gesture toward the Wesson Academy mug in his hand and clap a Southern belle palm to my chest.

Pixie dust swirls all beneath my skin. Ida has sent me Hot Sub Guy with a cup of coffee, and I love her for this. *Mental note: Buy that woman something purty. And probably Lilly Pulitzer.*

"Nick." He takes a tentative step in, striped dress shirt crisp and bright against his dark skin.

"Ida's got you on coffee duty? That's not fair." There's a lilt to my voice.

Stop it.

"Well, I'm in for Radcliffe and it's time for third-grade Spanish, so . . ."

"Ida's making sure we're getting our money's worth out of you?"

"Exactly." His dimples deepen, two inviting recesses that make him seem just boyish and nonthreatening enough to convince me he's absolutely dangerous.

"Miss Wallace?" a girl calls from across the room.

"Yes?" I say back, but I don't turn around.

I glance at his long fingers, bare and cupped around the mug. Nick isn't wearing a ring either.

"What did this girl do wrong?" she asks.

I shoot him a look like *No rest for the wicked, amirite?*—but when I twist back, sweet little pigtailed Lorelei Hunter is standing by my laptop, head cocked like a springer spaniel.

deafening record scratch

She indicates the screen with her tiny fingers. "Well, it says here she's getting spanked. My mom and dad said spanking is bad and no one should do it—and it says here that she's being bad, so I just wondered what she did to deserve that..." She looks like she's about to cry—

—and I feel like I am.

I 'roided-up-linebacker my way to my desk, but it feels like slow motion. Complete with a low, monster-sounding *NOOOOO* dragging on in the background. I shove a few tables out of the path and finally dive onto the offending device. Snap the top closed and hover over it, panting and sweaty. #myprecious

"It's a story," I say to the class, to Nick. Straighten my jacket. Smooth the stray wisps of hair that have wandered out of place. "A story about always listening to your parents and teachers, and following the rules."

Yeah. That's it.

"Or you'll get spanked?" Lorelei asks.

"Teachers aren't allowed to spank us." Grayson huffs.

GOOD LORD, CHILDREN—STOP SAYING SPANK*!*

I've clapped my palm over my forehead now, my headache returning. "Of course teachers are not supposed to...do that. You don't have to worry about that, guys. None of us would ever spank anyone."

Nick narrows his gaze at me from across the room and starts coughing with laughter.

I catch the giggles too, and my body quakes with it. I'm trying so hard not to snort in front of this gorgeous dude.

The kids? Goners at this point. They don't even know what they're laughing at—they're just laughing because we're laughing—but I need to rein this in.

Now.

"Girls and boys..." I silence them with a wave of my hands. Bibbity bobbity *BE QUIET.*

Even I'm impressed.

"Can anyone remind me what I've said about reading over someone's shoulder or looking at my computer screen?"

"*Don't do it,*" they all chant.

"Right."

A hand in the back flies up.

"Yes, William?" I sit on the stool at the front of my class and fan myself with last week's spelling quiz.

Is it hot in here?

"Can you tell us more about your story?"

"Oh yes," Nick says. He crosses his way to the back of the room and leans against the bookshelf like he owns the place. "I definitely want to hear more about that."

I sputter and then grin through a glare. Take a breath, for composure. "Okay, sure. What do you want to know?" I can make some crap up on the spot. No prob.

Jimmy-with-Perpetual-Kool-Aid-Lip's hand shoots to the ceiling, but he doesn't wait for me to say his name. "What else is in it?"

"Yeah, Miss Wallace." Nick sips my coffee. The muscles in his well-defined calves are evident as he crosses one leg over the other, all slow. "For instance, I'm wondering: Are there any...colors in this story?"

I narrow my gaze in confusion, and the kids riff off this idea.

"You should put pink in it!" one of the girls says. I'm too distracted and my adrenaline is whooshing around on high alert too much for me to see who it is.

"And blue?" someone else asks.

"Why not?" I shrug.

I should not have requested coffee; I should have requested vodka.

"How about gray?" Nick calls from the back.

And I quirk an eyebrow his way. Did he see the elephant drawing too?

He continues, amusement touching his cheekbones. "Like, how many shades of gray do you think you could feasibly put in your story, Miss Wallace? Forty-nine? Fifty-one?"

The room explodes into excited chatter, and I give up. Walk swiftly to Nick's spot.

"Gimme that." I rip the mug from his hands and chuckle. "You trying to get me in trouble?"

He scrunches his face and touches an index finger to his chin in faux consideration of that. "Something tells me...you don't need my help in that area."

Big smiles and then he makes his way toward the door, but he spins on his heel just before he reaches it. Gives his fingers a snap. "By the way—Deborah told me this morning she wants me helping you guys with set design on the first-grade play, so here." He reaches into his pants pocket for a Post-it pad and scribbles his number as he talks. "I used to build sets in high school and for a few other schools, so I'm happy to offer my services."

Before I can respond, he slaps the digits into my hand, he smiles again, and then he's gone.

*   *   *

"Get. Out!" Valerie shoves me—but in a playful, hasn't-had-sex-since-the-millennium kind of a way. At this, her sunglasses slip halfway down her nose, the picnic table wobbles, and Quinn *tsks* at her tea, which sloshes near her iPhone.

"Hand to God," I say, making the gesture and preparing to swear on anything they put in front of me. "And get this." I tap Quinn's forearm from across the table. "No ring."

"Well, he's got a girlfriend, I'm pretty sure." Quinn's scrolling through her Twitter feed, her hot-pink fingernails tapping away on the phone screen. Then, just as astutely: "Let the girls have a turn!" she yells toward the cluster of boys hogging the merry-go-round.

"Is it, like, a club or something? Are there, like, meetings all you attached people go to, where you find ways to torture your single friends? How do you know he's got someone?"

Her attention is now on me. "Ida told me." She shrugs.

I nod. "Legit source. Ida knows fricking everything. Lemme text her real quick. Just to see—"

Me: Mr. Greene?

Three seconds later.

Ida: Attached.

"It's just as well." I do a sweeping *Ain't-no-thang* gesture. "Now, let's focus. We're here to make a mockery of my social life while also performing recess duty—and, by gum, we're gonna mock me and waste time. Who's with me?" I fist-bump no one.

Valerie swats at my arm. "Creating your Spark profile is not a waste of your time. It's a more efficient use of your time."

Hmm. I like the sound of that.

"Okay. If we're gonna do this, we're gonna do this right," Val starts, and I get lost in her ambition for a moment. I can't help the goofy grin taking over my face.

This woman is a mother of four (five, if you count Mike), a teacher to twenty-five, and she still has time to give a shit whether or not her stupid friend dies alone.

If that were me—

My throat goes raw.

I watch her rearrange herself so she's sitting cross-legged on the bench, all comfortable, just like she's sat since we were kids.

If that were me, would I be half as good a friend?

I cough away the answer to that and wave off her speech. "Yeah, yeah, yeah. Here's the deal. I am perfectly content living out my days on a beagle farm."

Quinn cracks a smile long enough to join us back in reality. This is her favorite dramatic end to my life that I've come up with, and she usually eggs me on when I start talking about it.

"The girl has a point." She pretends to approve. "It's better than being a cat lady. It's...innovative."

"Exactly. I'll be a hoarder of beagles. And they—"

Nate Tomkins rushes our post, his face the same hue as the red paint on the swing set. "How many more minutes?" he asks, and Valerie gives an amused little chuckle.

"Of recess or of your time-out?"

"Both," he wants to know.

She looks at her watch, and it glints in the midday sun. "About fifteen till we go in. As for time-out..." She glances at him over her sunglasses. "You promise not to throw pencils—or anything else, for that matter—at Charlotte?"

His lip quivers as he lowers his gaze to his tiny Sperry Top-Siders, which are ever untied, the heat from this interrogation seemingly too much for him. "Yes."

Her tone returns to Minnie Mouse bright. "Then I think we're good." She musses his dark hair and he makes a beeline for the field before she can change her mind.

"Now then." She's back to business. "We need a strategy." From the depths of her emergency bag, Valerie produces a planner she's apparently bought for this. It's pink and puffy and has red hearts sewn to it.

"What in holy hell—"

"Someone gave it to the girls for their third birthday." She flips it open with fervor and gazes at the thing like it's her firstborn. "They can't even write yet. They won't miss it." She dismisses my laughter with a flick of her pen. "I've already taken the liberty of writing down some of the things that have been wrong with your previous guys."

On second thought, maybe Valerie has a tad more free time than I thought.

"Oh, really...?" I snatch the notebook from her and start to skim. "'Mark Smoley was a narcissist'?" I look up at them through an eye roll. "Are we really going back as far as high school? Because we'll be here all fall."

A conceding nod. Valerie grabs the book and flips a few pages. "College? Grad school?"

"You didn't even know those guys!"

Quinn fiddles with the end of her braid and deadpans, "That's what they all say."

The two of them bicker about when to start—which failed relationship or failed date of mine is the worst—and I see Daniel.

Tall. Jason Segel–like, in fact.

The *gentle giant*, as Quinn likes to call my type.

I crack a smile at this.

I hope they don't start in on my relationship with him because I don't really feel like getting into all that today.

I haven't thought about Daniel much in the six years we've been apart because I haven't allowed it. The news all but killed my older sister. How could I do this? Bridget had asked, ad nauseam. And after only five years of marriage? But the answer to that was and is always: I was young. Isolated, after I moved to Indiana for him. Sure, I could write and not worry about teaching, but the pressure of that? Of living on someone else's dollar? And without my family and friends around to cry to when the writer's block days hit? Brutal. I don't know why it always felt like that, but it did.

You should have been able to cry to him, everyone said. *You shouldn't have had to move out there.*

They had all the answers.

But that's what we did. And I could never talk to him for some reason. I don't know.

I had always wanted kids, but something about the way we were together made the thought of having kids with him feel like a life sentence. And when I realized that, I knew I had to go. And fulfill my lifelong dream of living in Bridget's basement for two years while I crawled my way back into teaching.

Yanno, just like we'd always talked about growing up.

I reach for both my friends' hands.

"What are you doing?" Quinn frowns at me like I've cut her in line at a Sam Hunt meet and greet.

"Just hold my hands, you morons." I stretch my fingers.

Squeeze.

"This is all a bunch of crap, but I love you guys. You know that? I love you. For helping me land this job. And for putting up with my bullshit."

We're quiet a moment, and all of a sudden I realize Quinn's crying.

"Nooooo," I say, swiping some tissues from my purse pack. Her mega-mascara's going to run and there'll be no turning back.

"That's why I want you up there with me on my special day." She sniffles and dabs at her eyes.

"I know." I pat her arm. "I just don't—do—weddings. I can't. I'll buy you the most obnoxious thing on your registry, though. How's that?"

"Yeah, that's the same." She tosses the Kleenex ball into a nearby trash can. Score.

"How are things"—I wince—"going with the wedding planning?"

She starts nodding. "Pretty good. We have all the major vendors taken care of. The stuff that's left is mainly about the details—salmon or chicken?"

"Definitely steak," I say.

Valerie gasps. "What? You know how she feels about red meat!" Quinn's eyes start to well again, and I clap both hands over my mouth. Pop a squat next to her.

"See? This is precisely why you don't want me there. Trust me." I play with Quinn's braid.

"Getting a tad offtrack, don't you think?" Valerie is all checklists and cattle prods right now.

"Fine." I pout. "I'll download fricking Spark."

"Yay!"

Checklists, cattle prods . . . and annoying little claps.

They huddle around me, and we wait in silence as the percentage it's ready crawls across my screen.

"Oooooh." A gaggle of girls have somehow materialized and are swarming us with their curiosity.

I clap my phone to my chest. "Yes, ladies?"

"Whatcha doooin'?" asks the ratty-haired one from Quinn's class, whose name I can never remember.

"Checking our stocks," I say. "It's a bear market, and the Dow isn't looking very encouraging."

She squints up at me like I'm speaking Swahili, her green eyes narrow. "Bears?"

"Exactly." I blink at her. "Now go play, you guys. Recess is almost over!" I shoo them with my phone, and once they scamper reasonably out of earshot, we're back to the task at hand.

"It connects to your Facebook profile, so it automatically takes certain things from there," Val says.

I raise my brow at her. "For a married woman, you sure know a lot about this dating app…"

She swats at my arm, and the pretty lights on my screen entrance us.

Rae, 34

"So much for giving myself a fighting chance."

"What do you mean?" Quinn looks up. "I found Phil when I was thirty-three…"

"My competition is chicks in their twenties. You're right— easy peasy." I give a snort.

"You're old enough that you know what you want," she protests.

"Translation: old enough to call them on their shit. Guys don't like that."

"Ty said he did…"

I nearly spit out my Diet Dr Pepper and just look at her.

"Okay—bad example." Valerie gives a passive-aggressive shrug and focuses back on my phone.

We scroll through my Facebook pictures, since those are apparently the only ones you can add to Spark.

"Let's see. Me and Billie...me and Billie...me and the Heat mascot...me and Billie."

"You cannot put pictures of you and your dog on there." Quinn crosses her arms.

"Just because you're the devil and you hate animals..."

"You don't want to come across as a weirdo," she says.

"Um—obvi. But let's compromise. One picture of me and Billie. Deal?"

She begins to shake her head, and I glance from her to Valerie.

"Look, ladies, if he doesn't like dogs then I'm not going to like him anyway, so we might as well be forthcoming about the fact that I have an animal."

"Fine. Deal." Quinn glances at her fingernails and rolls those copper eyes of hers.

"Should I put in there that she sleeps in bed with me?"

"No!" Like they'd rehearsed it.

We sit awhile in quiet, save for the tapping of the screen and the occasional *ding* of an e-mail coming through on one of our phones. We're searching through my pictures, and it's like a museum of bad decisions, bad haircuts, bad eyebrow waxes, times before I *discovered* eyebrow waxes...

Although I had cropped out the guys, deleted pics of old boyfriends, of Daniel, etcetera, I still remember who I was with the night I wore that sleek, fuchsia, off-the-shoulder number. Likewise, I recall just who got me those flowers on the mantel in the background of that shot of Billie begging for a pizza slice.

Just before I'm at the point of slitting my wrists with a piece of the wood-chip ground cover, Valerie pipes up.

"We have to do something about the rest of your photos. These are—really sad, Rae-Rae!" She cackles, and it's so late in the day, it's contagious to all three of us.

"What's so funny out here?" Ida saunters up to the picnic table, bringing with her a light, citrusy scent of body spray and a bag full of Hershey's Kisses.

"Nothing." I straighten up. Give a sarcastic throat clearing. "We're doing a lot of serious work this afternoon."

She glances at me over her glasses. "Right. And I'm Mother Teresa."

The cleavage show she's putting on says otherwise, and we all crack up.

"Did you like my little gift to you today?"

"You deserve a raise, my friend." I wink.

"Too bad he's got a girl. Mm-mm-mm." She shakes her head and shiny waves cascade to her waist.

"Why, Teresa of Calcutta—I never thought I'd hear you say that." I clap a hand to my chest.

"I'm fifty—I'm not dead!"

Another burst of laughter. The kids are staring.

"He's pretty hot for her too," she continues. "Showing me all these pictures on his MyFace or whatever it's called."

"That's…nice." I reach for a Kiss. "You sure you don't have anything stronger in there?" I make like I'm about to put my head in the bag.

Quinn and Valerie fill her in on the torture they're subjecting me to, and after she stops making fun of me, we do another round of Kisses.

"Thirty-four, divorced, and no kids…" Ida taps a finger

against her lips like she's trying to figure it all out. And then, almost jazz hands. "You're like a unicorn."

"Yep—that one dying in the woods in the first Harry Potter film. Given the choice between me and someone brand-new? Whose name is, like, Brandi—"

"I think they're all forms of Katelyn now," Ida corrects. "My advice? Stay single. You can watch whatever you want, eat whatever you want—"

She leans low, and I have a new respect for guys. Not looking at her boobs is like avoiding a solar eclipse. No wonder so many don't even try not to do it.

"*Do* whomever you want—" She says it behind her hand, like it's a secret.

"Why, Mrs. Papadopolous—I do declare—"

Ida yanks her hands back like *Just sayin'*. "By the way, I'm taking Graham Mitchell for dismissal," she adds, and she's gone as quickly as she came.

I look at them with a shit-eating grin. "See? Now it's two to two."

Valerie: "Ida doesn't get a vote."

I concede and we pore over the rest of my Facebook photos, then choose a few acceptable ones from this decade.

"You need to take some more," Quinn says. "That's your homework for tonight."

I flip her off behind my phone so the kids don't see—even the ones who can't seem to peel their gazes from whatever it is we're ever doing—and she snaps a quick pic of me.

"Yes! Can I pleeeease use that one?"

"No fuck-you fingers. That's a rule." Valerie scribbles that down.

"Just fuck-me bangs?" I flip them down over one eye and

open my mouth all Marilyn Monroe. Touching my face and neck like even I can't keep my hands off me, so how could anyone?

"You look pretty, Miss Wallace!" Sophia shouts from the four-square area (and promptly gets hit in the butt with the ball).

"Thanks!" I laugh.

"Muuuuch better," Quinn says. She snaps another shot when I'm not looking, and I wave her off. "What? Candids are great!" She takes a few more.

And before I know it, Valerie's blowing the whistle, and I'm saved by the bell.

*   *   *

CHAPTER 4

The thick breeze beats against my face, my ponytail, as Billie trots beside me, keeping up with my pace. My chest pounds as I pad along—more slowly than usual, but I'm making the effort nonetheless.

This used to be the time I called my mother and caught up on events of the day. When she'd tell me about the latest on *General Hospital*, who was sleeping with whom, what killed-off characters returned from the dead that week.

But now it's quiet reflection time. Part of my routine. Get home, shovel in something that takes five minutes of prep, and take Billie for a jaunt. Nod at the other folks with their dogs. Yank Billie away from discarded fast-food bags and posts male dogs have peed on.

And then a flash of Daniel saying I'm a decent runner.

Ha. Yeah, right.

I smile like I always do at those kinds of flashes. A pang hits me in my side—or maybe that's just a stitch from being out of shape.

At any rate, I complete the rest of the loop at a walk; and by the time my girl and I get back to my place, I'm ready to derail it all with a glass of wine or six.

"Those tests can wait until tomorrow to be graded, right?" I say to Billie and indicate my teacher bag, barfing up papers and slumped over on itself like a drunken hobo.

She just looks at me with those big brown eyes and gives a giant yawn. Goes back under her blanket. Nothing changes.

Tonight, however, instead of sprawling out on the sectional and binge-watching some *Game of Thrones*, I fire up the Spark app and take a gander at what we've got on my profile so far.

It doesn't look half bad, really. I know it's totally stupid to think, but at least I look decent. That's all that matters with these things, anyway. I doubt any guy's going to read what I've written regardless—especially if he doesn't like what he sees.

I fiddle my way through the settings a minute and then go into my "discovery preferences."

"This is where I can find someone tailor-made for me. Oh boy!" I use my best little-girl-from-a-fifties-movie voice and swing an arm. Billie just snores.

People within fifteen miles. Ages thirty-five to forty-one.

Men seeking women.

Swoonsville.

I ease back some grocery store pinot grigio while it toggles, and suddenly: There's a dude.

Bill, 37

Longish ratty hair. Icehouse beer in hand.

I get *real* close to the screen and close one eye. Try to picture running into "Bill" at a bar—and I instantly know I'd ask for the check and file past him without making eye contact.

He's got that *To Catch a Predator* quality down pat. Which, I guess, would keep me safe because of said thirty-fourness, but still. I don't like him. I don't like his stupid face.

Before I realize what I've done, my thumb has pressed the red X at the bottom of the screen, and then? The most glorious thing happens.

A graphic stamps across his forehead. It says—in red letters, no less: NOPE.

All caps.

And just like that, Bill and his Icehouse are gone.

My breath catches.

I think I'm in love!

I feel like I've just taken a hit of something. My heart rate quickens. My chest is light. I'm a little woozy—and I've only had a sip of wine, so it's not that. It's from this superpower I now have.

I sit up and fumble through my home screens to my texting app.

Me: You mean I can just hit this red X and that ensures I'll never even have to talk to these people?

I grip the phone and stare at it like it's the fricking Holy Grail.

cue the angel choir

Laaaaaaa!

Valerie: YES! You can only talk to someone if you've both swiped Right!

Me: You may have created a monster...

Quinn: You're not supposed to be Sparking! You're supposed to be taking more pictures. And we are supposed to have a say in your choices!

Me: Too late—I'm addicted.

Quinn: And swipe, don't hit buttons, Grandma!

Me: Dude—whatever. As long as it says NOPE across his face, I'm happy.

Valerie: You better be pressing the green heart for LIKE on some too! (Swiping Right!)

Me: I'm sorry—I can't talk right now. I've got selfies to take.

I send them a douchealicious one. Duck lips. Peace sign. Sultry squint.

Quinn: Remember—we're not trying to hook Kanye here...?

Me: Speak for yourself. Good night!

As I plow through the guys who fit my Very Specific Criteria, I begin to notice most of their profiles aren't as complete as mine. With this app, you can write as much or as little as you want, and most seem to write little.

I, on the other hand, put that I'm divorced and included a few details about myself because, on the off chance that some poor schlub and I do both happen to swipe Right and can, therefore, communicate, *if we so choose* (God, I love the passivity of it all. It's so noncommittal!), I want him to know straightaway that I'm divorced. So if he's one of those shrunken-ball CrossFit trainers who scares easily and he judges me based on marital status, he can feel free to weed himself out of the equation before I even have to.

It's bad enough having to say it—but being judged for it as well?

I'm gulping down wine. Voracious for more faces! Gym selfies! Dudes holding fish! Guys jumping out of airplanes! That's-My-Sister-with-Me shots! Those-Aren't-My-Kids-I-Just-Love-My-Niece-and-Nephew pics!

I'm losing the feeling in my thumbs, yet I've never felt more alive!

I'm giddy for Gamble Profiles, wherein the main pic is of four guys

and one is really attractive

and two you probably wouldn't kick out of bed for eating crackers

and one looks like Roddy McDowall's character in *Planet of the Apes*...

and then you click it so you can see more photos!

And the next two are of the same four guys!

You still can't tell who is the holder of all your Spark dreams, but you really, reallllly want to know because by now you feel like you know these guys playing cornhole, doing some choreographed line dance at a wedding, tailgating at a Jaguars game—because you've been through so much together!

Until you finally get to the last photo...

and there's Cornelius, all on his own, with a golden retriever.

Because, of course, that's the one whose profile it was. *Get off my screen, you damn dirty ape!*

NOPE.

I'm drunk with power—and good ol' pinot greezh.

I wake up on my couch. Sweaty. Dried drool at one corner

of my mouth, and still holding my wineglass in one hand, my phone in the other.

#klassy

I wake the screen. Eleven thirty. Not too shabby.

You're out of matches, says Spark.

"Tell me about it," I say. And then I nod out of respect, like *We had a good run tonight, Sparky.*

On the way to my bedroom, my phone buzzes in my hoodie pocket.

The Tongue: Hey

I almost fall down the stairs, I snort so loud. I consider ignoring the Lip Licker for a moment and toss back a few pre-emptive Advil that I keep on my nightstand, as per my custom. But then I think better of it because Valerie and Mike are our mutual friends and because I hate being text snubbed.

And I'd like to think I'm not that much of a jerk.

I decide I'll make like Scarlett O'Hara and deal with his obliviousness tomorrow, so I send a quick message back.

Me: Zzzzzzz

That oughta hold him for now.

*   *   *

The waitress is taking our order. Ingrid. The one who says absolutely so hilariously that trying to get her to say it has become a thing whenever we come to this hotel for brunch. The most times we got her to do it in one visit was twenty-one.

Poor sweet thing, she has no idea.

"Would you like more coffee?" *She looks at us over her bifocals.*

"That would be great." *Jesse offers that molten smile of his.*

She gives a firm nod—purses her lips in concentration—like he's given her the quest of a lifetime and it's up to her to change the world.

Give me French roast or give me death!

She turns on her heel.

He catches my stare real quick, and a twinkle glimmers in his eye. "Oh, and Ingrid?"

I choke on a laugh as she scurries back over, apron tied high on her waist, because I know exactly what he's doing.

"Could we get some more cream when you have a chance?"

She raises her non-coffee-wielding hand and bobs her head somewhere between How could she not have noticed *and* How brilliant is this man who thought to put cream in the coffee. *Nothing would make this meal more complete.*

"Aaaaabzuhlootly. You got it." *Pivot. And she's off.*

His hearty laugh warms me from across the table. He's winning our little game so far this morning.

"Oh, like she wasn't going to say it that time." *I toss a limp wrist.*

"Not impressed, eh?" *He cocks his head, his dark stare intense.*

"Not with that," *I say, all sassypants.* "It's impressive I have you the entire weekend, though."

He glances back at his breakfast, a big ol' pile of crabmeat and poached eggs plated to perfection. The sweet hint of the crab entwined with the warm smell of butter curls in the space between us.

His tone is suddenly serious. "I know you've been worried."

"That's not the word for it—"

"Stressed then." He meets my gaze. "There you are at your sister's, and here I am, still living at home."

My eyes start to well. I massage the tightness from my throat when he puts down his fork and reaches his big, tanned hand across the table for mine.

"Hey," he says, his voice liquid. "We're in this together. That's how we fell in love in the first place. Right when we were both going through such a difficult thing. I don't know how I'd survive this divorce without you."

I let him touch me, but I'm careful not to look at him because I don't want any tears to fall.

Instead, I offer a laugh.

"I know it's not exactly the same situation for you," I say. I break away as he begins to smooth his thumb across my knuckles but continue the thought. "Jonah's only four. It's—complicated."

He grunts. Takes a moment.

"You know what isn't complicated, Rae?"

I hear the smile return to his voice before I'm able to glance up to confirm. I know what he's going to say.

"You and me."

Yep.

"You know where my heart is. Where I want to be. What I'm working toward."

They're just words, but they make me all toasty inside. And it's been a long time since I've had toasty. Or even room-temperature bread, to be honest.

"A year from now?" he continues. *"It won't be this hard. You won't be at Bridget's anymore...we'll buy that little place in Myers Park..."*

I'm silent. I focus on the clink of silverware on elegant china. The plink of jazz standards spilling in from the Colonel Sanders–looking guy playing the baby grand in the lobby.

"Honey. Look at me."

I oblige.

A part of me knows it, even now as I watch his eyes swim.

Fuck this guy. Seriously.

But I want so much for this to be real. Need for it to be—

"Soon," he says. And every part of me but that little pebble of worry in my gut believes him.

Ingrid's back just in time for me to blink away the last of the moisture in my own eyes.

"Thank you," I say to her.

"Oh, aaaaabzuhlootly, miss. Aaaaabzuhlootly."

And we erupt into merriment once again.

*   *   *

CHAPTER 5

That stupid dream impedes my ability to make myself *not* look like I went thirty-four seconds with Ronda Rousey last night. It takes all of what little energy I can muster to shower and dress, to do my hair, and I have to wait for some of the puffiness under my eyes to go down before I can even think about performing a makeup miracle.

I'm forced to be one of those people I hate—pumping the last remnants of mascara gunk onto the wand and working some magic on my eyelashes at red lights. I'm just finishing up when I catch a glimpse of a blue hair next to me sipping from a travel mug. She scowls in my direction.

"Why, yes, I am doing makeup in my car," I say to her but really to my reflection. "Why don't you take a bite right out of my ass?"

However, instead of staring her down, I smooth on a smile as warm as the forecast for this afternoon and pull into Dunkin' Donuts. #namaste

When I get to school and I'm through potpourriing the

teachers' lounge with my morning score, the smell of fried dough and yeast—and coffee—permeates the air and lulls me into what I hope isn't a false sense that today is going to be a good day. I stand back and admire my masterpiece.

"What's the occasion?" Valerie flits in, flutters her fingers over the boxes.

Scoff. "Um—hello? Maybe I'm just a nice person?"

All the trolls in the room offer laughs.

"Hey!" I curl a lip and shove three chocolate-glazed Munchkins in my face hole.

"So did you find anybody good last night?" she asks.

"'NOPE,'" I quote my favorite new app and throw my head back in a mouth-full guffaw.

"You're being too picky." She wipes her hands on her khaki skirt. It's already got dry-erase marker smudges on it. "At lunch, Quinn and I will find someone who is swipe-Right material."

"If you say so, but my research last night caused me to develop some rules."

"Such as?"

I'm ripping into a chocolate éclair, and I begin gesturing wildly with the pieces. "For example, if they say they like music." I slip into Dude Voice. "'Music saved my life.'" I throw her an eye roll.

"So?"

"Hear me out. Like, if there's any picture of the guy near a microphone…with a drum set…holding a guitar…anything of that nature?" I sweep my forearms, mangled éclair carcass and all, into an X.

"No music lovers. Got it. You're holding out for someone who hates all joy." She gives me one of her signature frowns.

"It's not that."

With my clean hand, I grab hold of her pink argyle sweater a bit more intensely than I meant, and she yanks back and laughs. "How much sugar have you had this morning?"

"Not important. Look. You have the documentation right there in your creepy-stalker—I mean really sweet—*Rae's Love Life* notebook. I've done the musician thing, right? A couple of times, in fact..."

My gaze blurs into middle space, and I get lost in a college memory. Zachary Willis's calloused fingers plucking me all over like a—

Valerie boops me on the nose with a napkin.

"Right!" A couple of blinks. "I'm just saying. If you're in your thirties and you're still in a band? You probably also still live with your mother. And if your band is actually good? And, like, touring? Then you're probably letting lots of chicks play your instrument. No, thanks—I'm good."

Her face goes through a whole metamorphosis in three seconds. From grimace to glower to—snorting with laughter. "Dammit—you're right. So what else is on—or off—the list, for that matter?" She fishes in her giant purse and produces the sad tome right there.

"That was the most obvious one I came up with last night because there were so many offenders. How about..." I drum my fingers on my chin a minute. "Shirtless selfies?"

"They post shirtless selfies?" Her eyes become the size of French crullers, and the hue of her cheeks begins to match her sweater.

I laugh. "Only about every other freaking one. Wanna see?"

It feels just like we're sixteen again, paging through our yearbooks and judging our classmates, as we're giggling over profiles. NOPE. NOPE. Maybe? NOPE.

And then Quinn enters. She's a hurricane of fall fabulousness in leggings and a plaid flannel shirt.

"Thank the Lord for fried dough." Her razor-sharp pumps cut across the carpet, and she drops her bags to the floor with a huff.

"What's the matter?" I ask, pouring her some joe.

"Don't even ask." She blows her side bangs out of her eyes as she roots through what's left in the DD boxes.

Val and I exchange shrugs.

"And no more Spark until we can all do it." Quinn points a plastic knife my way before she obliterates a sesame-seed bagel with the strawberry schmear. "And since we have play rehearsal today"—she seems to remember we're at work because she does the guilty glance around, smiles at the math tutor, and lowers her voice a tick—"I say we grab drinks afterward and do it then."

"I'm in," I say and slam-dunk my napkin. Launch my arms straight toward the fluorescents and rock out on air guitar. Kick!

"No guitars, remember?" Valerie teases, and I continue my victory dance backward out the door.

When I get to my room, my line o' kids already stands patiently outside.

"Gooooood morning, dears."

Maybe I have had too much sugar.

But I don't have time to ponder my caffeine-to-doughnut ratio because the handshake processional begins. Deborah says she likes us to perform this morning ritual so that the students can feel more "official" and "professional" when they get to school— *It's like they're little businessmen and -women!*

"How many cups of coffee do you drink a day, Miss Wallace?" Emmaline Johnson looks up at me through her cruelly ginormous but totes adorbs glasses, her hands clammy.

"Never enough, my love. Never enough."

Once the Pledge of Allegiance and the announcements are through, it's time for reading.

"Today, guys, we're going to read a book."

And the wiggling begins. The hands.

"Yes?"

"What book will it be?" They all want to know in twenty different ways.

I smile. "It's one of my favorites. It's called *The Giving Tree*."

Discussion rolls its way through the class like the wave at a Rays game. I chuckle and grab Shel Silverstein's classic off the top of my filing cabinet.

They love when I read aloud, and I love it too. They're so quiet. Mesmerized. And although the words I write are very— *very*—different from the kinds of things I read the kids, it's seeing this magic at work that makes me ravenous to finish my manuscript. The bond that forms between us when I read to them. The way the words, no matter whose, have them spellbound.

I walk to the stool at the front of the room. "I want you to listen as best you can and then, when we're done, we'll talk about it and do a short assignment, okay?"

This idea is met with an uproar of enthusiasm, which never fails to surprise me. Prior to the divorce, I taught junior high, and there was no getting those kids excited about anything. With first graders, they are so thrilled about learning; it's a totally different ball game every day.

I begin. "'Once there was a tree, and she loved a little boy—'"

Just as I'm about to get lost in my own excitement in sharing this with them, my e-mail notification *dings*, and everyone flinches.

"Are you going to get that, Miss Wallace?"

"I don't know, Benji. Don't you want to—"

Dammit. They know me so well.

I put up the one-minute finger, hop off the stool, and scoot on over to my desk to see what fresh hell this is.

Dear Author,

And there it is. I didn't think I had any query letters left floating out there with agents.

"Anything good?" Marcus asks.

I laugh. "What did I say about minding your own business, guys?"

They singsong: *"Do it!"*

I shake my head and take a breath. A rejection, first thing in the morning. Beautiful.

Thank you for considering the Wright Agency for your work.

Unfortunately, with fiction, we have to really love something in order to take it on—it has to really be "wright" for our list—and this does not quite fit.

That said, your writing is strong, and we encourage you to query us with future projects or consider other agents for this piece, as their tastes may align better with your work.

Have a great day!

Joseph Wright

I chew at the insides of my cheeks. Press my lips into a line.

This is one of those times I wish I had the balls to actually have a flask in my desk.

But I don't.

So I dig in my front pocket for a couple of Tylenols and knock 'em back with a sip of java.

Breathe. You can do this.

I turn off the volume on my laptop, check my phone to make sure it's on silent as well—delete the e-mail from my app on there too—and mosey back to the stool by the white-board.

"Where were we?" I say, bright. Wave a wand like it never happened.

Soft giggles popcorn around the room, and it only makes the pit in my stomach deepen.

"The tree loves the boy," they answer.

"Right."

And so I read. Choking back emotion, my throat suddenly raw, I read.

I've read this story a handful of times to previous classes. And although the words never change, it's never quite hit me like this. No matter how much the tree gives and the boy takes.

But I have to press on and keep my voice on an even keel.

Teaching is like that. People expect you to be Maria in *The Sound of Music* or Mary freaking Poppins—or, really, any form of Julie Andrews where she's singing to children and enriching their lives. Any whiff of being a regular person pops the idealized teacher bubble that folks have and ruins everything for them for some reason.

So I press on. Spoonful of sugar.

And, really, someone should call the Academy for my performance, because the tree keeps giving and giving and the boy keeps taking and taking, but not one of my kids would ever be able to guess how broken I feel inside because my voice doesn't break at all.

Not even as my mind drifts to the e-mail, to the months I spent on that stupid manuscript. Not once.

I'm mouthing the words and turning the pages, and I'm getting hot in the face. And pissed at Shel Silverstein, come to think of it.

But my tone stays focused.

" 'Come, Boy, come and climb up my trunk and swing from my branches and eat apples and play in my shade and be happy' …"

But now this miscreant is too busy to climb trees. He's asking for money. What in the actual—

Have some self-respect, tree. This boy is shitting all over you!

When we get to the part where he chops down her trunk, I concede my Oscar because my vision does begin to blur. But I press on, wishing I'd chosen the other option—*Love You Forever*—and then I realize books suck and maybe I need to be writing picture books or chapter books for first graders that don't make you want to blow your brains out at the end.

" 'I have nothing left. I am just an old stump. I am sorry.' "

The kids laugh at the word *stump*—are they even getting this?—and it takes everything I have not to chuck this book out the window and peace out.

But I don't.

Instead, I suck in a breath, close the book, and push a smile across my face.

"So what did you think?" I ask, folding my arms across my silk top.

"Can we read another one?"

I chuckle. "Not right now." I stand and start my teacher pace through their worktables, weaving in and out of the Vera

Bradley bags and trying not to trip. Or to marvel at the fact that their parents buy them Vera Bradley bags.

"So," I begin, "why do you think the tree kept giving and the boy kept taking? Take a minute and think." I glance at the clock and watch the second hand tick away. Something in the repetition soothes me, and I zone out for a moment, but All the Feels are back when the minute's up.

Stupid Wright Agency.

"Now. Turn to your table partners and tell them what you came up with. Why did the tree keep giving?"

Their excited conversations buzz in my ear, and a sense of calm washes over me.

"Because it loved the boy, like you said at the beginning," Maisy says over the hum.

"Good—let's build on that." I cross to the bookshelf and straighten the jagged stacks of thin easy readers. "Do you think the boy loved the tree?"

They take a minute to discuss and then come up with the idea that, no, the boy did not, in fact, love the tree. This is not right and it's not wrong, and it's lessons like this that make me drift back to my college English classes.

I just smirk and indulge them and go on. "Interesting. Do you think the tree knew this?"

"*No*," most of them chant.

"I do," Ashley pipes up.

"Yes?"

"I think the tree knew, but it didn't care. It was true love."

Bless her little heart.

I press my lips taut and cross to the window. Look out at the cluster of cypress trees right outside. All at once, I wonder if Silverstein's tree was in the cypress family.

"I like that," I say, returning my attention to Ashley's platinum pigtails. "And you know what? There's another name for that. Unconditional love. Have you ever heard of that?"

This is met with an uproar of confusion, little faces scrunching this way and that, but I explain further.

"Unconditional love is when you love someone—or something, really—no matter what. No matter what he or she—or it—does to you."

"You mean like how you love your family?"

Ashley's on fire today.

"Exactly." I punctuate her correctness with a point of a finger. "But you can even love a thing—have a dream or something—and love it, no matter how hard it is to do sometimes. You ever do that? Try and try at something—a sport, maybe—and you're not that great at first, but you keep going and you keep practicing because you love it and you get closer to your goal, and you get better?"

I know the parallel I'm drawing and I'm not sure if it's Great Teaching or Incredibly Narcissistic and Making Everything All About Me. But I suppose no one will know either way, and that's the beauty of being the queen of your classroom, so what's the difference?

"Do you, Miss Wallace?"

The question pulls me from my reverie. I sit on the edge of my desk and pull my laptop to my chest like it's a teddy bear. "I do. It's writing." I smile. "And no matter how difficult it is, I know I'll never be able to give it up—and thank you for reminding me of that, guys. Because it isn't always something I can remember." I drift to a stance. "That stuff isn't always easy to remember, is it? So let's remember to be the tree—not the little boy. Give all we can. Love with all we are. No matter what. Even if we become an old stump in the end, we still have use."

They giggle once again.

I close my laptop and work my way to the board. As I scribble down the writing assignment, the dry-erase marker squeaks, and the anchor in my stomach has gone weightless. I giggle right along with the kids. *Stump* is a pretty funny word after all.

And I might just be an old stump, but I sure as hell am not sorry. Not for any of it.

*   *   *

CHAPTER 6

But that query was old. That manuscript was old." Valerie flips the ends of my hair, and I offer a small smile, the air thick with beer and deep-fried hugs.

"I know. But it still sucks, getting a form rejection like that."

"You don't know—"

"'Dear Author'?"

"I get it. It was a shitty way to start the day."

I put my hand over hers for a second. "I know you don't understand my obsession with publishing—"

"It doesn't matter, Rae-Rae. It's your dream, and honestly, I just wish I had one."

Before I can delve into that little nugget, Quinn shows up with three pints of love. "Next round's on you." She hands me mine.

I raise the glass in approval, and we all take gulps like we're sorority girls trying to outdrink our sisters at the ten-year reunion.

"So what's going on with Phil?" I ask since all Quinn did

during play rehearsal was talk on her phone outside and pace around the courtyard.

"Oh, you know." She waves it off. Takes another sip of beer. And gets lost in the menu. "What kind of delicious grease shall we consume?"

I cut my stare to Val, and she just shrugs.

We manage to avoid all real conversation until after we order—mostly tales of e-mail woe: from helicopter parents to REPLY ALL work chains that no one even remembers who started anymore. (The point being, no one GAF about when Joanne Testaverde has recess duty or lunch duty or when she takes a shit for that matter, so why are we all being informed?)

I'm mainlining chicken nachos, and my friends are making me laugh with their Problems. They're checking their phones every six seconds—Mike even has to FaceTime Val just to make her feel like a bad person for not being there to feed the kids dinner for, like, once in her life.

I snatch the phone from her clutches, tingly with bitterness and beer.

"What's that, Mikey? Hiiii, Mikey!" I wave, kind of like a mental patient.

"Hi, Rae." His tone has an edge to it, and he runs a hand through his sandy hair. Not sexy—annoyed.

"Valerie's being such a good girl," I continue, "and if you could just let her stay out a teensy bit longer because she's with her best friends in the world— Say hi, Quinn." I point the phone her way and she does a distracted flip of the wrist in the middle of finishing pint number two. "I personally guarantee she'll go down on you tonight, once all the kids are asleep."

Valerie gasps with laughter and starts grabbing for the phone.

Mike's face lights, and he almost looks how he did the night we met him at that dive bar. Hair Hugh Grant–floppy over one eye. Dorky. But confident. His features now slightly rounder than they were.

"Very funny. They're never all asleep," he says just as Val reclaims her phone.

"Sorry, hon. I'll be home in a little while. M'kay? You can do this."

A snorting fit ensues. I love when she stands up for herself. Even passive aggressively.

But it's just nice to hear her be real for once, instead of spewing out sunshine all the damn time.

"It's like no one's allowed to be in a bad mood ever anymore. Yanno?" I hiccup. "Oops—askew me."

"What are you babbling about over there?" Quinn gives me the side eye.

"We'd better get to the Sparking before we get too drunk," Valerie says.

"Too late." Quinn giggles, and I order us another round. What the hell.

"I want you to know that I hate both of you," I say.

"Well, that's too bad. You're stuck with us. Now take out your phone."

"First up. 'John, 35.'" My thumb hovers over the red X.

"Give. Me. That." Quinn rips the phone from my hands and looks at it. "Why is he a no? He's got a nice car—look at that beautiful Beemer. Oh, I love the green. Let's see what his other pictures are." She clicks.

"This is going to take for-damn-ever if you're going to analyze every single one."

"You have to 'like' five guys before we can leave," she says and holds up her hand. "Got that? F-i-v-e."

"Is this what it feels like to be in your class?" I smirk, and she ignores me.

She and Valerie flip through John, 35's pictures for a few minutes and then they come to the conclusion that I came to—hello—in three seconds. That John, 35, is probably a douche because his main pic is of him and his car, and Who Does That?

"But you were almost fooled." I wag a finger at Q and then let it hover over the red X. "Shall I do the honors?"

She shoots me a finger back and then obliges on her own.

NOPE.

We go through this a few more times. It's a blur of faces and voices and judgments, but—thank God—we're pretty much in agreement about all of them.

"How about him? He's kinda cute…"

Nose scrunch. "Hipster beard."

"Okay, this guy's main photo is of LL Cool J."

"I mean, the ladies do love Cool James…"

"Do you think there are some women who fall for that?"

"Based on the kinds of humans I encounter on a daily basis in life? I'd say yes. Yes, there are women who fall for that."

They're flipping and flipping and I've taken to laying my head on the table. "Like, how is it possible that this is my life, you guys?"

They ignore me.

"What about this one?" Quinn asks.

I study the profile. Squint at it. "No."

"Why not?"

"You can tell he thinks he's really good-looking. He loves himself. This isn't just a case of 'Oh, I'm a dude and I found a couple of decent pictures that make me *not* look like a murderer.' This guy—this Steve—he's posing for them. He's got this pose perfected. He's done it a hundred times."

"It does kinda seem that way," Valerie says, taking a pull of her dirty martini, to which she's now switched.

"Kinda?" I laugh. "And, I mean, a man doesn't do that. A boy does that. A guy who just wants to fuck something does that. Can you imagine your dad working on his truck and ever being like 'Let me take a picture of myself while I strategically wipe off this strategically smeared grease from my strategically set jawline'? No. Not even when he was thirty-six years old. A real man is not vain like that. Not one I would consider dating, anyway. It's one thing to care about your appearance. It's another if you care more about that than the girl you're with. I'm not at a place in my life where I feel like competing with some dude's watch collection. Sorry not sorry."

Silence from the two of them, and I take that as a mic drop.

Valerie pretends that didn't happen, and she's on to the next. "What about this one?"

Lip curl. And then: "Converse."

She knits her brow at me. "Huh?"

"Converse sneakers. No."

"Aw, I think that's cute." Quinn stretches out her words in a whine, not even looking at the guy but at her own phone, which she hasn't been able to part with all evening.

"Yeah, you know when that was cute? High school. Next. And here's another one." I reclaim my phone. "'Work hard/play hard.'"

"What's wrong with that?"

"It's like the douche-bag motto. NOPE. And when did everyone get so 'laid-back'? I'm not laid-back at all! In fact, I want to put that on my profile. 'I am as stress riddled as they come. Totally uptight.'"

"Don't." Quinn lowers her thin brows at me.

We're making some real headway here. How are there this many single guys around, and how are they all this disappointing?

"Gah!" Valerie frowns. "I meant to swipe Right on that one. But it won't let me undo it." She taps at the screen. "Well, they now have a thing where you can pay for Spark—an *upgrade*, they call it—and if you have an account like that, you can have more Right swipes, they say. I guess they limit those? And you can also undo a Left swipe."

Quinn laughs, her focus still on her device. "Something tells me that's not a feature you'll be needing."

"Ha! No. Like, if you're swiping Right so many times that even Spark's like 'Whoa, there, slick. Slow down,' you should probably reexamine your life. This is how one can distinguish between the just plain single and the single and desperate."

"Aw, look at this one. He's got a dog," Valerie croons. "You love dogs! Look how sweet!"

Eyebrow raise.

I consider him.

He only has that one picture. Him and a pit bull something-or-other mix that's insanely smushworthy.

And then?

"No."

"What?" They screech to a halt and gape at me. I might as well have just gutted the dog right there on the table, Ned Stark style.

"Look at the size of the dog…Now look at the size of the guy."

There's a full five-second lull as they do. Quinn is even paying attention now.

And they close their frickin' yap holes. Allow a moment of silent respect because there's no way they can dispute it.

"I never would have even thought of that, but you're totally right!" Quinn marvels up at me, her stare glistening in what looks like admiration but might just be alcohol.

"I'm not trying to discriminate based on height. I'm no runway model, of course." When they—shockingly—don't protest, I continue. "But it's not like that's a Saint Bernard or Scooby-freaking-Doo he's holding."

"No, you're right. He's definitely not riding all the rides, if you know what I mean." Val winks.

"Not this one, anyway." Thumb to clavicle, and they chuckle.

We're kind of loud, but we're pretty much the only people in here—Thursday night must not be senior citizen night—so thank God we don't have to bother with respecting others. Alex the bartender glances at me every now and then, a smirk sliding across that hot mouth of his every time.

"I didn't think I'd say this"—Quinn picks at the last of her fries—"but this is harder than it seems like it'd be."

"That's what she said," I say. I just can't help it.

Valerie snorts and tries to smack me but misses. "I agree, but still."

There it is.

"Don't you think you're being a little judgy, based on very little information?" Another one of her frowns.

I take a breath and prepare to blow their minds once again. It seems a bit ridiculous that I have to explain this to my best friends—especially Quinn, who was right where I am, and not too long ago—but whatever. I'm a teacher. I educate.

"Not really, no. But I'll prove it to you if you want. If I have to."

"How?"

I talk with my fork. "I'll let you swipe Right on five people, and if we match up, I'll meet them."

"Even if you would have vetoed them?"

I sigh. "Yes. And you will see that these seemingly superficial details are actually indicators. I'll even be more lax in my swiping on my own. How's that?"

"What's the catch?"

"The catch is, if I'm right, you have to admit it. And lay off. And maybe...buy me something nice." I smile at my quick addition.

They exchange a look. "Okay."

"And I don't have to be in the wedding."

Quinn rearranges herself in her chair and crosses her arms. "You're just going to sabotage it. Be judgmental and not even try."

"I promise I won't." I set down my fork and grab her hand in both of mine, a tad more dramatic than I intended, but whatever. "I mean, what's the worst thing that can happen for me? Really. I might meet someone nice and give him a chance? Fall in love?"

They both grin.

And I spit the Amstel Light I've just gotten back into. "Okay, I couldn't keep a straight face anymore. I'm sorry! But you know what I mean. And you can trust me. I promise I will try. As long as you promise to actually see and acknowledge the truth, if I'm right."

And then: *ding!*

A text comes up. A photo, with a message to accompany it.

The Tongue: Hey, girl. Where you been all week?

He's wearing the tightest of V-neck tees, gray workout shorts, earbuds hanging slack around his neck. His head's cocked to one side, the phone visible in his bathroom mirror, his too-sculpted brows knit in what I guess is supposed to be his version of puppy dog eyes.

"Aww! Ty!" Valerie's hands fly to her heart. "Write him back," she singsongs, her pity for him grating in my ear.

"You put him in your phone as *The Tongue*?"

I wave off Quinn's question and shake my head at no one in particular because—balls—doesn't anyone get it?

Me: Busy, busy...

"That's mean." Valerie shoves a fry in her face.

"How is that mean? Look, if he doesn't sense the tone—"

The Tongue: Too busy for this?

Another picture.

Valerie gasps, eliciting worried glances from the waitstaff, and Quinn spills half her drink.

"Is that—"

His manhood plunging angrily out of the fly of a pair of suit pants, his face beaming with what can only be described as pride in the background. He's even pointing to it, as if it's unclear where the recipient is supposed to be looking.

They burst into laughter, but I drown them out as I scrutinize this dick pic. This ever-perplexing, unsolicited assault on my eyes.

There's something different about this one. Something—

"Rae?"

Lightbulb!

"What is it, Rae?"

"He just straight-up sent that bathroom selfie. Now he's in a suit at the office hanging brain?"

They exchange horrified stares.

"What we've got ourselves here, ladies, is a recycled dick pic. I'm sure it's not the first of its kind, but this is definitely unprecedented for me."

More gasps that give way to laughter.

Me: Sending me used pics, are we?

There's a pause. We hold our collective breaths. What can he possibly say to that?

And then:

The Tongue: Haha, busted.

I turn to Valerie. "I want to thank you again for setting me up with Ty..."

"I'm so sorry." She snorts until she's choking. When she finally regains her composure, she shrugs. "What am I supposed to do the next time I see him? Oh my God!" And then she's back to wiping tears of laughter with her napkin.

Once we recover—and it takes *a while*—they're a little more game to listen to me.

"So regarding this little experiment, we'll see who's right. I don't want to, like, ruin your whole world or anything, but most guys out there..." I gesture toward the phone. "And I'm not saying this in a bitter way, I want you to know."

Although, when you're thirty-four and single and you're

talking to Marrieds or people in relationships and you say *I'm not bitter*, all this does is convince them of your bitterness.

"Single guys, maybe," Quinn interrupts and bares her insecurity teeth.

"I'm not saying Phil. Or Mike. For Christ's sake," I snap.

Why is Quinn doing this?

She gives me a slow blink, like I'm supposed to *watch it* lest I wake her temper or something, and they continue their search.

I scowl into my beer.

What's happening to Quinn? It happened to Valerie so long ago I've forgotten a time when she was just Val and not Val-and-Mike-Who-Share-a-Facebook-Profile.

But Quinn? She's different. At least she was.

I see her the night we decided to shake Plantation off our shoes and go to Ibiza. We had originally wanted to go to Ireland because we had just finished watching *P.S. I Love You* and there was that hot Javier Bardem knock-off from *Grey's Anatomy* waiting for Hilary Swank. But we settled on Ibiza because Quinn had a friend we could stay with there and we were poor schoolteachers, after all.

"That could be us!" she said, standing on her bed and brandishing a half-empty jar of *queso* we'd just opened that night. "Let's do it."

Or maybe the jar was half full?

We were thirty. Divorce survivors. It was fresh on the heels of Jesse disappearing from my life, and she'd just come off a broken engagement.

"Who needs retirement money anyway?" was my response.

And just like that, we said a big *Eff you* to Plantation and got out of Dodge for ten days.

One of the first nights there, we took in a few umbrellaed

something or anothers at this beach bar around the corner from where we were staying, and Quinn got very serious.

"We are fearless," she said.

It was like a battle cry. A promise.

I raised my glass at her. "And we are feared."

She played with the ends of her hair, extra glisten bouncing off it in the glow from the hanging lights. "That might be true, but screw 'em. If women fear us, it's only because they're jealous they're stuck. They're worried their men want us. If men fear us, it's because they're not really men. We are strong. We will fight. We will win. And you know what? They should fear us."

She was like a tiny, clean, non-blue Braveheart as she threw back a shot of vodka and wiped her mouth with her arm.

I offer a sad smile at the memory. Where's that person now?

I realize I'm pouting into my empty pint glass, and they're chattering away like happy little monkeys, all giggly because they've already chosen a few people for me and they're so excited.

When they pick the last of the five, Valerie motions to Alex for our checks. "We aren't trying to set you up for failure, Rae-Rae. We took your 'rules' into consideration."

"Yeah, you just happen to have a better eye for them than we do!"

Maybe Quinn hasn't forgotten. Maybe she remembers all too well.

But why try to pretend it all away? Is she that insecure with Phil that she has to dismiss my single life away? She was down here in the trenches with me not so long ago.

I know nothing about Phil. And I don't think he'd cheat. But Quinn knows as well as I how sleazy guys can be.

Married, engaged, attached.

Just because she's found the love of her life now, my cynicism is wrong? Unwarranted?

I hatch a silent plan to teach the two of them a lesson about men. Not only am I fairly certain I'm going to clean up with this reverse-Spark plan, but I'm also going to show them I'm not crazy. I'm not just being cynical. A good man is hard to find, and I'm not being too careful. Or too judgmental.

And then I think, *What the hell do I know about planning anything—I can't even plot my own book*...and I decide maybe I should drink more.

*   *   *

CHAPTER 7

The night air ghosts across my hot cheeks, my forehead, and Alex's mouth tastes just how I thought it would that first night I saw him, when I was with Ty. Like Altoids almost covering up the cigarette he probably had during a break. But good. Smoky and dangerous. Like making out with James Dean.

"How'd we even get here?" I ask, breathless, in between crushing kisses, but the truth is, I don't care.

He's suctioned to my lips as if the last time he's screwed someone from the bar Bruce Jenner was still Bruce Jenner and he'll be damned if he lets me go for one second. His hands mess through my hair. His grip, tight on my waist.

I'm only slightly concerned as his tongue searches my neck, my ear.

Godddd.

But what's a(nother) hickey? That's what they make infinity scarves for, right? Hooray, fashion!

My pulse rushes in time with whatever's coming from the

EDM club down the street, and my back aches against the brick wall in the alley as he pushes me against it.

"You wanna get out of here?" It's a low growl. A purr.

That hint of an accent tickles deep in my ear, and the sensation waves right through me. All the way down to my feet. My toes curl in my kitten heels.

I answer by pulling him closer, and my breath catches. I'm helpless to escape his grasp. Desperate for him to hold me even tighter. I want more of him. Want him closer. It's too late. There's no other way.

Somehow, we get back to my place and I'm fumbling with the lock like a goddamn custodian, the echo of keys jangling all through the hallway. It's not that easy to open the door with a bartender attached to your face—but we finally make it in. Barely.

Once we do, shirt be damned, he's all abs and shoulders and pecs. One knot of muscle after another in delicious-looking black boxer briefs.

"Hold, please." I stumble into the kitchen and hurl some treats in Billie's general direction. "Here, girl."

I catch her disapproving stare and toss another biscuit onto the fire. "Don't say I never gave you anything. And when's the last time you got laid, huh?"

"What?" Alex calls, and it sounds like he's already in my room.

I kick off my heels, fling my purse somewhere in the vicinity of the couch, and pad across my place until I reach the open door.

"Gee—make yourself at home." I slide on half a grin.

"Get over here," he says, and he lassos me with that dark stare that drew me in from across the bar a few nights ago.

I knew as soon as Quinn and Valerie said their good-byes and we locked gazes—it's starting to come back to me now—that he and I would be here, or some variation of here, before long.

Moonlight spills in through the sheers and highlights all his gorgeous definition, every ripple, as he swims in an ocean of Egyptian cotton.

The moment I get there, he yanks my blouse overhead, and there's a little *rip* as it comes off in one swift motion.

We both laugh.

"Hope it wasn't expensive…"

But I shut him up and shove him down to the mattress.

I can feel the buzz in the mere inches between our bodies as I linger over him. How much he wants me. His eyes, a shade of wild as he drinks me in. He clamps both his hands over my ass and pulls me to him. He holds me there and I let him do it because he's so hard. Distractingly hard.

But I only let myself be distracted for a minute.

I've completely sobered of alcohol now, but I'm drunk with power and I want to torture this poor Alex in the best of ways, just because I can. I'll fulfill his little bartender dreams, but when I say "say so." My way.

My bed, after all.

I slide down his body, and when he realizes where I'm going, he gives one soft whimper, which he seems to silence as quickly as it came on.

I finally smooth my hand over his body, and the anticipation has all but throttled him. He grips the sheets on either side of him. Breath labored. And I'm so pleased with myself I can barely stand it. I bite my lip to keep from self-congratulatory laughter.

When I'm face-to-face with my destination, I slide my hand down it—give it a glide—

and it does this weird jerk to the side thing. Like a spasm, whenever I pull down. It twitches and yanks back like he's having a dick seizure, and upon further inspection, I see that something's not right.

OH THE HUMANITY.

Either some doctor botched his circumcision—

or he was born like this or—

something.

I don't know.

But before I can examine further, my grip is released, and the offensive appendage springs like a doorstopper.

Is this why he's bartending? To pay for dick plastic surgery?

And then—

The acrid taste of the sliders I shoveled in earlier climbs its way into the back of my throat, tangy and chunky. I wax on, wax off my arms like the Karate Kid on E and thrash out of the prison of my sheets. Spike them to the floor.

"Are you—"

But I'm flailing my way into the bathroom and then I'm bent over the porcelain savior and puking up everything I've ever eaten in my entire life. Purging everything—except the image of...that.

Some things you can't get rid of.

Now his fingertips are like eels at my shoulders, and I'm cringing at his every touch.

"Too much to drink?" He kind of...chuckles, and I'm hot with anger, sick with my body turning itself inside out.

It couldn't possibly be him or his Frankenstein penis. It's got to be me. Something I did.

I push myself up and wipe my lips, dab at the sweat from my forehead with a length of toilet paper.

I'm too tired to argue. "That must be it," I croak. "You'd better go."

After a few moments of dumbstruck silence, when I realize he hasn't budged, I turn my watery eyes on him, and he's standing there in the doorway, all wounded looking.

But at least he's got his boxer briefs back on.

shudder

"I'm really sorry," I say.

And I am. I'm really sorry he's going to make a lot of girls vomit with that thing, because the rest of him is really kinda spectacular.

But a warning would've been nice?

"You don't want to just wait it out?" I can hear the *Oh fuck* in his voice.

I consider that for 1.3 seconds, and I'm about to speak—but I get another flash in my mind of how that thing Night-at-the-Roxburied. Right in my face.

I retch again and again.

Puking for all the times in my life I should have puked and didn't. For all the times anyone ever needed to. I'm the Jesus Christ of puking. Purging for everyone's sins.

I press my eyes closed at the fucked-uppedness that I just thought that and bask in the embrace of cool ceramic—

until I hear the front door click shut.

*   *   *

CHAPTER 8

The kids are at their special classes, and it's the first time all day I've had a moment to just... think. I inhale and take in a lungful of *eau de* my room: sharpened pencils and Expo marker. Planning's done for the week, parent e-mails are answered, and I'll be damned if I'm going to let this hour slip by without working on my manuscript.

I open the file. Skim through the last ten pages.

YASSSS.

I can do this, this time. I'm a warrior.

I drain the cold remnants of my fourth cup of coffee, and I'm ready to go.

Before I realize it, I've been *tap, tap, tapping* at the keys for a solid forty minutes when the buzz of my phone breaks my concentration.

A small yellow lightning bolt icon has appeared in the top left corner of the home screen.

Looks like I've got a Spark match. Or Google is somehow telling me there's an incoming storm?

Maybe both.

I breathe in deep as I click it—Which one of Quinn and Valerie's white knights will this be?—and then his face pops up.

Anthony, 36

He has dimples. Deep ridges on either side of his face.
Not bad at all.
And he's one of the few who's written something in the pro-file area.

Likes: Fitness, craft beer, baseball, and traveling. Dis-likes: Moody people, prison tattoos, political correct-ness, and poor grammar.

I tap an index finger to my lips at the last two dislikes.
Hmm. I could be onboard with this. But I flip through his pics, just the same. No reason to get too excited yet.
Dark hair. Buzz cut.
Good shoulders.
I wonder who that hot blonde with him in this wedding pic-ture is, but that's okay. I'll allow it.
Things are looking pretty decent, so I alert my fairy god-mothers.

Me: Just got my first Spark match. Huzzah.
Valerie: YEEEEEEEEE
Me: What do I do?
Valerie: Now you can message each other! You've both swiped Right!

Me: Shouldn't I wait for him to—
Quinn: *headdesk* MAKE LIKE NIKE AND JUST DO IT.

I snarl at my phone, then go back to the app.
Really, Anthony, 36?
My thumb hovers over the keyboard a minute. I really wish he'd write first. I don't want to seem desperate.

Me: Fine.

I chew at my bottom lip as I type out three renditions of *Hi* but ultimately settle on:

You had me at good grammar.

My stomach tightens as I hit SEND.
When he doesn't answer right away and I can't get back into the writing, I check out more man options.
Seven of pretty much literally the same guy in different packaging. Plunging V-neck tees. Into the outdoors.
NOPE. NOPE. NOPE.
I shake my head at the screen, and then a gleaming smile stops me cold.
A Taye Diggs look-alike I'd know anywhere.
I check behind me. Like he's there and somehow knows I'm looking at him.
He has written simply *I'm down for whatever,* and the whole time I flip through his pics, my hands tremble. Like some assassin is about to take me out for stumbling upon his deepest, darkest secret.
His are a bit like modeling pictures, and I'm not sure how

I feel about that. Ordinarily I'd be turned off by this—I'm no model and I certainly don't need some guy who's prettier than I am, or someone who's going to judge me by my lack of thigh gap—but I can't peel away my focus.

A staged candid of him laughing, his big back against a tall fence, one hand gripping the metal, the other running through his close-cropped hair.

A belly laugh captured at juuuuust the right moment.

A shot of him on a motorcycle. Taken from a low angle. He's glancing at something to his right this time. Hint of a smirk. It's sexy as hell, and I feel more like I'm paging through *GQ* than looking at a dating app.

These pics are what other guys are trying to achieve but aren't because these are obviously professional shots.

It's douchey, yes. But they're so well done and he's got such an Isaiah-Mustafa-in-those-Old-Spice-commercials swagger, I don't care.

He looks amazing.

Biceps better than the girls and I imagined through the dress shirts he wears to school.

My heart hammers.

Ugh. *Stop it*.

I should just go back to writing. Channel this heat creeping up my neck into my manuscript.

But I can't focus. Can't look away.

And I can't keep this to myself, obviously.

I burst from my chair and trip my way to Quinn's classroom. I stick my head through the doorway and hang on the threshold.

"Valerie's room. Now."

When we clomp our way in there, Val jerks her attention

toward us and the assignment she was writing on the whiteboard goes from crooked and messy scrawl to squiggly limp-dick-of-a-line once I spill the news.

"Are you serious? Hot Sub Guy?" Quinn sits on the top of a student desk and rests her elbows on her knees, her copper eyes wide.

We huddle around her, and I bring my phone back to life.

Nick, 35

Collective gasp.

"But I thought he had a girlfriend—"

"*Shh!*" I race to the door and peek into the hall.

Not suspicious at all.

I shut it and then press my back against it like we're in a lockdown drill and I'm saving all our lives.

"Maybe it's old." Val does a slow pace in front of her desk. Her eyes glaze a bit as she reasons it out. This blows her blissfully-ignorant-about-ugly-things little mind, apparently.

"Maybe." I humor her but can't stop the arc of an eyebrow.

"It could be," she snaps, and I cut my stare to Quinn, who remains silent.

"Of course anything is possible…but come on, you guys. Do you see?"

They're both stricken with such looks of despair, I feel bad. But only slightly.

The panic? excitement? fear? of discovering those pics vanishes and is replaced by a different type of burn beneath my chest.

"You can't possibly admit I'm right about guys?" I don't bother to control the edge to my voice. I just stand there, expectant of an answer—a validation—that doesn't come. Quinn turns away, and I toss up my hands.

"Unbelievable," I mutter.

And storm out.

When I get back to my room, I slump into my desk chair and just sit there. Swiveling. Staring at his profile.

I'm down for whatever, he says.

Yeah, I bet you are.

Hot for his girlfriend my ass.

I swipe Right.

Not a second later, my phone buzzes, and my blood turns to arctic winter. I didn't think he'd swipe Right on me. Particularly since I'm sure he'd have recognized me.

But when I check the notification—one eye open—it's Anthony, 36, responding to my message:

You had *me* at you're hot.

*   *   *

I'm fumbling with my phone and giggling like a moron when I take Billie for her nightly jaunt around the complex. I'm also thoroughly enjoying being That Girl walking and texting. Usually I want to plow down That Girl with my Camry, but I'm seeing things in a whole new light.

Growth!

Anthony, 36, and I spent the better part of the afternoon messaging, and he picked it back up again this evening. Talking everything from which recent box office flops were the floppiest to which presidential candidates, if elected, would have us hopping the next plane to Timbuktu. It's been fun.

Not that I admitted that to Quinn when she asked about him earlier and not that it means a goddamn thing.

I've also learned this Anthony has never been married, he hasn't fathered a fleet of children, and his longest relationship (which ended over a year ago) was just shy of the three-year mark.

All good signs to me.

Maybe I shouldn't be so hard on my friends and their dude choices. Maybe I *have* been too picky.

Him: So what are you doing now?
Me: Lounging around in trashy lingerie, obvi.

I snort.

And then a pang of anxiety, because of course.

I flutter my thumbs across the keyboard.

Me: *looks down* Oh, wait. Nope! Walking my dog and wearing sweats. #mistaken
Him: I could get onboard with that.

"Dammit," I say, and the little boy whizzing by on a scooter does a double take.

I wave. "Oh no—not you. Sorry! Carry on..."

Awkward laughter.

Him: Do you have a kik account?

I pause and blink at the elephant ear caladiums dotting the perimeter of the buildings like a line of deep purple pom-poms.

Me: No, and I don't Snapchat either.
Him: Haha, why not?

I'm getting winded as I drag Billie up the last hill.

Me: Because I'm not in high school? Listen, I'm sorry if I
sent you the wrong vibe with that lingerie joke, but I'm not
gonna sext you, or whatever they're calling it these days.

My pulse quickens.
Guess this is it?
I hold my breath.

Him: No, no—I just meant it might be nice to move this
off Spark. It's a little annoying logging in to the app every time, no?

Too judgy indeed.
I snarl at my screen—and at the prospect of my friends being
right.

Me: Ohhhhhh. Gotcha. Well, why don't we just text
then?
Him: That's essentially what kik is. A way to text without
giving out your phone number.

I laugh.

Me: What, are you in the CIA?
Him: Let's put it this way. There are a lot of crazies out
there.

Me: Right. So does this mean you've been burned by the online thing? Because I hear you. But I'm not "a-scared." I daresay we should maybe even—gasp—talk on the phone. My fingers are getting tired anyway. #thatswhatshesaid

Here.

And I send my phone number before my brain can catch up with the tickle of something unfamiliar his cynicism gives me.

I rub at my chest.

What the balls is that—hope?

But then there's no answer. For like five minutes.

Billie and I have made it to the top of the hill and she's panting away and I'm sweating both from out-of-shapedness and from my one second of not being careful. I look at How Freaking Long that message was and choke back some self-loathing.

Five minutes isn't the end of the world, of course, but there's a politics to texting, I learned after the divorce. When you're having this back and forth and then, all of a sudden, Dude goes silent...and you've been the last to message...

Bzzzt.

I practically slobber all over the phone.

Him: OK, so I can't in good conscience text or call without telling you first that I'm locked up. Don't worry, I'm not a stalker or dangerous in any way. But I won't lie and have you find out later. I was enjoying our conversation, and if you still wish to talk, I'll fill you in all the way.

I blink.

Who shot who in the what now?

Home girl and I have made it to the sidewalk outside my place, and I sink to the curb. The concrete is chilly through my yoga pants, and I read the message again.

Once the proper synapses fire, a surge of HOLY SHIT brings me to my cross trainers.

Me: What are you saying to me right now? You're locked up? How are you—what are you—

I send it, and my head is spinning. There's no way for me to delete the message with my phone number. Stupid Spark.

Stupid Rae. Stupid, stupid, about-to-be-murdered Rae.

My fingers are electrified with fright. Betrayal.

Me: How are you messaging if you're in prison? Seeing movies that we were talking about? Etc...

Why am I even engaging this guy? But I can't help it. I need to know. This is not something I anticipated and my curiosity gets the better of my judgment. I haven't seen my judgment all fricking day.

Him: Prison has changed. We get cell phones snuck in for exorbitant amounts of money. We just have to be careful. Hence the kik account.

Hence. I'll give him *hence.*

And I unmatch. Just like that, Anthony, 36, is out of my life. He may or may not have my phone number, but I can't worry about that right now.

I heave my stupid, stupid self inside and jump on the ol' laptop to research everything I can about Spark's terms and conditions, privacy—and dive into a vat of vino.

*   *   *

I will never live this down.

Sarah's had me telling this story all morning, all afternoon. To everyone we know. Everyone we don't know. The fifth-grade reading specialist. Her mom, over FaceTime.

"At least he was honest…So many guys aren't these days," she says, chuckling into her microwave macaroni and cheese like she has any clue what guys are like these days.

I stop my fork midair and just look at her.

"You're right. He was eventually honest. But, call me crazy, I'm still holding out for—yanno—not prison."

The regular cafeteria dwellers—who never say anything but just shove their faces full of whatever is in the hot lunch line—offer snickers of condolences. I'm pretty sure they don't believe half the things they hear me talk about, and I'm pretty sure I don't care.

When Valerie makes it in, she's wearing a frown that says she knows not to talk about it. Gives my arm a loving little rub.

We sit in silence, the sound of someone chewing a banana somewhere in the room lighting my insides on fire, and Valerie catches my gaze.

All of a sudden, she's insta-laughter. Snorting. Nearly choking on her egg salad.

"What?" I demand. I've caught the chuckles now too, though. I'm too slaphappy from not sleeping at all last night to even function. "What are you laughing at?"

She gives an exaggerated shrug. "I don't know…What do you think I'm laughing at?"

I swat at her forearm. "Not this again. You know this is a thing!"

"Miso-what?" Sarah crinkles her forehead at Val.

"Sound sensitivity," I explain. "The hatred of sound."

"No one was even talking." Sarah shakes her head and stares back into her gluten-free pasta.

"Doesn't matter—Rae-Rae goes all Hulk if she hears someone chewing. Breathing. You name it."

"Isn't the old-fashioned term for that just being a bitch?" Amusement touches Sarah's freckled face.

"Look it up! Science!" I protest, but they just keep laughing. "Aw, you people are worthless." I get up and toss my tray.

"Don't forget we need to do some planning for Quinn's bachelorette weekend," Valerie says. "You wanna come to dinner tonight?"

*   *   *

CHAPTER 9

I walk right into Valerie and Mike's kitchen like I always do. No doorbell, no knock required.

"Honey, I'm home," I call through the toy monsoon they call their living room, and I'm like Santa Claus and the Publishers Clearing House people rolled into one as I stride in with two armfuls of Chinese food.

Valerie cheers and the kids are beside themselves with glee that silly old Auntie Rae is here.

Click.

Val snaps a photo that I know is going on Instagram before I can even say hello, and then she whisks the take-out bags away.

The twins, Amanda and Mae, attach themselves to my thighs. "Auntie Rae! Come play with us!" they say in unison, like they do a lot of things.

But it's not like in *The Shining*. It gives me the warm fuzzies, and I scoop them both up into my arms and cover them with long-overdue smooches.

"Either I'm in way worse shape or you guys are getting too big to be picked up."

"Noooo." Amanda giggles, chubby hands to mouth. "We're only three." She flicks the fingers up like a pro.

"If you say so." I shrug, and they're all smiles and screeches and heart-melting squeezes as I tickle them into oblivion.

"Are you staying over?" Jakey wants to know from the bottom of the stairs, never taking his fourth finger from his mouth.

I give his staticky, sandy hair a pat as the twins are yanking me to their bedroom to show me their *Frozen* dolls.

"Not this time," I tell him. "Next time I'll bring Billie and we'll plan for it, okay?"

He jumps up and down, already in his Spider-Man pajamas, and he follows us upstairs like we're a kid caravan.

On the way, I peek into the baby's room. Blue walls split with a fire-truck paper border. Empty wooden crib glistening in the soft overhead lighting. Rocking chair complete with a teddy bear in the corner.

Such a big, beautiful home. So full of kids and chaos. And quiet moments like these, with a kid attached to each appendage to warm you and love you.

"Where's Frankie?" I ask.

"Dad's got him, in the office," Jakey says, his free hand now wrapped around mine.

I start as I peep inside the dark office and glimpse Mike looking like Schroeder from Peanuts cartoons, all bent over his computer, back slumped like Quasimodo. Frankie's giggling and blowing spit bubbles in an ExerSaucer thing. Bouncing to the nineties rock Mike has pouring from the speakers.

"Hey, you," I say, and he minimizes whatever window he was looking at on the screen and jerks toward me.

"Oh, hi, Rae." He does this exaggerated stretch, like he's ninety-six or ninety-seven, or some ancient tortoise from the Galápagos Islands, and his gaze snaps back to the computer. All business once again.

I'm barely able to sneak Baby Frankie a kiss on his fat cheeks before his siblings are tugging me toward the twins' lair again, and no matter how much merriment, how many giggles, Mike never cracks a smile or has a second glance for any of us.

I set my jaw but then slather on a smile of my own, since I seem to be the only one who notices or cares. Maybe Valerie is just out of fucks to give or she doesn't even have time to realize it with all she's doing to keep the family afloat.

Or maybe she's too tired from all the energy she expends posting photos of family perfection on Facebook. I don't know.

We're three pages into the Curious George book Mae handed me upon entry when Valerie appears at the door, half a grin painted across her porcelain face. "Dinner's all set up."

The kids groan like they rehearsed it, and we laugh.

"Sorry, guys. Knock, knock," she says to Mike from the doorway.

"I'll be right down," he answers, rounded back still to us.

"Want me to bring Frankie?" She makes a silly face at the ten-month-old, and he erupts into wet-sounding giggles.

"Naw, I got him."

She throws up her hands and does the ol' wide eyes at me like *I don't know what's all up his ass* and shakes her head. Drapes a lazy arm around my shoulders as we descend the stairs.

"What do I owe you for this feast, my love?"

I toss her a limp wrist. "Don't worry about it. I'm sure I owe you thousands from all the dinners I've mooched off you over the years."

True story.

She gives me a side squeeze and then we split off, each lifting a twin into a booster seat. I retrieve Jakey's sippy cup of what I'm guessing is milk from the kitchen counter.

Just as I expected, the table's been set to perfection as well—her plates are part of her set of everyday china from her wedding, and they actually match—with adults' orders set in our respective places; each take-out container full of fried rice placed on a diagonal to the left, each complete with a fortune cookie and chopsticks laced through the thin wire handles.

"Nice touch, Martha Stewart." I offer her an eyebrow, and she snorts.

"Martha Stewart wouldn't have served leftovers to the kids... but thank you. I try."

Click.

Another Instagram treasure before we dig in and ruin her display.

Mike comes down when I'm about halfway through my mu shu pork and the kids have long since finished picking at their chicken fingers, their eyes now aglow with tablet screens.

"It's probably cold," Val says, wiping her hands on her napkin.

He shrugs without looking at her. Plops Frankie into his chair.

I try to continue with our conversation about Quinn, about school, but I just feel stupid in front of Mike. All the fun has been sucked from the room once he's in it, and I wonder why this is and if it's my fault. Does he hate me? Or is he always like this? So instead I start to ask him some questions. About his family and about work mostly.

And he does answer. He actually makes eye contact here and

there as he pours hot mustard sauce all over his beef and broccoli. I guess computer systems sales really does it for him.

And then he catches me off guard. "Think you'll go out with Ty again? He seemed to dig you." He glances up at me and shoves half an egg roll into his mouth.

My own mouth has gone dry because I honestly had forgotten Mike was somewhat involved in that fix-up too.

"Um—" It comes out guttural.

"He sent her a . . ." Valerie glances at the kids and then seems to think better of finishing that sentence. Shakes her head. Collects herself. "We're trying a new experiment," she begins again, catching my eye and bailing me out.

God bless her.

Mike gives an eye roll to his plate. "Yeah? And what's that?"

Val dishes on Spark, and each new detail she divulges shrinks me more and more until I'm small enough to run around the table and hide behind my fortune cookie.

Or so I wish.

"Auntie Rae's getting married?" Jakey must be half listening, still sucking away at that finger.

"Ha-ha—no," I say, shoveling in some rice.

"Are you ever getting married?" he singsongs, like the kids in my class do, and I cough up a bite of pork.

Before I can answer, Mike does it for me.

"She *was* married, buddy."

"You were?" The confused little five-year-old rips his gaze from the screen and fixes his big shiny blue eyes on me.

I sit with my mouth hanging open for I'm not sure how long. Still hearing Mike's She was *married* and overanalyzing the intonation of the *was*. That cloying emphasis he put on it.

Just what was that supposed to mean?

"She was, buddy, yes. Go back to your game." Val's tone is sharp. Val to the rescue once again. She taps at Jakey's tablet screen with a perfect fingernail and screws her mouth into a frown.

A moment later: "I don't think we need to be having that conversation with the five-year-old, do you?" She *tsk*s in Mike's direction.

We finish the rest of the meal in relative silence until I start asking the twins a bunch of ridiculous questions about their lives, like what their majors will be in college, how many kids they think they'll have, how much they contribute to their 401(k)s, etcetera, which elicits giddy laughter from them both. A sound that warms the otherwise drafty kitchen.

I won't stop yapping.

But it's in the name of changing the subject and taking the heat off me and my failed marriage as fast as possible. In the name of trying to keep my mind off the tension I feel. The stiffness.

"What's your fortune say?" I ask, tearing into my cookie.

"'The greatest risk is not taking one,'" Val reads. "What's yours?"

"'If winter comes, can spring be far behind?'"

"Ooh—I like that." She beams. "Save that one."

"It's not even a fortune," Mike chimes in.

"He's right. Neither of those is. How about you, Mikey boy? What does the universe have in store for you?" I lean on the table, sarcastic enthusiasm dripping from my fingertips.

"'Your fortune is as sweet as a cookie.'" He snorts. "Um, yeah. This is crap."

Val smacks his forearm.

"Oh, the kids aren't even listening."

I crack a smile—*Like father, like children*—and start clearing the plates.

*   *   *

I offered to help put the kids to bed, but Valerie wanted to do it.

"Stay down here. Relax," she said with a smile and handed me a giant glass of malbec like the excellent friend she is.

And so I sit, with my legs up under me on their Restoration Hardware leather couch, and thumb through Facebook. "Like" the two pictures Val somehow had time to tag me in when I wasn't looking. And sip the lovely wine. The sounds of Mike rinsing dishes, the *clinks* of cups and plates, the *clonks* of plastic on plastic echoing in the space between us.

As I do so, all these questions run like computer code in *The Matrix* in front of my eyes while our dinner exchange claws at my insides.

What had Mike meant by telling Jakey I *was* married? Was that a judgment? Or was he simply telling his kid the truth when he had asked?

Was I being defensive?

And, furthermore, was Valerie's swoop-in meant to rescue me . . . or was that a judgment as well?

I don't think we need to be having that conversation with the five-year-old.

What did that mean?

When I can't take it anymore, I rise from the couch and join Mike in the kitchen. "Can I help?"

"Nah, it's okay" is his response.

"You sure?"

He doesn't answer. But he's generally like that, so I try not to read into it. Just lean my back against the counter, pop a knee—socked foot against a cabinet door—and take another swig of wine.

"Listen, I'm sorry about Ty. I don't know if you're close to him or whatever. He was a nice enough guy. I just…"

He shakes his head, a grimace forming at his mouth, but his focus is still on the Captain America cup in his hand. "I told Val it was a bad idea. Ty's not right for you, I don't think."

I quirk my head his way. "No?"

"No. But I think you could do a lot worse." He suddenly faces me. "I don't know what it is you need—let's be real. But I just didn't see it. So don't worry. I'm not mad if you're not seeing him again. Okay?"

"Okay." All I can do is blink at all of this articulation coming from the Mikester.

"He wants to settle down, have a family. You don't." He shrugs.

I listen to the rush of the faucet as I take that in.

What does this guy think he knows about me? Sums me up with one shrug.

And then: "I don't?"

"Aw, I don't know." He makes a face like he's sorry he said words. "Seems like you don't. You kinda had that before and didn't want it. And now you don't really seem to go out with the same guy more than a few times. Don't ask me for dating advice. I don't know what I'm talking about."

I'm clutching the wineglass like it's Mike's neck and praying it doesn't break in my hands.

"Is that what Val says about me?"

"Is *what* what Val says about you?" asks Val as she enters, wiping her brow with a languid hand.

He laughs. "Nothing. Just making an observation." And then he dries his hands on the fall-themed towels and vanishes back upstairs.

For the next hour, Valerie and I pore over details of Quinn's bachelorette weekend. All the while, my interaction with Mike plays on a loop in my head.

But I can't say anything to her because he's her husband. You can't say anything about someone's husband. You can't even really say anything about someone's boyfriend ever, if you still expect that person to be your friend. That's just how it works.

As much as I would hope she'd side with me or at least commiserate with me, or tell him that was a jerk thing to say and He Barely Knows Me, it's tricky with people's significant others because…well…there's always the chance that they won't side with you. Years of friendship be damned.

And I don't think I could take learning she's not Team Rae about this. Not tonight. So I just stew silently and keep planning the weekend.

"The *Magic Mike* experience?" she repeats, nearly spitting out her vino when I say it, a sparkle in her eye.

"To be clear, we're not talking about your Mike." I indicate the upstairs with my glass.

"Why ever not?" She feigns a wounded look, those doe eyes blinking in mock astonishment, fingertips of her free hand perched over her heart. "Obviously, every day's the *Magic Mike* experience for me!"

We both crack up, and then I say, "Focus! There's no room for discussion of marital bliss right now; this is a GD wedding." I spend the remainder of the evening cackling my way through every last idea while Valerie just blushes—but never once does she suppress a half grin.

*   *   *

Curled up on the couch with my phone and shiraz this time, I twirl my fingers through Billie's fur. Soft strokes and the sweet, fruity sips help to dull the ache I've felt since Valerie's kitchen.

Maybe Mike's right. Maybe Val too. Maybe they're in their kitchen right now, talking about how picky I am and how I threw everything away to bring a different guy home every night. Because that's what I did. That's exactly what I did.

Right?

My glass is drained before I even know it, and I bring the device to life. Check my teeth with the camera function, and they gleam a beautiful shade of purple.

And then I swipe.

I swipe and I swipe Right on lots of guys I ordinarily wouldn't because maybe everyone is right about me.

But I don't want them to be. I'd have the house, the marriage, the babies—but I just don't want to do it with the wrong person.

I wanted Daniel to be right. But he wasn't.

And as sad as that made me and as hard as it was to let that go—to go out with people who are not as good as he was—yeah. That hurts.

But two (or one thousand twenty-two, as it were) wrongs don't make a right.

I have to stop this worrying about what Mike thinks. He doesn't know me; he doesn't know his own wife.

Swipe, swipe, swipe, swipe. Like a bloodthirsty banshee ravenous for her next kill.

Swipe, swipe, swipe, swipe.

Matching just about every other one, but who has time to message?

And then Spark tells me:

You're all out of matches.

#sadface

I wipe sweat from my forehead.

"Well, I guess that's good for a night's work," I say to Billie, who just huffs in response and turns so her ass is in my face.

And I can't help but agree with her.

*   *   *

CHAPTER 10

I skedaddle into the main office to check my mailbox—nothing—and Ida stops me with a look.

"So what's this I hear about a date tonight?" she drawls, all cat-eye frames and boobs pointed my way from her spot at the front desk.

"Geezus—lower your voice. I'm going to kill Quinn and Valerie," I whisper, giving the lobby a look-see for any other respectable humans who might somehow use this information for blackmail.

"What's his name?" The lilt to her voice scoops through the air, with no mind to my request for discretion.

"Andrew. He's a dentist. Forty. And he used to be fat."

She chokes on her coffee. "Was that his tagline?"

"Ha-ha, no. But I'm taking this as a good thing. Because look." I fish my phone out of my pocket and show her the screenshots I've saved of my first Spark date.

"Gurl" is all she says.

"I know!" I take a second and admire the strong jaw. The

purposeful scruff that adorns it. The way he fills out an Under Armour polo.

Then—*ahem*—I'm back.

"Ordinarily, I'd steer clear of someone this pretty because we really haven't messaged that much. He just…wanted to meet."

"How do you know he used to be fat, then?"

"Facebook," I say with a wink. "But I think the fact that he used to be fat means…maybe he's not so full of himself that all he cares about is how he looks. Like maybe he's humble, from former not-so-perfection. I don't know." I flip through the pics again.

Dayum. I hope so.

"Or maybe it means he's super into himself now. Because of *present* perfection," comes a deep male rumble from the recesses of the mail room.

I recognize the swagger of that voice—and freeze. "How long have you been in there?"

"Let me see this guy," Nick says, taking it upon himself to pluck the phone from my fingers. He makes a bunch of grunty sounds like *Hmmm, maybe,* and I'm grasping for the thing back and he's holding it up and out of my reach and I'm sweaty with panic.

"Now, children," Ida says with a chuckle, and we both snap to attention.

He tosses my phone to me, and I fumble but do catch it.

He puts up his palms. "Whoa, I didn't realize you were such an athlete. Nice catch, 'Rae' Lewis."

"Yeah, you're lucky I caught it, or you'd be buying me a new one, Nick…Jonas," I say to his back. That crisp blue dress shirt struts away.

Palm to forehead, and Ida cracks up, a loud chortle echoing its way up to the rafters.

"Hey, wasn't Ray Lewis a murderer?" I spit.

"Charges were dismissed," he tosses over his shoulder.

He's barely out the double doors, and I spill to Ida that I saw him on Spark.

"Gurl" is all she says again. It's all she needs to say.

"I know—how humiliating is that? So he has to have seen me and swiped Left then because we never matched up, and I thought he had a girlfriend, and dear God. Can you just fire him?"

"Sorry, honey. That's above my pay grade. Besides, he's real nice to look at. You will just have to deal."

With that, the phone starts to ring, and Ida moves an acrylicked hand to get it.

"Have fun with Used-to-Be-Fat-Andrew tonight," she adds with a wink.

*   *   *

My hands are shaky as I grip the shot glass. I get to the joint fifteen minutes ahead of time so I can decompress some before Used-to-Be-Fat-Andrew arrives.

I swing my bare legs off the barstool and flick through my messages until I reach my group text with Quinn and Val.

Me: Remind me never to do this again without talking to the dude more.

A few seconds later,

Quinn: You'll be FINE. You don't have that much time to be pen pals. The wedding is four weeks away!

"Don't remind me," I say to the bartender. A girl.

"Pardon me?" she asks, diamond stud in her nose winking in the track lighting.

I smooth on a smile, the Fireball whiskey working its magic already. "Nothing. I'm ready to close out."

I recognize Used-to-Be-Fat-Andrew, DDS, right away as he strides into the place at exactly eight o'clock. He's wearing a gray sport coat, dark jeans, and some sort of man boots. He looks more lumberjack than dentist, really.

I'm not complaining.

"Very punctual" is my opening line as I glide off the barstool and slide my hand into his. "Should we do the awkward first-meeting hug?"

Blue eyes sparkle down at me as he grips my hand and takes in my dress.

"Absolutely," he says with a wide grin, and he wraps his other arm around me.

Swoon. I can smell his Man Soap, and I'm giddy as it swirls in my nose.

"You must be Rae."

"Your table is ready," the hostess says with a smirk I want to slap off her twenty-year-old face, but whatever. I'm on a date with this and she's working tonight. Rae 1, Hostess 0.

As we await the appetizers, he sips a Bud Light draft. I get it. He used to be fat. He's quiet and fidgets, and I thank baby Jesus that I had the brilliant idea of getting things started early with the alcohol because it's helped me not fidget. And not avoid eye contact like he's doing.

But his nervousness is kinda cute.

"So on a scale from one to ten, how much of a deal breaker is it if I don't floss as much as I should?"

He lets out one strong *Ha*—a Shaquille O'Neal of a *Ha*, really—and leans back in his chair, one ankle resting on a tree trunk of a knee. His open jacket reveals sweat marks under his arms as he takes another sip of beer.

Supes adorbs. I probably shouldn't enjoy making men sweat this much, but I am who I am.

I lower my voice a tick. "Is that cliché to ask?"

"You're funny. No." He smiles back. "And that depends...What are we talking here? Every ten years?"

I run my tongue over my front teeth and scrunch my face at him. "Not that long!"

"Good!"

For the next hour and a half, we cover all the basics—he recently bought out his father's practice, born and raised in Florida, blahblahblah. I'm doing the witty banter thing and he's receptive to it, but he's not lobbing too much my way by the time entrées are set out in front of us.

And then we get onto past relationships—in particular, our most recent ones and What Happened There. When it's his turn, his light, kind of doofy but charming demeanor changes.

He stares out into middle space, his eyes glassy, the candle in the center of the table reflecting in them as he speaks.

"She was...younger than me."

"Like, how young?" I ask. #inquiringmindswanttoknow

"Twenty-five."

"You're really slumming it with me, then." I snort.

I wish I hadn't said it—why do I always do that—but I can't help it.

"I was with her for five years. On and off the last two."

"Were you engaged?"

He shrugs. "No."

"Live together?"

"No."

I laugh, a little uncomfortable. Red flags start to wave over his used-to-be-fat head. "How come?"

He looks right at me, intense. Like he's having a fight with her right here. Like he's looking at me and I'm her. Shiver me timbers! I rub at my arms and say nothing. Just let him answer.

"I wasn't sure she was the one. You know?"

"I suppose, yeah. But after five years? How come you were on and off for two?"

He leans in, large forearms peeking out of rolled sleeves now, giant hands I can't picture fitting into mouths gesturing wildly as he speaks. "The breakup just never really stuck for long. Like we'd be broken up and then she'd call me and we'd get together for lunch because we missed each other, and before you knew it, we were back together. Just like that." He snaps his fingers, I guess for effect.

I get it. Trust me, buddy.

I signal for the server—*Another, please?*—and sit back as Andrew describes this toxic relationship I've seen, experienced, a million times. His face is so full of hope when he details the good things about her—and then it flashes something sinister when he talks about their problems. Petty junior high shit that I can't believe a forty-year-old guy would put up with. Or do.

But then again, she's in her twenties.

And he used to be fat.

He doesn't know I know this. About my Facebook research. But I feel for him. Poor fat Andrew from the stories he tells.

After a...while, I decide this guy's way too emotionally invested in these stories. He's being like I am when I relive something—but I'm a writer with a memory that's way too long. I haven't seen anything like this in another person before. For a writer, sure.

But still.

He's not a writer. And it's probably not good.

Third drink comfortably tingling its way up my legs, I'm done with this ex story. Hell, I have an ex-husband and I don't have half as much to say as this guy does about that relationship.

"So tell me"—I might have cut him off, but I'm beyond caring at this point—"when did this end, officially?"

He wraps his hand around his glass. "Two months ago."

I press my lips into a line. Oh.

"How do you know it's over? That this is the time the breakup 'stuck'? Five years is a long time."

I squint like I'm trying to make sense of it all. It's a valid question.

"Because." He scoots his chair in and smiles. His face relaxes, a whisper of a wrinkle or two smoothing across his forehead, and he grabs his fork. "The last time I tried to contact her and get together, she said no."

Any remaining pixie dust I had swirling around in my heart for him fizzles, and I just focus on my fettuccine.

*   *   *

He's not ready. He's nowhere near ready, I text the girls when I get home.

Although he did say he hoped we got together again and he did give me a peck on the cheek, I knew I wouldn't be seeing him again. Nor did I want to.

Quinn: Aw, why not??
Me: He's not over his ex. Poor thing thinks he is, but he's definitely not.
Valerie: Okay, okay but... DB?

I laugh at her persistence.

Me: Too early to tell. But I suppose I couldn't quite characterize him as a douche bag based on this date, no.

It's late, but I've already walked Billie and I'm not altogether unwound from the evening, so I sink into my garden tub in hopes it will loosen my muscles, slow my thoughts. The water is hot enough to turn my submerged parts pink. Hot enough to hurt. And it does. But, damn, it also feels so good.

*   *   *

The images glaze over with the fog of film noir.

That crappy little karaoke bar packed with writers from the conference. Famous writers. Not-so-famous writers. Writers whose work will never be published. All of us alike. All of us tipsy. Clustered around rickety high-top tables and sloshing our craft beers on the splintered wood.

That travel writer from Sacramento, the one who knows how good-looking he is, grabs the mic like he's David Lee

Roth. Soft lights misting down his slicked blond hair. He looks ethereal. Otherworldly hot.

But he sounds like a bag of cats being swung over someone's head.

I crack half a smile at the irony.

He keeps jerking his thumb up to the sound guy, like More volume, why won't this guy give me more volume? *His voice juuuust a note or two sharp of the melody. Either he doesn't know or he doesn't care. I have to respect both.*

His audience pretends to like the arrogant, terrible rendition of Def Leppard's "Pour Some Sugar on Me," so he just keeps smiling. Singing. Eyes closed as if he's Joe freaking Elliott himself.

After a few painful minutes, I peace out for a smoke. It's a chilly September and I'm in chilly Boston, so I hike up the collar of my short trench coat and sip my drink. Rest the pint glass against my cheek as I listen to the sounds of passersby and conflicting muted music from adjacent bars.

"Got a light?" comes a voice to my right.

I cut my stare his way and narrow my gaze. "Hold this." I hand him my beer and snatch the cigarette from his tanned fingers, a grin tugging at my mouth.

"So that was pretty rude," he says.

"What was?"

"You left in the middle of my song."

"You noticed that, didja?" I take a deep drag to light the cig and present it back. "A peace offering."

"I did notice."

"Sorry. I hate eighties music."

The tinge of a frown colors his features, and he scrunches his brow. "You hate men?"

"I'm married," I answer, a chuckle escaping as I exhale, interrupting a smooth stream of smoke.

I'm technically married.

Daniel and I are three months into our separation, three months away from divorce. I'm three months into sleeping on Bridget's futon.

But this guy doesn't need to know any of that.

"And I like to think I don't hate anybody," I continue, struggling to stifle the lilt in my tone. *"Your singing, on the other hand…"*

"That bad, huh?"

He clutches at his heart and I take that opportunity to sneak a peek at his third finger. He's married too.

"Yep," I answer, steady stream of smoke this time, and he doesn't bother holding back his laughter.

"See what I mean? Rude."

"What's rude is disturbing someone while she's smoking, making assumptions, and not even disclosing your name."

"Hmm. Noted." His smile deepens, and he takes a step closer, his shoes crunching on the damp pavement. *"Jesse,"* he says. *"And I'm sorry."*

I face forward, still leaning a shoulder against the sandstone. Looking out over the street and the cloud of smoke I emit, I repeat the name.

"Very good. And you are?" Another step in.

The air buzzes between us, as electric as the bug zapper flickering a bright purple over the scene.

I look up at him through my eyelashes. What a smug fricking dude.

But I can't help but let his stare draw me in. He knows what he's doing. He knows exactly.

I don't.
"I'm Rae," I say. "I'm a writer too."

*   *   *

I emerge from the tub feeling relaxed and sleepy. Until I see I have three missed Spark notifications—one message from Used-to-Be-Fat-Andrew, which I ignore; one match, with Nick, 35; and one message from him as well.

Nick, 35

Apparently we matched while I was taking my bath and apparently he's messaged me. And apparently OMFG!

Him: Okay, instead of Rae Lewis, how about Mike Rae? Although that's kind of obscure. Rae Rice? Your skillz were nothing short of impressive today.

He sent it eight minutes ago.
Before I can even get the rest of my robe on, my fingers are flying over the screen, and I've sent the reply.

Me: Uhm. It's Jerry Rice. #nailedit
Immediate response: Oh, there's a Ray Rice. #Googleit

And I do. And goddammit.

Him: Admit it. You only know Jerry Rice from Dancing with the Stars.
Me: I admit nothing.

There're a few minutes of lull during which I get all the nightly routine stuff out of the way—if he could see me now, all head-toweled and face-creamed—and then he messages again.

I can hear the swagger in his words.

Yes, his words swagger.

Him: Date with Mr. Used-to-Be-Fat must not have panned out. You're home pretty early, no?
Me: That's DOCTOR Used-to-Be-Fat to you, and I was home by ten. #backtothedrawingboard

I linger over the app for a solid thirty seconds and then something in my chest yanks me back.

Me: Hey, aren't you...attached? What are you doing on Spark anyway?

I can't resist.

But his answer is immediate.

Him: My profile is old, actually. But when I heard you talking about Spark this afternoon, I thought I'd sign on and mess with you. #consideryourselfmessedwith Besides, you never contacted me about when you want to discuss the set.
Me: The set—right! Are you available tomorrow after school? We're having rehearsal.
Him: I'm your man! And it sounds like, after tonight, you're gonna need one!
Me: Har har. Well, as much as I'd love to stay and hear

all your theories on why my date was Destined to Fail, I
need to get my beauty rest. You subbing at all this week?
Him: Time will tell . . . See you at rehearsal.

But I stare at the design in my ceiling for a spell and wait
for my heartbeat to slow down. Why does talking to him make
me so nervous? I didn't do anything wrong, say anything wrong.
The only thing wrong is how succulent he looks in his suit
pants. Because that just ain't right.

I stare and I stare, wondering with each passing minute what
he would have said next, had I not shut down the conversation.

Why he messaged at all.

To mess with me, for real? Because I hadn't texted him about
the set?

I decide I'm reading too much into things.

But, dammit, why can't I just effing find someone who can
banter like that, who's as sexy as that, who is not, in fact, attached like that?

What am I sending out into the world to deserve this, and
do I have the energy to wade through it all?

Probably not.

Everything haunts me long after my eyes drift shut and into
the morning when I sneak back onto Spark to see if that really
happened last night. Long after I message Andrew back while I
zigzag through traffic. Long after I get to work late (again) and
zigzag through the parents' hundred-thousand-dollar cars.

Through small talk, through kids in the hall, through e-mails,
through lessons.

Off to zigzag my way through another day.

                    *   *   *

CHAPTER 11

At rehearsal the next day, Val and Quinn leave it to me to do all the directing, and they simply act as kid wranglers, which is exactly what I need them to be. If not for them, Damian Adler (aptly named—why do parents still name their kids Damian??) would be lighting things on fire backstage and Jenny Linn may have succeeded in climbing up to the rafters this time.

I've finally got the first scene staged and we're running through the blocking when Nick comes in—and, of course, derails all the discipline and focus I've worked so hard to create, as anyone new, any distraction, any reason to lose focus, does in first grade (in any grade).

"Mr. Greene!" It's like Justin Timberlake himself has graced us with his presence, except for the fact that these kids probably don't know who that is. Kids are yelling, other kids are screaming because their friends are yelling, and they're all running around like they snorted some kind of bath salts during their afternoon snack.

Quinn and Valerie have given up their duties in light of this new stimulus, since it seems there's nothing to do but allow it to run its course—a quick and brutal downpour before the storm lets up.

We watch him as he raises a long finger to his lips and grins. "Hey, guys."

And, like he's performed some kind of hot-guy voodoo on them, they begin to settle down.

"Can you all sit for me for a minute?" He glances at me. "That okay?" he asks.

I gesture toward him like *Be my guest.*

He continues. "Did you know that Miss Wallace wrote this play you're performing?"

Even though I absolutely did tell them, their faces brighten with the excitement of hearing about it for the first time. Ella Ryan lets out a "Wow, really?" that is audible above the murmurs of enthusiasm.

"Yes, and did you know it's true?"

"What do you mean?" she wants to know.

"Well, what's it about?" he presses.

"Native American tribes in Florida," a few of them chant on top of one another.

"Right, and so these are actual cultures that actually originated here."

This is met with more oohs and ahhs.

"It's a part of our history. Which is particularly cool to me"—he turns back toward me a sec—"because I'm usually a history teacher. I've taught history at other schools."

"Very cool," I chime in and join him at the front of the stage. "And let me know if you guys have any questions about anything in the play. Kind of goes along well with what we've been studying in social studies."

"Miss Wallace?" Madison LaRue waves her hand high.

"Yes?"

"Can I go to the bathroom?"

"I hope you can…"

She just looks at me.

"Go right ahead, sweetie." I snort. "Now let's get back to it."

When the kids have settled into their places and we've started scene three again, Nick joins me, Val, and Quinn at the center of the auditorium.

He sits in front of the three of us and flips around, face full of concern. "Hey, I didn't mean to 'mansplain' to them why the play was cool—which it is, by the way. Deborah gave me a copy of the script. Good stuff."

"I didn't think you were."

"Naw, and we're used to having kids listen more quickly and attentively to male teachers than female teachers, no matter who they are. It's just a fact of education. No matter how much they respect us—which they do," Quinn says.

"It's the same at home even," Valerie chimes in. "My husband doesn't say too much by way of discipline or direction, but the minute he does, they're giving him their rapt attention."

"Well, then… I'm sorry?" He winces. "But I'm also glad to be of help?"

"Good answer." Quinn pats him on the arm. "I can tell you've been trained well."

After the next scene is over, Valerie and Quinn supervise the kids while Nick and I pore over the set design.

"It's a simple concept, really," I say. "This is first grade, and our budget is, like… a dollar."

"I got this. I'll draw up some things and we can talk about them at the next rehearsal."

"Sounds good."

"Yanno, I did read the script," he says, tongue flicking across his gleaming teeth.

"Yeah?"

"And I was really impressed."

"Oh, you're a theater critic now?"

"I'm just saying…*Indigenous People of Florida*? Not a topic most first-grade plays tackle. I'm not even sure I could pronounce *indigenous* when I was in the first grade."

"Or now." I laugh. "Well, I happen to think these kids can handle more than what we give them, you know? Not that I want them to grow up too fast, but I don't think we should baby them either. We should challenge them. Hold them to high standards. Because when we do, they rise to the challenge."

"Are you always like this?"

"Pretty much."

"Good. I like that."

We hold a stare a little longer than is comfortable for me, and then it's back to the Apalachee scene.

When I get home, I send him a text:

Me: Thanks for your help today, Mr. Greene.
Nick: My pleasure.

*   *   *

The next few days are a blur of Spark messages and dates. I've never been more exhausted, mentally and physically, but I've also never felt as powerful and desirable as I do right now.

"So who's on tap tonight?" asks Sarah when she stops by the

lounge to grade during her break and pops a squat next to me at the table.

"Gross," I say and then crack up at the insinuation. "I have not given a blowie to a single one of these guys, you filthy animal—let alone have I even wanted to make out with any of them. In fact, the whole thing has been The Worst so far."

"It was just a question." She bats her eyes. "But if you're not having any fun with these guys, why are you doing this? Why the date marathon?"

I shrug into my pile o' papers. "It's a sociological experiment."

"And?"

"And"—I hook an eyebrow at her—"I'm learning a lot. For instance." I put up a *One second* finger and scroll through to tonight's bachelor of choice. "Tonight, there's Barrett. A marathoner. He does Ironman races too. 'I eat a lot of kale, but I do enjoy a burger every now and then,' he says on his profile. See? He's down to earth." I snort.

"Are you going to take up running?"

"Ha. No. But I don't seem to be getting anywhere following my rules, and I promised the girls I'd venture out of my comfort zone. Bend some of my Spark rules to appease them. There's got to be someone who's wedding date acceptable. And what's so wrong with going out with someone who's healthy?"

I stop at the sound of a jaunty little whistle making its way toward us from down the hall, and then Nick struts into the lounge. He masterfully pulls off a pink dress shirt like so few men really can—despite what their significant others tell them. He's whistling absentmindedly, in a way that feels like it's not absentminded at all, and I both love and hate him for it.

I've thought about him since our little encounter at play practice, but I haven't seen him since then, and of course my worst fears are being realized—I'm flushing to what has got to be a deep shade of berry at the mere sight of him.

Kill me now.

"How's it hanging, ladies?" He breezes right past us and parks his *nom*able *tuchas* over by the coffee station.

"We're fab-ulous," Sarah says, a flirty little drag leaking into her response. "Sixth grade taking it easy on you today?"

His eyes bug and he hooks a finger under his collar like he's letting out some steam. "Man, twelve-year-old girls will say anything. Sheesh!"

"Between them and Ida, you have to be feeling pretty good about yourself this week." I laugh.

"I don't know about that, but that Ida sure doesn't let up, does she?" He's shaking his head at the Keurig, a deep smile exposing those gleaming teeth.

"She's harmless," I say. "But if you think she's going to let you escape easily, you'd be wrong." I gesture with the purple pen I'm using for grading.

He laughs. We all do.

Actually, the sound that comes out of me is more like the chattering of a rabid capuchin monkey, but it's the best I can do. I'm all fluttery because he's in here, and I'm pretty sure my face is a few degrees away from catching itself ablaze.

I'm like a sixth grader myself; and the more awkward I am, the warmer I get. My entire torso is, like, steaming through my blouse. Why in the Sam Hill did I wear this unbreathable fabr—

I just want him to leave.

Idaaaaaaaaa.

My attempts at mental telepathy aren't working, and so

Sarah makes small talk with Nick while he waits for his java to brew, one arrogant leg draped over the other. His gestures are animated as he speaks.

"I suppose I'd better be getting back to the lions' den," he says when his coffee is ready, and he begins his mosey on back toward the door. But before he's gone, he does an about-face.

It catches me off guard when he snags my gaze for such a split second that I'm not sure it even happens. But then there's no mistaking the knowing twinkle in his dark eyes.

"You have yourselves a lovely day, ladies." He's all dimples and double finger points in ironic douchiness (or is it just that I want it to be ironic? I don't know) and he flips back around, waggles a few fingers at us behind his back, and disappears.

Once he's gone, Sarah's mouth goes agape and she starts hitting me. "Whattttt was that?"

"Whatever do you mean?" I'm rubbing at the sore spots her gel-manicured fingers are leaving on my arms.

"You turned bright red the second he came in here and your snarky little Rae comments were conspicuously at a minimum. Spill."

I run my tongue along my teeth and gauge if Sarah can be trusted. I don't want to tell Valerie and Quinn about this yet— I just want to bask in the excitement of...whatever this is...a crush? For just a liiiiiiittle while longer.

But I need to process it with somebody!

So I grab Sarah's hands like a middle schooler. This is who I am today. I've accepted it.

And I spill.

When I'm done dishing on, really, the nothingness of what has happened, she leans all the way back in her chair and twirls the ends of her platinum waves. "Oh. It is *on*."

"But it's not on. It can't be on. He has a girlfriend. Don't encourage me!" I can't contain the smile forcing my mouth as wide as it will go, and I'm giddy with laughter.

Maybe telling her was bad because now it's, like, legitimizing it.

"I heard he made it up," she says, her gaze a dare. A challenge.

"Where'd you hear that from?"

"Just a rumbling among the fourth-grade teachers…"

"Regardless. Work is work," I say, firm. Hoping to convince myself.

"Well, then you'd better hope this Barrett is a welcome distraction tonight," she says into her tea, "because it seems pretty *on* to me."

I throw her an eye roll, and just as I do, my phone buzzes.

"Oh. My. God." She screeches. "It's him, isn't it?" She's practically pulling my arm off as I'm shushing her like some old school librarian.

Palm pressed into the air to calm her, I confirm, failing miserably in my attempt to look annoyed. "It's him."

"What did he say?" She's whiny and we're ridiculous and adorable (I mean, probably) and so, *so* annoying, but we don't GAF.

Until I do, because Quinn saunters in with her leather teacher bag.

"What did who say?" Suddenly she's all copper eyes in my face, and I have to yank my phone away and set it facedown on the table.

"The guy I'm seeing tonight. Barrett." I set my jaw at Sarah and give her a side eye, and I pray to jumping Jehoshaphat that she's catching what I'm throwing.

This answer seems to appease Quinn, though, and Sarah plays along with "Ooh—where's he taking you?" so my blood goes back to normal human speed and I calm the hell down.

"We're just going to a beer-tasting place."

"He's not feeding you?" Sarah hitches an upper lip, Elvis style, and returns her attention to the math tests in front of her.

I chuckle. "I actually have no idea. We're meeting at six thirty, so I've got to fly like a bat out of hell to get home and take care of Billie. Shave the ol' legs. You know—"

"You're shaving your legs this time? *Muy* impressive!" Quinn and Sarah cackle like the bitches they are and smack each other five.

"What's this? I don't like this new little alliance." I gesture between the two of them with my grading pen. "I always shave my legs before these dates. How dare you. Even for the ones I know are going to be bad."

They're still laughing, and I decide to change the subject.

"Where are you off to, missy?" I stab at Quinn's bag.

"I have to go meet with the cake lady real quick. Hot Sub Guy is going to watch my kids until I get back. I just ran into him in the hall. Pretty in pink if I ever did see it!" She fans herself.

Sarah is squeezing the circulation out of my leg under the table, and I'm choking back the urge to full-on guffaw.

Middle schoolers indeed.

"Oh?" is all I can muster. I bite down a tad too hard on my bottom lip.

"That sounds fun," Sarah says, doing better than I am at holding it together.

"Fun, annoying. Potato, potahto. Don't get married." She tosses a limp wrist at us, blows me a kiss, and then she's out.

And part of me stews as I watch her leave.

Don't get married. Seriously? Who the hell is she trying to convince she's so cool? Sarah? She damn well isn't doing it for me.

But the fakeness to her tone—her very air of blasé—leaves a bad taste in my mouth for the rest of the afternoon, and I can't even enjoy the texts Nick sends, which are all hilarious things Ida has done today or surprisingly suggestive things sixth-grade girls have said to him (I might need to have a talk with their teachers!).

Sarah grilled me when Quinn left: "So now you're lying to your best friends?"

But I just can't deal with their judgy comments right now.

This is the first fun I've had in a long time. And I know it's just flirting and I know it can't go anywhere but #godddddddd.

*   *   *

Barrett is already inside the brewery when I arrive—has already paid for himself and is a few "tastes" in before I even get there—so I am already somewhat disenchanted with him when I have to shell out my own twelve bucks to get in. I mean, #independentwoman and all that, but still. Really, pal? He is deep within the crowd of yuppie thirty-somethings and nowhere near the entrance waiting for me. Swoon. And I have to play a less-fun version of Where's Waldo? amidst plaid button-downs and sloppy corporate attire, loose ties and rolled sleeves. Girls who've shed their blazers and are now allowed to expose their shoulders to whomever they want.

But there he is, in the middle of the beer line, and pretty accurate to his pictures online. Six foot something, band shirt under a short-sleeved button-down. A little more Nordic look-ing than my usual jam, but still.

Win.

It has finally stopped raining. Once I'm properly sampled up and we've been reasonably acquainted, we make our way out-side to the patio—picnic-style tables nestled beneath a ceiling of white-light strands. If it weren't for the humidity, it might be pleasant, but my jean jacket and the air all but choke me as we find a quiet spot to talk.

And we do.

He's pretty chatty, though I'm not even sure what all he's talking about. I try to be interested in his race stories just like I'm sure he's trying to be interested in my writing stuff.

We each nod as the other speaks. We drink. We refill the commemorative pint glasses we get to keep.

"So tell me about your divorce," he says. Kind of suddenly. And with all the nonchalance of *Tell me about your day.*

This topic takes the hops out of my—Who am I kidding? I know nothing about beer. But seriously. I've known this guy thirty minutes and I'm not really ready to talk about my divorce with him. Something about the fact that he wants me to talk about it right now claws at my insides.

Inner she-beast fighting to get out again?

The bench I'm sitting on is damp, and I can feel it through my dress—the same black dress I've taken to calling my first-date uniform because I've worn it every time I've gone out this week (All hail, Febreze!). I can feel the wetness through the jean jacket I'm now sitting on, the air almost gooey in my lungs, and it hangs around Barrett and me, between us, like a clothes-line of dirty laundry he's apparently wanting to air right here, right now.

I ease back the lager something or other—bring me a vodka soda any day—and it leaves a skunky taste on my tongue.

But I think it's supposed to be that way.

Regardless, it buys me a second before I launch into the college essay version of my divorce that I've gotten so good at rattling off, I'm sure I sound unaffected.

You know, like a serial killer.

His response is simply: "We all have our things. Don't worry about it." And he smiles.

And I'm put off by that too. Because fuck this guy. I don't need his validation and I don't need his sympathy.

What I need is a goddamn menu and another skunky beer.

"You know what I'm looking forward to?" I ask, tone bright.

"What's that?" He leans in, pale blue eyes blinking a sluggish, alcohol-addled blink.

"I can't wait for when we're all microchipped, so when meeting people, someone can just go *scan wrist* and save, like, hours of backstory. Because I'm really tired of explaining mine."

He laughs, but I'm kinda serious.

"It's not so bad." He touches my arm. And then: "You want to try that wheat beer?"

*   *   *

Well? Nick writes midway through the evening. When I felt my phone vibrate from inside my purse during Barrett's story about how his company's monthly quotas work, I had thought maybe it was going to be Quinn and Val, but alas. I was wrong. I had wanted to check it…but I waited like a good girl until I excused myself to the restroom.

Meh is all I respond, because it's weird chatting with him about my dates. But then I'm just buzzed enough because there is zero food at this beer-tasting place, and I had run home so quickly after school for Billie, I didn't have time to eat even a precautionary banana or cereal bar beforehand.

> Me: I think this is like one of those meet-and-greet dates. Never experienced one before. Have you ever done that?
> Nick: I'm not sure what you mean?

But then I realize I've been in the bathroom a scooch too long when the girl who came in after me has come and gone; so instead of answering my new text pal, I head back out into the wild and search for Barrett's shaggy hair.

"You ready?" he says when I return to the spot where we've been parked for the last hour and a half.

"Um—yeah?" I swipe my umbrella from the bench and toss it into my purse, my stomach rumbly-tumbly and hoping he's about to suggest dinner. Not because I'm so interested in him but because I don't really have an opinion yet and holy hell I'm famished all of a sudden.

My phone vibrates again, and I put my hand on it. *There, there.* I don't know. I'm fuzzy around the edges and in need of grease and carbs. Stat.

"Where did you park?" Barrett asks, a hand at the small of my back, and I can't tell if it's affectionate or, like, pushing me the hell out the door.

I gesture toward my Camry with my phone when we get closer, and he says that's great because his vehicle is near too.

Jeep. Totally fits.

We walk in silence and I'm wondering what it was I did to make this dude want to leave an hour and a half in. Not that

I'm all that broken up about it, but still. I thought I was a delight.

"This is me," I say, fumbling to retrieve my keys.

"I had a nice time," he says, and he leans against my driver's side door. Kind of familiar for my tastes. Expression unreadable.

I locate my keys. Yes!

"I hope we can get together again sometime," he says, and he wraps his arms around my shoulders. Starts to rub them in firm, confusing strokes with his long, investment banking fingers.

"Wow, you're . . . really gettin' in there" is all I can say. I don't even know where it comes from, but I'm so perplexed by the brevity of this date, the haze in his stare, the evenness of his tone—and now this weird back rub?

My stomach is screeeeeaming at him—*Get your mitts off her shoulders and put some food in me!*—when he leans in for a kiss.

"Really?" I ask. And my tone isn't bitchy. It's straight-up confused. It's like I don't even have control over what I'm saying. Words are just coming out when food should be going in.

He chuckles, and his sudden forwardness—based on no real chemistry in this ninety-minute whatever-this-was—grates on me.

"What do you mean?" he asks, a grin tugging at his thin lips

"I just . . . wasn't sure what you were thinking. You're hard to read, I guess?"

He somehow takes this as an invitation and kisses me. There's nothing spectacular about it. Just lips pressing lips. No fireworks, no sparklers—no Fourth of July bang-snap things, even.

He pulls back, and a lazy smile crawls its way up his face. Creases his eyes at the corners.

It doesn't strike me as a real smile. But what do I know? I've known this guy ninety minutes.

"I just—had to do that," he says.

It sounds like he's quoting some terrible movie and suddenly my disdain for him electrifies my whole body. It's like he's saying this because it's what he thinks he's supposed to say. Like that's charming.

Furthermore, it's friggin' eight o'clock. If he digs me all that much, he'd want to go somewhere else where we could talk more. Eat. Spend more time. Get to know the wonder that is Rae.

Again, I don't care, but, like, what is this guy pulling?

"Thanks again," I say before I get into my car.

But even that pisses me off because what exactly am I thanking him for?

"Oh, did you pay…?" was his only acknowledgment when he noticed the pint glass in my hand when I first found him. With a dot-dot-dot at the end of that thought and nothing else.

Damaged, Nick explained once I elaborated on the state of my date, back in the sanctity of my apartment.

Nick: He's probably a serial online dater so he doesn't want to spend the money or the time, and he probably orchestrates these quick dates to see if he's interested and then tries to get the person into bed.
Me: He didn't ask me to go anywhere else, though…

Not that I gave a shit. But still.

Nick: Well, it doesn't sound like you were too receptive, hon.

I smile at the memory of my candor.
Wow, you're... really gettin' in there.
Yeah, I'm the best.

Me: You think he wanted to sleep with me?
Nick: ...*gives you a look*
Me: What look is that?
Nick: Of course he wanted to sleep with you.

After a few minutes of pondering:

Me: Dudes be crazy. *soaks self in alcohol*
Nick: How about soaking yourself in nourishment instead? You eat anything yet?
Me: PSH. I put in a pizza the second I walked through
the door. You don't have to worry about me, Mom.

Too late is Nick's response, and I sit and stare at that message
a lot longer than I should.
And then:

Me: So a little birdie told me today that your girlfriend is
fictitious. True or false?

I can't help myself.

Nick: Damn, blunt! I like it! That rumor is true. I actually
just got out of something recently, but I find it's easier
to say you're attached when working in a school. There
are always the Idas, there are always distractions. I find
if I say I'm in a relationship, people tend to take me a

little more seriously. Not that I think I'm all that whatever or anything, but it's hard being a guy in a school full of women.

Me: Oh, I feel so bad for you. How brave of you to get out of bed every day. #pleasehearthesarcasm

Nick: Fair enough, LOL.

Me: How come I'm the lucky one who gets the truth?

Nick: Something tells me you're different. And I think we could be friends. Didn't want to lie to you.

Me: I'm different, all right. Haha.

*   *   *

CHAPTER 12

Friday afternoon can't. Come. Fast. Enough.

"You guys leaving straight from work?" Sarah asks, and I can hear the hurt seep into her voice that she wasn't invited to this bachelorette weekend in Miami with the big girls.

"Yes, ma'am!" I say, crumpling up a paper towel and launching it into my desk trash can. "Two nights of pure unadulterated fun. It'll be just like college. Except, you know, we're a hundred years old now. Thanks again for watching Billie for me." I hand her my spare key. "And just remember—no questionable fluids on my sheets. Or couch."

She smacks me. "Billie and I are going to have a snuggle-icious weekend. You're the one who's going to have to worry about questionable fluids. Keep your phone on you at all times, please! And probably hand sanitizer."

I hug her and pepper the air with kisses—klassin' it up—and then I'm off to grab my chicas after afternoon car pool.

"Why are you driving my car? Or, I should say, why am I

letting you drive Phil's car?" Quinn asks as I guide her into the passenger's side.

"Because I'm in charge this weekend, ladies. And what I say goes. Make sure you thank Phil for the use of his Porsche Cayenne. I'm sure we'll fit in quite nicely this weekend. It's bigger and safer than my car and I'm sure it'll be just the ticket." A beat. "And now that we're done with the safety portion of the weekend, I'm also driving because—hello—I'm here to ensure you have a good time." I look back at Val. "Both of you."

"Can we tell her now?" Valerie's voice quivers (with excitement? terror?) from the backseat.

"Tell me what?"

"What Rae's got planned for you…"

"Don't blame this all on me." I glare into the rearview mirror. "You personally okayed everything on the itinerary."

"There's an itinerary?" Quinn sounds disappointed.

"Well—I mean, Valerie was involved," I say, and we burst into laughter as we make our way down I-95.

*   *   *

An hour later, we arrive in South Beach. The ocean is an endless stretch of teal that makes one wonder why anyone would settle for a pool at all, ever. The beach sprawls—a flawless white. Were it not for the aggressive afternoon sun, the scene might look like a winter landscape, frosty blues and whites painted across a canvas.

At the sight of it, Quinn squeals when we roll up to the hotel, so I feel pretty good about my life choices.

"What's first?" She's practically licking her lips, doing stiff little claps like if her fingers touch all the way she'll either break a nail or her hands will explode.

The excitement in her voice almost makes this price tag worth it. Heh. And when the girls clutch each other and screech at each new amenity, it lights me from within.

The reflective marble that shines almost liquid in the lobby, the smell breezing its way through as we traipse over to the bell-hop station.

"It's almost like…cotton candy heaven!" Val says, closing her eyes and taking a dreamy whiff like she's guest of honor at the damn Wonka Factory.

"They pump special aromas into the air-conditioning, it said online," I say, and I feel like Willy Wonka himself as I hand the last of my bags to the bangable bellhop. He's not orange, but he's got a golden glaze from the sun, and I'm guessing that's where the metaphor ends.

"Here's hoping there aren't hallucinogens in it…" I throw the guy a look and he smiles, Mario Lopez dimples popping out to say hello.

"Here's hoping there are." Quinn bites her bottom lip as she unapologetically stares at his ass, and we follow him to the elevator.

"What's the occasion that has you beautiful ladies joining us this weekend?" A. C. Slater presses the button for the second floor. I had wanted to get an ocean walkout, but Mike wouldn't agree to the upgrade, so Valerie and I had to settle on an ocean view.

First-world problems.

"This girl right here is getting married in three weeks," I say, tousling the ends of her wavy hair, "so we're spending some girl time together."

His smile deepens. "Well, let us know if you need anything. I'm Armando." He holds open the elevator door with a sun-kissed arm, and we all file out.

"Will do." I hand him a fiver and give a quirk of an eyebrow.

"A suite?" Quinn gasps when we reach it, and tears well in her copper eyes as she takes it all in—the marshmallowy king beds, the sparkling glass shower, the size of the private veranda.

"Nothing but the best for my girls this weekend." I drape a lazy arm around each of them.

"Okay, but you sound like a madam," Val says.

"Will you lighten the hell up?" I ask, producing a flask from the wicker purse I scored just for the occasion.

And—uh—the flask too.

I offer it to her. "Do you trust me?"

"Famous last words," she says, yanking the thing from my fingertips. "Not ominous at all."

*   *   *

Much to my utter delight, we are sprawled out in cabanas near the pool not thirty minutes later. Okay, I get the allure of this particular pool—endless frothy waterfalls that soothe like bath-water when we dip our feet.

"Oh, Sven." Quinn wiggles her fingers at the Thor-looking cabana boy. "We're ready to order when you are."

"Is that his name?" I'm already feeling my sips from the flask so I can't remember if he actually told us that or if Q's just de-cided he looks like a Sven.

Side note: I've never really had a thing for dudes in banana hammocks, but I'm starting to understand the appeal as Sven strolls his way over in a deep green one.

"Does it matter what his name is?" She rearranges her enormous, floppy sun hat and looks at me over her equally giant shades.

"Shh!"

We all laugh and laugh and laugh.

Quinn—my Quinn—is back. And I can't wait to spend this weekend with her.

I turn to Valerie, who looks amazing swathed in a classic black swimsuit with the sides cut out. Gold hoops at each hip. "You are rocking the hell out of that monokini, girl. Where did you get it?"

"Preach!" Quinn toasts her with the piña colada Sven has just set before her. "Especially for having birthed all those babies. How many again?"

"Oh my God. You're drunk already." Valerie snorts, but it's loud enough that I can tell she is well on her way too, and this is already the best weekend ever.

"What's on tap for this evening?" Quinn takes a swig through the straw.

"Maybe Armando." I immediately lose it over Sarah's joke from the other day.

And then I straighten up. Take a glorious swig of my daiquiri. Its strawberry goodness electrifies my taste buds and sends a chill right through me as it goes down.

So smooth.

"We have to stop being such vultures," I say, feeling a pang of guilt for lusting after every piece of man candy strewn about the lovely candy dish that is this pool.

"Why?" Valerie yanks back, and I love her for this. "When have they ever stopped?"

I give a conceding shrug and answer Quinn's question.

"Tonight, Valerie and I thought we'd pamper ourselves. Grab some dinner and get massages and pedis at the hotel spa. It's open twenty-four seven, baby."

"That all sounds like a dream, but—eww!" Quinn grimaces. "Who's getting a pedicure at four a.m.?"

I squish my face at the pretty pink umbrella in my drink. "That's . . . probably not what people are getting at that time."

"Yeah, they're probably getting handies." Val snorts again, and we all crack up.

*   *   *

I stay under the sheen of a light, continual buzz that leaves everything just a little fuzzy around the edges. And gleaming. Like an Instagram filter.

"So Barrett? He's a no-go?" Valerie drags out her words and then emits a long groan of pleasure, which, to be quite honest, has been making Quinn and me a tad uncomfortable for the last forty minutes because they sound like sex noises. We keep sneaking each other the ol' wide eyes and then trying not to laugh.

That said, the deep-tissue massages are so luxurious I have had to stifle my own sex noises here and there, so I can't be too critical; these chicks really know what they're doing. And I'm actually somewhat relieved they gave us women instead of men, because with the way my two besties seem ready to Turn Up, I'm not sure we wouldn't get kicked out of this joint if they had dudes massaging us.

"Which one is Barrett again?" I ask, and she swats at the air just out of reach of me.

"Probably," I say. "It was just weird. No chemistry, really. But he was trying to force there to be. Nick said—"

Shit.

"Nick as in Hot Sub Guy?" Valerie wants to know. She's at Eleven in an instant.

"Yes, he moonlights at Quiznos," I deadpan.

"Is Quiznos still a thing?" Quinn smacks her lips. "Now I'm hungry."

"Yeah, well, I was too, and that's one of the reasons Barrett's a no-go."

"I don't understand. You were talking to Hot Sub Guy about your date?"

I wave off the masseuse. "Thank you," I say. "That's good for me."

She gives a small smile and GTFO. This girl totally gets me.

"No, I wasn't talking to Hot Sub Guy about my date," I lie. Sit up. Tighten the towel under my armpits. "I was talking about it to Ida, and he happened to overhear. And then he put in his two cents."

That's . . . almost true?

"What did he say?" Quinn's starfished herself and her masseuse girl is making faces but is ultimately being amazingly patient with the three of our tipsy asses.

They must be used to it.

I trace the cushy piping that lines the massage table with a lazy finger. I don't make eye contact with her. "He said that Barrett was probably just trying to sleep with me."

"Duh," she says, and her massage is over.

I give a sad half grin. Blunt Quinn's my favorite. I've missed her.

"I could have told you that. But, I mean, if he wants to fuck you, he's got to feed you, amirite?"

"Oh gawd." Head in my hands. "Are you girls sure you want

to do cocktails at the beach bar? I'm afraid we're going to get ourselves arrested."

"*Ay dios mio*. Yes."

And that settles it. After shoveling our faces full of gourmet burgers and duck-fat fries at the hotel's five-star restaurant, I consider myself to be killing it here so far. Everything is within walking distance, I'm keeping us hydrated and well fed, and the girls seem to be having the weekend of their lives.

In no time at all, Valerie and I are doing a white-girl version of the sexy salsa dance Quinn has perfected. She's Sofía Vergara in a sequined miniskirt, and she spins flawlessly in time to the music all over the parquet wood floor. A few of the resident dance instructors have taken to us (because *obvi*) and we're all Julia Roberts laughs and glamorous hair tosses and ambitious shots of tequila until it's way past our bedtime.

As we're gliding back to our hotel, heels in our hands, the warm breeze sifting our hair out of our faces like we're a trio of goddamn goddesses, I can't suppress a sigh. "This is better than Ibiza. I mean, that trip was amazing, but what do you think?" I turn to Quinn, who looks to be floating over the cool sand squishing beneath our feet rather than walking on it.

"I agree. It's way better. Because we're all together. All three of us. Like it always used to be." She puts her arms around Val's and my middles.

"And, you know, there's not that horrible business with those horrible men to think about." Valerie snorts.

"Indeed not." I nod.

Wind still strong, we keep sliding over the sand, in what— let's face it—probably looks like choreographed rhythm.

And then, Valerie: "I was jealous." Her gaze is fixed on her bare feet, but she keeps walking. "That you guys went, I mean."

We take a few more steps in silence, the waves crashing in and out the only soundtrack, and a feeling of sobering eeriness creeps over me.

"But you have Mike," I say. Cautious to stay every bit the Positive Patty about their guys and looooooove this weekend.

"And the kids, yes, I know. I'm aware."

There's something a little heartbreaking in her tone. The moon spills down the length of her hair. Her milky shoulders, exposed.

"We haven't had sex since before Frankie was born. I don't even want to."

There. She's said it.

I've suspected it for a while and I've certainly made my jokes about it to Quinn and to Sarah on occasion, just with all her stupid Rodan + Fields posts on Facebook and the portraits of Pinterest perfection... but to hear her admit it now, out loud, makes me ache for my friend. My Valerie. Who genuinely enjoyed men in college. In high school.

How is it that she can be married—the ultimate goal for all of us female folk, right?—and be as horrifyingly miserable as I know, deep down, she is?

I've always hoped I was wrong, but now she's said it. No turning back.

"You're just drunk," I offer, an out.

"So what?" She rounds on me and then pulls back just as quickly. Softens her tone. "He's not a bad person," she says.

Quinn plods along wordlessly next to us.

"He's just—"

"You don't have to do this," I say. I stop, toss my shoes to the ground, and squeeze her to me. "Just—let's order room service. Sleep it off."

"I'm not a teenager," she snaps over my shoulder, still clinging tight. I can feel the desperation in her grip.

"I know. I don't think anyone's saying that. Are we, Quinn?" I give her a look like *A little help here?*

"Of course not," she chimes in. "But it's late."

"Sure." Valerie shrugs. "But if I can't talk about it to the two of you, who can I talk to about it?"

"You can talk to us anytime. Sure—let's talk," I say.

But just as suddenly as the conversation came on, Valerie makes a beeline for the ocean, the wind tossing her hair all about, and she's kneeling. Throwing up.

"How about a health-care professional?" Quinn quips.

I give her a frown and then go help our friend.

*　　　*　　　*

It isn't anything half a dozen Gatorades and one extra-large room service pizza can't cure.

Not too much later, Valerie is cozy and snoring in her room, and Quinn and I are lounging on the balcony and smoking cigarettes we bummed from Armando because we're idiots and like to do this sort of thing when we've had a few too many cocktails. That was just how we asked him for them too: "Hey! We're idiots and like to smoke when we're drinking—mind if we snag a few?"

"Think this is better than Ibiza now?" Quinn's long eyelashes glint in the moonlight as she stares off at the inky ocean.

"I do," I say ironically because #wedding, and she laughs. I take a deep drag and watch the smoke disperse against the night sky. "So she emoted. So what? She probably won't remember it in the morning. Or she'll pretend she doesn't. You know Valerie."

I keep it breezy, but the weight of our friend's words sticks with me, anchors me to my spot, and it's difficult to feign being upbeat. I don't know how Val does it all the time if this is how she really feels.

"So what are we doing tomorrow? I'm so excited!" Quinn's words don't quite match her dusky tone, and the two of us just sit in utter relaxation. Utter non-movement, for what could be hours, for all I can tell.

"I'm not so sure you're up for it." I give her the ol' side eye and throw her half a smile.

"BASE jumping?" Her eyes bug.

"Hell no. Strip club."

Her laugh is light and its echo dances off the balcony and disappears. "I fucking love you!"

"Ha—I wasn't sure how you'd react. But I figure we should do it once before we die, right?"

"You've never been?" Her voice goes up at the end and it somehow tells me she has.

Or maybe she thinks that's how I spend my weekends now.

"Why do you guys think I'm, like, this crazy party girl? No, I've never been," I say and take another drag.

"Tomorrow night will be a blast." She nods, and her lips curl upward like the Grinch's before he's about to steal Christmas.

*   *   *

CHAPTER 13

Showers and a greasy breakfast do us a world of good the next day, and Valerie's back to her usual chipper self. Not a mention of last night's conversation or a gloomy moment to be spared. We're catching up on our phones and working on our tans until our dinner reservations at eight.

"Vitamin D is just what the doctor ordered." Valerie fans herself with an *Us Weekly* she's been thumbing through all afternoon, and Quinn and I can't contain our laughter because #penisjokes.

Midway through the swordfish and pumpkin farrotto, my phone buzzes. I cringe a little inside because Nick messaged me last night and I ignored it.

Nick: Big weekend plans?

And I just couldn't take the implications of that question. Or worry about whether or not I was reading too much into it. Which I probably was.

But when I bring my phone to life, I see it's a Spark match. It buzzes again.

"What is it? What is it?" Valerie's practically salivating all over her fried okra.

"It's...James. Thirty-eight." I feel a blush bloom across my cheeks as I realize this one—this is a guy I swiped Right on the other night during my Spark free-for-all. And, I daresay, he seems great. "Nothing offensive or questionable about his profile at all. Provided he is, in fact, real, this could be my date to your wedding. You know, if I meet him and don't hate him."

"Gimme that." Quinn's snatching for my phone, but I'm holding it out of her reach.

"I didn't even read the damn thing yet," I bark.

"Well?"

James: Hello. It's me.

"What, is he doing Adele?" I scrunch my nose at the screen. And immediately write back.

Me: I was wondering if after all these years you'd like to meet.

Bzzzt.

James: To go over. Everything.

"This is so lame, you guys," I say. But I laugh. And there's a tickle in my chest.

"Let me see him," Quinn practically yells. She nods in what looks like appreciation after she sees and hands the phone back.

"It's cute! Write him back again!" Valerie bangs her fork on the table like a toddler.

Me: They say that time's supposed to heal you, but I ain't done much healing.

A few minutes go by before his next message comes through, and the tickle I'm feeling starts to hedge toward panic, but he replies.

James: OK, enough. Sending the first message is the worst, but thanks for playing along. I'm James. Which I'm sure you've gathered because I can tell you're not an idiot.

Wide grin.
"Oh, James," I say to the phone and to the girls. "I do believe we might have found ourselves a winner."

*   *   *

We stay fuzzy and fizzy just like the champagne, which has been our drink of choice at the restaurant. And, if we're keeping score, with brunch. Because #bellinis, obviously.

The champagne is probably why I say yes to Armando when he suggests we "beautiful ladies" take a limo this evening to The Dude Ranch, our destination for fine male entertainment. But he insists it won't cost that much more, and this James Spark and his wit have had me reeling all day, so I'd probably have agreed to just about anything.

We pull up to the strip club and snag the attention of every man, woman, and child—okay, there aren't children there, I don't think—waiting in line. A Mr. Clean type with a clipboard and some Secret Service–looking wire attached to his ear waves us over.

"We're the Wallace bachelorette party?" I say, inspecting my nails. Ain't no thang.

He runs his meaty fingers up and down the list. "Are you Rachel Wallace?"

"I am, but—"

"Go right in."

"Damn, VIP!" Quinn trills as he opens the door, and we enter an explosion of music. A champagne popper of sound.

"Is there a mechanical bull?" Valerie peers up, down, left, right. Like all her senses are being stimulated at once and she's about to spontaneously combust.

Cacti! (Seems dangerous…)

Split-rail fences sectioning off private dance areas! (Authenticity!)

"Valerie, this place is called The Dude Ranch. Of course there's a mechanical bull. Isn't there?" I ask the shirtless cowboy who's just sidled up to us with a drinks menu. (Helloooo, Dolly!)

"Surely there is, little darlin'," he says, and he tips his hat. Gestures over toward the far end of the place, where a group of salivating spectators has already gathered.

"So polite." Before I can stop it, my hand is magnetized to the cowboy's chest, and I snap it back. "I'm sorry! I'm new!" I say, slack-jawed. "You're not going to kick me out of here, are you?"

He chuckles a good hearty hombre chuckle and clutches me to him. "You're allowed to touch," he shouts over the bump of the music.

He smells way better than a cowboy. I mean, probably.

"Whom do I talk to about the *Magic Mike* experience? We're that bachelorette party—"

"Just the three of you?"

"What can I say?" My hand back to his chest. "We're old. We're the last ones."

"Age is just a number, little darlin'." Another hat tip. "And we'll take good care of you in here at the Ranch. Now, who's the bride? You?"

I laugh and laugh and laugh until I can't breathe, the lights, the confetti, the ranch hand making me dizzy.

"I am." Quinn steps forward and does *Ta-da* hands.

"Good," he says, still looking at me, piercing into my cold, black heart with those baby blues.

I know it's all pretend, but holy hell.

And then he takes Quinn by the hand and we all snake our way through the crowd after him.

*   *   *

I'm holding my stomach because it hurts from laughing. I don't remember the last time I laughed this much. Unless they've pumped this place full of nitrous oxide, it's from all the Vodka Red Bulls we've switched over to (always a good idea)—we've kind of been drinking like it's the end of the world—and all the ridiculous attention we're getting. All the hilarious things the strippers have made their patrons do. Made Quinn do. At one point, they pulled her up onto a fake tractor, said they were going to plow her, and made her lick A.1. Sauce off this dude's washboard abs.

I was so horrified for her (and slightly jealous) and so entertained by Valerie's hoots and hollers next to me that I was literally gagging on glee.

I take up residence at the bar and opt not to try the

mechanical bull since I like my neck how it is—unbroken—thankyouverymuch, but Quinn and Val really hold their own. Valerie beats every other woman in the joint in terms of time held on, and she wins herself something that at the moment I can't recall, even though I only pretended to take the last three shots we've been offered (poured them right into the plastic cactus plant when everyone else took theirs, because I'm afraid this place could be the death of us—and, after all, I promised they could trust me to take care of them).

But my time as an observer comes to an abrupt end as I hear the emcee, Cowboy Steve, summon me onto the stage.

"Our lovely bachelorette wants to share the love," he croons into the microphone. "Let's get the rest of her party up here and have ourselves a good old-fashioned rodeo!"

"*Yee-haw*," screams the crowd.

As the spotlights start their search, I feel my face redden. Call me crazy, but I don't think there's going to be anything *old-fashioned* about this rodeo. There's no escape. Cowboy Steve and Quinn are thick as thieves now—thick as rib eyes—and they scour the crowd for Valerie and me.

I'm scrambling to get away, clawing my way to hide behind every chick in the place, when all of a sudden something drops over me and cinches at my waist. I glance down and clutch at the spongy ropelike thing. It's a rope made of pink Lycra. And then, with a *whoosh*, I feel the heat and I'm blinded, the spotlight flooding me in white.

I flip back toward the stage, my eyes wide—every gaze fixed on me—and I realize I've been lassoed. I'm being pulled onto the stage.

The crowd is losing their collective mind. And their shouts—*"Go! Go! Go! Go!"*—have me dizzy. I squint my way through the sea of rabid women, and the music vibrates through me. I am powerless to stop this cowboy from pulling me onstage in one swoop of a solid arm.

I wobble as he sets me upright and I steady myself using his biceps. Blinking like it's going out of style, trying to retain my balance. To orient myself.

As the purple dot in my vision from the spotlight dissolves, I start to take in what's around me. Hundreds of women jumping all over themselves from the floor, spilling their drinks, pushing and shoving to get closer to the edge of the stage.

Valerie too has been Lycra-lassoed, and she's being lifted onto the stage by another hombre in brown leather chaps. Her face is lit up like Vegas—and it's then that I think to check out the cowboy who's got me.

He's wearing black chaps, jeans peeking out from underneath, and a tight flannel shirt, rolled at the sleeves. It's unbuttoned halfway down and exposing glistening pecs that are the stuff of Tyson Beckford ads—

When suddenly that thought gives me a chill.

Tyson Beckford.

And I think to look up into the guy's eyes.

Penetrating eyes with a hint of what looks like sheer terror widening them. It probably mirrors my own.

His grip loosens a moment and I almost fall to the floor, but we hold each other's gazes even as he catches me. Helps me stand on my own as recognition sets in and his terror turns to what looks like amusement, with a quirk of a smile.

A familiar twinkle in his warm, dark eyes almost makes me lose my balance again. My mouth can't form words as Nick glances down at me.

"Howdy?" is all he's able to say as he shrugs, a shit-eating grin sliding across those lips, and a new song starts. The strippers wind the ropes around each of us, and I'm dizzy from it all.

Nick—

He spins me.

—is here.

Spin.

Two spins this time. Alternating ways.

"You know, you're just asking for girls to throw up on you," I shout. And I hear his deep rumble of a laugh between beats.

"Is that a warning?" he asks and spins me again. "Don't worry—it's almost over."

"So you're—"

But then he crushes me to his chest, warmth flooding me like I just chugged a fifth of, well, something, and he sets me down on a stool. I steal glimpses across the stage, at Quinn and Valerie now, who are getting the same treatment—and *whap!* Off comes his shirt, the wind from the impact blowing my side bangs off my forehead in its wake.

Five strippers—the three of them with us and two more filling the space in between us all on this huge stage—engage in intricate choreography, the likes of which Usher and Justin Timberlake could only aspire to. They're boy-band precise but half-naked so it's way better. Or worse? Break-dance twirls— holding themselves up with one arm—weaving in and out of the three of us "little darlins" in a rush of testosterone and AXE Body Spray.

Somehow—osmosis?—they rip their jeans out from beneath their fringed chaps.

"Did you just pull your nads off?" I shout at Nick, unable to contain myself, hands glued over my mouth in laughter.

He just gives me one of his looks and shakes his head as he

throws the discarded article of clothing at me and dances to the edge of the stage.

Panic prickles in my chest as we get to the finale of the dance (I've seen *Magic Mike*—what the hell are they going to make us do?), and the fear must be evident on my face because, as the strippers unwrap the lassos and outfit us in leather vests and cowgirl hats, and one has Quinn strapping on a saddle, Nick gives me a reassuring little squeeze.

"How strong are your thighs?"

"What?" I shriek.

He laughs and lifts me up before I can register what's happening.

"Wrap your legs around my waist."

"Come again?"

"Just do it." He's got rough hands on me, positioning my legs, I guess how he just told me they should be, but all I can focus on is gripping them around his middle for dear life. He's walking me forward to the beat—I'm going backward—toward the edge of the stage, his strong hands at my back, gentle at my neck, as he dips me out over the crowd. A sea of horny bitches, who are losing their minds with jealousy, and me just trying not to slip down his now-slick-with-sweat middle.

He yanks me back up with one arm, and I'm flush to his chest. I feel his heart pound.

"You're stronger than I thought," he purrs, and he dips me again before I can respond.

When he yanks me back up, I can see the other cowboys, clad only in shiny, teeny speedos, with my friends.

Is that all Nick has on now too? I'm mortified to even look. I don't.

One is doing The Worm over Valerie, who is lying on her

back on the stage. Each time his body comes down, it's poetic. It's like stripper ballet. He lands so calculated, so gentle, just an inch from ever touching her. Valerie's body quakes every time he comes down, but she doesn't look afraid or horrified; the glow on her face looks like exhilaration. Quinn is riding her stripper as he bucks like a bronco, her legs fastened tight on either side of him, the saddle the only thing separating her from his back. It's all so over the top and hilarious, and each time Nick dips me over the crowd, I lose myself in laughter.

When we hit our final poses, silver confetti rains down on us, applause roaring through the club. I feel like Madonna, Janet Jackson, and Lady fricking Gaga rolled into one, given the wildness of the crowd and all the half-naked dudery.

And then the lights cut out, and I'm blind. I'm being ushered backstage, and I don't realize until we've made it to the green room (is that what they call it in strip clubs?) that Nick's got me by the hand and he's leading me to safety.

*   *   *

Quinn and I sink deep into a cliché crushed-velvet couch adorning the dressing area and sip Vodka Red Bulls while we await Valerie to finish redeeming her prize.

"Are we sure she's all right?" I ask Leo, Quinn's handler on the stage.

He and one of the other guys share a knowing grin.

"I'm sure Sylvester is taking real good care of her. Don't you worry." He salutes me.

"'Cause, you know, it's my job to get these girls home in one piece," I say, rearranging my legs underneath me.

Leo leans way in to Quinn. "Do you have any complaints, darlin'?"

Giggles bubble out of her still-flawlessly lipsticked mouth. "Not a one," she says. "Good for her for winning a private dance. That mechanical bull was no joke!" She sips her drink. "I'm sure she's fine. I feel like we're all friends here." She winks at Nick.

"Yeah, so do I. Funny…" I throw a glance at him too.

He's now in basketball shorts and a tee. They keep him a lot more covered up than the after-show wear of his cohorts, but I can't unsee what I saw on the stage.

And I keep seeing it, feeling his hands on me, as I sit here.

I try not to meet his eyes because I feel like he can tell. I feel naked in his stare. I feel—

"So now you know my little secret," he says. "You gonna make trouble for me at school?"

I guess his, well, nakedness makes him feel exposed now.

"Of course not," Quinn answers and swigs the last of her VRB through the stirrer.

"I can explain—"

"No explanation necessary," I say. "We know—you're putting yourself through medical school." I snort, and everyone laughs.

But, for a second, I get a wave where my stomach drops out from under me. Was that bitchy to say?

Nick chuckles in response and I decide it's probably safer to retreat into my text correspondence with James, who, it turns out, wants to meet up when we get back to town—yee! So I make like Taylor Swift and shake it off.

*   *   *

CHAPTER 14

We're just about packed and loading up on room service waffles when Quinn and I realize something's wrong with Valerie. She was quiet last night and she's been quiet all morning, which is like her sometimes, but I notice she won't meet my gaze as I offer her more orange juice, more butter, more banter.

Quinn just shrugs in my direction and offers up a toast with her juice. "Best. Weekend. Ever."

I'm feeling better than I thought I would the night after All That—thank God for late-night Taco Bell and Advil before bed—until Valerie jumps up from the table and races for the bathroom.

"Are you feeling sick, hon?" I call to her, flashing my teeth in a cringe to Quinn.

We hear her retch. We both grimace.

And then, a moment later: "I'll be fine," she croaks.

"If you want, I can call for a late checkout, to give you more time. Otherwise, we need to be heading out pretty soon."

"I said I'll be fine," she snaps.

I toss up my hands and reach for more bacon. "Okay."

As we descend the sprawling staircase in the main lobby and make our way to the bellhop stand, wrought-iron bannisters cool to the touch, Valerie's perked up a tad: She's upright, she's only a faint shade of green—sea-foam green, if you will—and she's got a to-go coffee in hand.

"It was fun, but I'm excited to get home," she says, wrapping her arms around herself and inhaling the rich steam coming from her cup of joe.

But when we get outside, a slew of cop cars parked wherever they damn well please around the perimeter stops us cold.

"What's going on?" Quinn asks Armando, who's wringing his hands over by his post, sweat dripping from his prominent brow.

"We were trying to keep this quiet, but with the police— everywhere—I guess all our guests are going to know." He lowers his voice and beckons us closer with a wave. "A number of cars were stolen from our lot last night."

Quinn drops her bag. Blinks. "How many?"

She reaches for her suitcase in what looks like an attempt to gain some purchase in preparation for Armando's reply.

"We are still trying to get a fix on the actual number and pin down guests who've been affected—"

"What about my car? The white Porsche Cayenne?"

But before she even gets the words out, we all know the answer.

He shakes his head. "I'm so sorry, miss, but it appears as though yours is one of the vehicles missing."

"Why are we just now being notified?" I blurt.

"I can answer that." An officer, clad in navy blue, steps forward.

"Because the car isn't registered to you. Are you a Miss…"—he glances at his notes—"Quinn Morales?"

"Oh my God," Quinn answers and she dissolves onto the pavement.

I sink with her, but then I realize she hasn't passed out; she's just horrified.

"Your fiancé, a Mister Phillip Hayes? He's on his way here since the vehicle is registered to him. Have you not spoken with him today? He should be here shortly."

"Well, no, I—I—" Quinn begins rummaging through her bag and produces her phone.

"I guess I can see why." The officer smirks at the smashed screen.

"How did this—" Quinn devolves into almost-hyperventilation, a mess of tears and erratic breaths. Val and I hold her from either side, there on the pavement, until Phil pulls up in his Lincoln, his nostrils flared.

"You mind finding your own way home, ladies? I think Quinn and I will probably be here awhile sorting this all out." Phil fixes his scowl on the officer and he doesn't look either one of us in the face as he lets Quinn almost knock the wind out of him with her embrace.

"Yeah, that's fine," I say. "We'll figure it out."

Valerie and I snag our luggage from the cart and make ourselves scarce over by the café.

"Can you believe that jerk?" I dig out my own phone, which seems to be in perfect working order. "No 'Are you guys all right,' 'How did this happen,' nothing. Just huffs and puffs and swears us off so he can find his precious car. Jeez."

"What are we going to do?" Val says, ghostlike, as though she hasn't heard a word I've said.

I hold Val even tighter, and my own vision blurs with moisture. But then I rally, because that's what you do. I give Val a
final squeeze and break our embrace.

"I know just what to do. Don't you worry. I'll get us home."

She nods absently, and before I can think better of it, my fingers start fumbling through my apps.

*   *   *

Valerie doesn't ask questions when I tell her we're getting
picked up in a more incognito, less cop-filled location. In fact,
she doesn't say anything at all, so we slog our luggage a few
blocks away to the diner on the corner and we sit outside on
the curb like a couple of vagrants. I saw her pop a Xanax when
we left the hotel, so I interpret that as a sign she's going to
her happy place—and I take to my phone to see if James has
messaged.

He has.

James: So about that drink . . . ? Provided you ladies are
not dead from the weekend, I'd like to take you to dinner tonight. Thoughts?

Oh, I have several.

I can't suppress the smile that spreads over my face, but when
I look up, goofy grin still stuck there, I meet Nick's gaze as he
arrives in some type of boxy Nissan. He must think my smile is
for him because it catches on his face too, and I get a sinking
feeling in my heart region.

But why, I'm not quite sure.

Luckily, we're not going to be able to make eye contact while

"How's your phone—can you call Mike?"

Her pallor flashes green again. "No. I'm not calling

"Okay, okay, calm down. What's with you today?"

She grips me by the wrist and pulls me to a more s
area. We stand there in silence for what feels like forev
eyes bloodshot and serious.

Finally, she's out with it in a spew of a whisper: "I had se
that stripper last night. During the private dance. I don't kn
that's what they usually do or if that's what he expected, but—

She's chattering on, when "WHAT?" erupts from me. I c
help it—I full-on shout it, and several patrons look our way.

"I don't know what I was thinking." Tears spill down her de
icate face, splotches blooming pink across her chest. "I haven
felt that wanted since—"

"Since Frankie was born, I know."

"Since college," she corrects. "And I know it wasn't real, but
he was just so—so—" Her gaze glazes over, and I can tell she's
seeing it, feeling it, all over again. Her cheeks flush deeper, and
her top teeth catch one corner of her bottom lip—

All at once she's clutching on to me and sobbing and I don't
know what to do.

I brush back her hair from her face and offer what I hope are
calming shushes. Pat her back reassuringly. Let her breathe.

"It's going to be okay," I say. "We won't call Mike. And I
won't tell anybody. Ever. Okay?" I pull back and stare her square
in the eyes, which swim with emotion. Hold her chin. "Not
even Quinn."

I glance over at our friend and Phil, and a sickness curls its
way around my insides.

My Quinn is gone. This weekend may have been the last
time I'll ever have with her.

he's driving, so we won't have any more of this. For at least sixty minutes, anyway.

"Nick is our ride?" Valerie makes an appearance in the land of the aware for a second before Nick has gotten out of the car to help us load our bags, and I shrug.

"I took a shot," I say. "We're kind of friends now, and I thought Uber'd be too pricey for this trip."

And she retreats back into her quiet land. Hard to read.

When we get into the car, it smells like coconut, the tree-shaped air freshener dangling from the rearview mirror doing its job. What is it with guys and those air fresheners? I glance around the rest of the vehicle for more clues about Nick. The whole thing looks like it's been freshly detailed, as in not a half-eaten bacon cheeseburger smashed at the bottom of a fast-food bag, not a pile of mail beneath my feet, not a crumb. Anywhere. I make a mental note never to let Nick see the vortex of horror that is my Camry. A couple of old CDs are in the door pocket, and I thumb my way through them as he drives. Mostly old-school hip-hop.

"Find anything you like?" he says after a while, sarcasm tickling his tone.

"I'm really more of a top forty kind of girl."

"Predictable." He offers a *tut, tut, tut* of his tongue. "What a shame."

"Sugarhill Gang? This used to be my jam." I flash him the jewel case.

"There's not a CD player in here anyway—don't hurt yourself," he deadpans. "So..."

"Ha-ha, right? Now what do we talk about for an hour?" I drum my fingertips on the center armrest.

"We could talk about your amazing survival this weekend..."

"We made it, yes. Pretty much. Quinn might not, though. I feel terrible."

"I bet! But it wasn't your fault, you know."

His voice is tender—almost like he's got his hand on my knee or like he's reached out to comfort me.

But he hasn't. Thank God. I need to get a handle on this crush of mine.

I let a beat go by as I watch a line of trees blur past the passenger side window.

"I know it's not technically my fault," I finally say. "But I feel like I'm going to get blamed for it."

"Why?"

I glance back at Val, who looks to be dead-to-the-world passed out, her head lolling to the side and bouncing with each bump of the drive.

"Because I just do. They always do this. Well, not always. But since marriage. Since guys."

"And this is why you hate guys?"

I laugh. "I don't hate guys."

He gives me a side eye.

"Okay, fine. But I don't hate all guys. Not always. In fact—" I chew on the corner of my lip for a sec. On a scale from one to ten, how weird is it that I'm discussing guys with Nick? But then the angel on my shoulder (haaa, like an angel wouldn't burn to death on my shoulder) or something akin to it wins out and decides it's fine to discuss guys with Nick because Nick is someone I work with, and we're friends, apparently. And maybe it'll help me put this schoolgirl attraction to him to bed.

"In fact?"

"Well, I might have met someone normal on Spark, and I think we're going out tonight."

He chuckles. "I wouldn't say you necessarily met me on Spark, and I haven't agreed to a date tonight, but—"

"Your arrogance is staggering."

"Thank you," he says, and I swat at his arm.

And when I feel his skin brush under my fingertips for just that second, I get a flash of last night. My legs wrapped around his middle.

Not helping!

My face gets hot.

Focus.

"Not you. Someone dateable."

"Ouch," he says, rubbing at his forearm.

"You know what I mean."

"Oh, so... not a 'stripper with a heart of gold' that you also happen to work with? Gotcha."

"I'm serious!" I smack at him again.

I can't help it. It's like I can't stop touching him.

Stop it!

And then somehow we're not talking about James or other guys at all. Somehow we're talking about school and Ida and how Valerie and Quinn and I met in high school and who both of us were in high school (him, student council president; me, debate team nerd) and how he came to be subbing at Wesson Academy.

"I was teaching up in Tallahassee, but then my brother got sick in the summer."

"Yikes. I'm sorry."

He presses his lips into a firm line. "Yeah. He's fifteen. And my dad's been gone about five years now—not much of a pension for my mom to work with and take care of Bryce and the bills, so I tried to look for a teaching job closer. Too late in the year for any jobs to be available, though."

I want to ask what's wrong with his brother, but the words trip on my tongue. I've paused just a second too long, and Nick seems to sense this because he bails me out.

"Leukemia. He relapsed from when he was really little. So I couldn't justify living four hours away when my family's here and they need me, you know?"

"That's awful, Nick. And how sweet of you."

I squelch the urge to reach out and touch his arm again—what is with me today? I just sit and digest all of this.

He's quiet until I ask, "Why Wesson?" and then he cracks the smile I haven't seen in a few miles.

"Easy. It's near my mom's place and it's the most expensive private school around. I figured it must pay its teachers pretty well too."

I snort.

"Trouble is, they had no openings either, so that's how I got on the sub list."

"So you generally teach history, you said?"

"When there are positions available, yes. But I've had to be creative to make money so far. Have to help Ma with all the medical bills." He pauses a minute. "I did a little modeling in college—shut up—and, well..." He clears his throat. "I hooked back up with my agent when I got here. He's the one who suggested this stripping gig." He shakes his head and half a smile splits the side of his face I'm now staring at. "I only do it here and there," he says, "and the money happens to be pretty stellar. So I'm kinda stuck at the moment." A beat. "I'm not just some dirty stripper."

His tone is light, but it's edged with a hint of something I can't put my finger on.

"And here I thought you were just trying to follow in

Channing Tatum's footsteps." I wink at him from across the front seat, and he laughs. "You don't have to explain to me," I say. And I feel bad he's defending himself.

"I know." He meets my gaze at a red light and a wave runs through me. This pull I haven't experienced...since I can remember. This flutter I can't suppress.

But it's back to chauffeur duty before I can acknowledge it or make it worse.

We sit in silence for a while, and an ease lays over me instead of the weird, stiff tension of the usual awkward silence when I'm with a guy I don't know particularly well. I get lost in thinking about it for a few exits. How it feels so natural. And it's fun. Nick's so easy to talk to. And even though I don't happen to believe guys and girls can be actual, real, non-friends-with-bennies friends, I start to think...maybe they can.

Before I realize it, the ride is almost over.

"What time is it?" Valerie asks as she stretches her newly awakened self in the backseat.

"Almost two," Nick answers. "Where should I drop you ladies?"

"Why don't you just take us both to my place? I can drive Val home."

With Valerie awake, Nick's and my banter comes to a close, and it dawns on me that I haven't answered James about tonight yet, so I whip out my phone and his message is still sitting there, with its arms crossed. Tapping a toe.

Me: So sorry—YES. Had a crazy morning/afternoon. Nothing the cops couldn't handle—heh. I'm only kind of kidding. What time and where should we meet?

James's reply with the details is swift and I'm still getting the fireflies lighting up my chest for him, so apparently I don't need to worry about this stupid attraction to Nick—but I notice I'm shielding my phone from the driver's side as I type.

Nick must notice too. He clears his throat. "Big date tonight?"

The question is like a bug zapper to the fireflies; they're dead in an instant.

"Yet to be determined," I say, forcing a playful hitch to my tone.

But my heart breaks a little with the admission.

The rest of the trip is all business—I direct Nick to my apartment complex, turn for turn. When I get out of the car and he's helped us out with the bags, the two of us linger a moment while Valerie's on her phone with Mike. Nick leaning against the back hatch, arms crossed; me up on the sidewalk and staring at my toes as I line them up with the grooves in the pavement.

I feel an energy between us. Like there's more to be said, but I don't have any idea what else to say. And, furthermore, I know I shouldn't.

James.

Breathe.

James.

I glance back up at Nick and he doesn't say anything either—just flashes that smile—so I offer a sheepish one in return and thank him for the ride.

Val and I are pretty quiet on the way back to her house too, and I'm not sure if she's making like *Fight Club* and we're just never going to talk about it...or this is supposed to be an understanding between the two of us like What Happened in South Beach Stays in South Beach...or if she and I will have some heart-to-hearts coming up because HOW CAN A PERSON HOLD THAT MUCH INSIDE?

But I can't bring myself to broach the topic of Mike or Sex with Stripper Sylvester or What This Means because it's all uncharted territory for us, and I don't want to drive her away.

So I just drive her home.

Before I've even backed out of Valerie's driveway, my phone buzzes, and I'm wondering if she's forgotten something. I glance in the back to see what's there, but there's nothing.

Nick: Have fun tonight. =P

It cracks me up, but it pins me down as well.
Couldn't leave well enough alone, could he?

Me: Do you always have to get the last word?
Nick: Of course, little darlin'. ;)

*   *   *

CHAPTER 15

Sarah seems to have taken great care of Billie; she's just how I left her—alive, chubby, and starving for love. Sarah's not here when I get in, but she's left a note for me, saying she hung around until one thirty and what a sweetie pie Billie is.

Duh.

I spend a long while making over said sweetie pie, who's as wiggly as a puppy at the sight of me, and then I decide to take her on a walk to get some of that excited energy out since I'm leaving to meet James this evening.

And, really, I just need to process the weekend.

I've texted Quinn about seventy times, asking about the status of the car, and she's yet to respond, so there isn't much to do but be alone with my thoughts and plod on, picking up beagle poop along the way. As one does.

*   *   *

James has suggested this new, swanky Italian place I've been dying to try. It's got a twenties vibe with its art deco décor, and they've been billing it as a wine bar, so count me in.

But my hands are a bit shaky as I straighten my hair. Smooth on my eye shadow.

I've really mixed it up this time—no first-date uniform tonight. I've chosen to wear a burgundy wrap dress that's more than a few shades darker than the rosé I've ordered but just as delicious. It hugs and hides where it's supposed to, and it's fun and flowy like I hope the conversation will be.

I twist on the leather barstool, and the wine is sweet on my tongue. I can't believe I'm drinking after last night, but I'm nervous this time—excited about this guy; I'm not doing it because I'm trying to numb myself to anything.

I need this to go well. I hope it does go well.

It's the first time since we started this little experiment that I've felt this way, and now that I feel I've somehow let the girls down, I've got to really try on this date. Plus, I might actually like this James Spark. I picked him, following my own rules and everything, after all.

And I've got to stop being lured by Nick. Why does he have to be so damn alluring?

I swirl the wine in the stemless glass and think about our conversation in the car this afternoon. #dree #mee

I take another slow sip.

Not dreamy. *Stop it.*

I ease back the rest of the rosé and dab my lips on a black cocktail napkin.

"That psyched to meet me, eh?" says a guy's voice, and warm fingertips graze my elbow.

I jump at the sight of him. James, 38. In the flesh.

Hummina, hummina.

He's got thick, wavy hair—dark, just like in his pictures. A crisp button-down filled out with what looks to be as solid a frame as his profile indicated.

That's as far as I get because he's asked me something. At least I think he has, because he's looking at me, eyes all big, like he's expecting me to answer.

"Should I scram?" He hitches both thumbs back toward the door, and I laugh.

"Who says *scram*? And, no. I mean, I just—"

"Relax." James chuckles and gives me a friendly little hug. "I needed some liquid courage too. Believe me. But thank God." He takes a step backward and gives me a once-over. "I don't mean to be a total ass, but I was pretty sure you'd be—"

I blink at him and throw on a sarcastic smile. "Sure you want to finish that sentence?"

"Yes." He offers a firm nod. "I was just going to say, I was pretty sure you'd be a catfish."

"Me?" I clap a palm to my chest, and I already feel the lilt skate into my voice before the words even come out. "Oh, I'm more piranha than catfish, honey."

"Is that right?" He looks amused, light brown eyes alight in the glow coming from the crystal chandelier.

He takes the seat next to me, orders me another glass of wine, himself a scotch.

"Is it 'Liquor before wine, feeling fine'?"

He scrunches his face to reveal a cleft in his chin, which he probably hates because everyone with one of those seems to hate them.

But not me. *Nonononooo*. I'm a huge fan.

"I can never remember," he says. " 'Beer before liquor, never sicker'? Something before beer is 'in the clear'...wine, 'feeling fine.'"

I hold up my glass. "I'm feeling pretty fine at the moment. And, yeah, I wish we'd have thought about those helpful little sayings this weekend." I laugh.

"Tied one on, did we?" His gaze is molten and his smile is infectious.

We finish our drinks at the bar while I give him the yada-yada version of everything, and I'm doing that thing where I'm kind of handsy, but he doesn't seem to mind. His forearm. His knee. His biceps. It all seems fair game.

"I'm surprised you made it out alive," he adds when I'm done with my spiel.

I think of Quinn and the car and a pang of guilt hits me right in the feels, but I spare him that little shit show for now.

He tells the bartender to add everything to our dinner tab— I love him already. But, for reals, for some reason it doesn't feel like he's doing it to impress me or to show how much money he makes. It feels like he's...doing it to be nice.

Where I'd ordinarily be suspicious of a move like that—what is this game he's spinning, doing it to be nice?—I realize I'm kind of mad as we make our way to a very intimate table near a fountain teeming with gorgeous koi.

And I'm kind of an idiot.

Because it's not a dick move. He really is just nice.

#weird

They dim the lights, I guess for the dinner hour, and I make the same crappy joke I always make when that happens: "Oh— everyone just got better-looking." But the floating candle centerpiece provides a soft, dreamy glow and my corny comment doesn't seem to faze him.

Once we're seated and we've heard the specials, I narrow my gaze across the table at this guy, whoever he is, wherever he's been all my life, my fresh French tips popping against the white linen tablecloth.

After a moment, he laughs. "What?"

"We'll see, pal." I smile through my squint. "We'll see."

He simply shakes his head.

Throughout dinner, he's the perfect mix of sarcastic and genuine, flirtatious and respectful, witty but not pretentious; I'm Goldilocksing the hell out of this date, and he seems to be juuuuust right. My phone buzzes twice and I don't even bat an eye—I'm so engrossed in James's stories about how he got into house flipping, how he and his brother handle the business, etcetera, that I don't even check to see who it is.

Until he excuses himself to the restroom, that is, and then I remember—oh yeah—I do wonder if Quinn and Phil made it back to town and if Valerie's drowning in self-loathing.

But when I see the texts are from Nick, I clear the notifications without reading them, and now I feel guilty that he's messaging me when I'm with James, instead of the other way around like it was this afternoon.

And that makes me feel good, actually. Like I'm finally doing something right. That I'm kinda into this guy and now I don't want to do anything to mess it up. Not even reply to Hot Sub Guy.

I can't help a smile when James returns, his gaze lingering on me the whole way back.

"Looks like there's a nice moon out," he says, glancing toward the picture windows. "You want to take a stroll through the square?"

And I do. I genuinely do.

"That sounds…absolutely perfect." I tuck the phone back into its pocket and offer a shy smile.

*　　　*　　　*

"And?" Sarah salivates into her Rambler bottle as we weave our way in and out of student tables in the cafeteria.

"I never kiss and tell." I wink and do a cheesy and dramatic leg kick like I'm Katharine Hepburn or Grace Kelly or, yanno, someone totally fabulous and demure and totally the opposite of me.

She huffs. "Since when? Pick up that grape, Thomas!"

"Nothing happened," I admit.

"Nothing?"

"Well, not nothing. We kissed for a while in this gazebo."

She stops and looks at me through her bangs. "Are you making this up?"

"No!"

"Who are you, freaking Liesl von Trapp?"

We're still laughing when Valerie and Quinn pass us with their trays, but their sullen expressions zap all the merriment right off our faces.

"How was your date?" Quinn asks, her tone sharp.

I'm surprised she remembers.

"It was okay," I say with a dismissive hand. "What happened with Phil and the car? I was worried about you. Why didn't you write me back?"

"I'm sorry." Her eyes start to well. "It was just a really draining day. I know it wasn't your fault."

"Do you?" Now my tone's the one tinged with Bitch.

"Yes. But of course Phil is upset—"

"He has every right to be, sure."

There's a stiff moment of silence and I can't help but think I could use a stiff drink.

Am I becoming an alcoholic?

#probs

"Listen," I offer at last, stirring some honey into my voice this time. "Let's have dinner one night this week, okay? Can we do that? Catch up on what all we need to do for the wedding—three weeks!" I squeal. "Since we didn't talk wedding stuff at all this weekend. Don't we need to, like, do final fittings of our dresses and stuff?"

This elicits a smile from her, and the mood has already lightened tenfold. "Yes, I was just going to say. Thursday. Can you both be there?" Quinn looks from me to Valerie, who looks pretty much the same but I know isn't the same.

"Yes," she answers, blue eyes wide and shining.

"And I do want to hear about your date. Do you think maybe this one might be your date for the—"

"Shh! Don't jinx it!" I laugh and then bring my voice to just above a whisper. "But, yes. He just might be."

Sarah groans from over by the table washer station. "Oh, puke. When are you seeing him again?"

"Tonight, actually. He sent me a 'Good morning' message before work and then asked if I was available this evening. So…he's coming over to meet Billie and then we're going to grab some dinner. Maybe watch some TV or a movie or something. I'm nervous."

"Netflix and chill?"

"Not the 'chill' part." I narrow my gaze at her.

"If you say so…but it sounds like you haven't 'chilled' in a while." She giggles. "When's the last second date you've had?" she asks.

And it takes me a minute of head scratching before I can figure it out.

"Nineteen . . . seventy-two?" I finally say.

Might as well have been.

* * *

I'm relieved not to see Nick at all today. I checked his messages when I got home from my evening with James, and although they didn't say too much of anything—just asked how the date was going and then joked about not divulging news of my stage debut over the weekend—I felt guilty. So I didn't answer.

And part of me felt guilty for not answering, but that's ridonkulous.

I still haven't answered.

Even as I sit at my desk while the kids are at recess and I stare at my manuscript and the words just won't come.

I catch myself glancing at the door every now and then, and I smack my hands to my blotter.

He's not here. And stop it.

My phone buzzes, and I freeze.

But it's a Spark message from James, thank baby Jesus.

James: Looking forward to seeing you tonight!

Swoony swoooons!

And, just like that, the words start to flow and I knock out a quick eight hundred of them before my break is over and I have to begin a new science unit.

* * *

While I pluck and primp in preparation for tonight with James, I think again about Sarah's question. When *was* the last time I had a second date with someone?

It was about six months ago, with this firefighter I saw a few times. I remember just how uncomfortable I was as we searched my Netflix queue for something to watch. I was actually sweating like I was taking the damn bar exam or something.

But I just felt like everything needed to be perfect. That if we watched the wrong thing, it would be a reflection on me and my tastes, a reflection on our overall compatibility. And I realized, halfway through all my clicking, that what we chose to watch was likely going to matter very little because he was probably just trying to sleep with me anyway.

Which made me even tenser and sweatier.

So, ultimately, I decided *Fuck it*, and I got my buzz on. And he did indeed try to sleep with me. And I was just so relieved not to have to worry about talking or making a fool of myself or, yanno, connecting, that I let it happen.

And I vowed never to Netflix and chill again.

Yet here I am, frantically surface-cleaning my whole apartment like the goddamn Flash; throwing my pile o' worn work clothes that's morphed into an unwieldy mess into my laundry room and shutting the door on it; dusting the tables, the mantel, my nightstands, around all the tchotchkes; cleaning the toilets; making my bed (do I even remember how?).

Adulting at its finest.

But I don't let myself feel bad; I've seen plenty a meme on the Interwebs to know I'm not the only slob in America. I'm average in terms of filth at the very least.

I'm putting the finishing touches on my outfit—cropped jeans and a top, since we decided it's going to be a low-key kind of night—when I head over to my liquor cabinet. All just half-empty bottles of things I should probably throw away because they're Lord Knows How Old, when I come across a mini bottle of Malibu.

Done.

I toss back half of it, and the sweet coconut flavor lingers on my lips. They tingle. I feel my half a swig burn its way into my stomach like a flame traveling down a long wick.

I scrunch my nose at the bottle.

Finish it?

But before I can once again unscrew the cap on my baby-sized beverage, a knock at the door makes me jump. Billie's bark is muffled beneath a blanket on the couch in a way I know means she was dead asleep. *Burrrrr!*

As I make my way to the door, I say a quick prayer to the heavens above that this dude's going to be okay with my dog. Because if he's not, I will hate him. Instantly. And there will be no recovery.

One time I had a date over for the first time, and he wouldn't even pet her. She kept wiggling and wiggling. Looking up at him with desperate eyes. *What am I doing wrong, mister?*

Because, of course, she'd be polite enough to call him *mister*.

And after my third, increasingly annoyed request that he just *Pet the dog. Pet her, and she'll leave you alone*, Dude's response was *See, I like dogs and everything, but—I pet them when I want to pet them. Not when they want me to pet them.*

cue the tire screech

I had never heard anyone say anything so bizarre or, let's face it, repulsive before, and, quite frankly, I saw the writing on the wall right there.

Valerie and Quinn even admitted, after their initial protestations that this remark was Not a Big Deal and I Was Being Too Picky, that someone who not only feels that way but *says* something like that to a dog owner he's trying to date is *prob*ably a jerk and *prob*ably has some control issues that go beyond when to pet and when not to pet animals.

Regardless, that was our final date—and the reason how a guy treats Billie is a big deal to me.

Here's hoping, James!

I fluff my hair one last time and open the front door.

"Damn," he says, a six-pack of fancy-looking beer under one arm. "I was about to turn back."

"You were not." I give an eye roll, but my smile and the flush in my cheeks I'm already sporting like a fourteen-year-old give me away. "Come on in," I say, holding Billie off with my right foot while he steps inside.

"Come here." He wraps me up in his free arm and plants one on me that almost puts last night to shame. It makes me remember why I put myself out there over and over (and over) again.

Billie's beside herself, her little legs pawing away at James's dark jeans, and he chuckles, mid kiss, and breaks away.

My stomach lurches. The time of reckoning is upon us.

"Aww, who's this little sweetie?" He bends down to greet her, seemingly unfazed by her lack of obedience training, and he gives her a scratch behind the ears.

And she's fine. Just like I told that other jackhole she would be.

When she disappears into the living room, I know she's about to bring him every smelly old toy in her basket, so I usher James into the kitchen and give him a mini tour.

"Nice of you to bring beer," I say, making room for it in the fridge.

"Well...I'm a nice guy." He shrugs, but it's not douchey; it's matter of fact. And he's right—he is a nice guy.

"Are you hungry?" I ask.

"Starving." At once, he's attached himself to me again, and I get lost for a second.

His kisses are slow. Sweet. He's not jamming his tongue down my throat. Not grabbing all over me. It's a nice change of pace. He follows it up with a little squeeze and then we part, his hands still affixed to either side of my waist like we're in a tableau from a Cary Grant movie.

#sigh

"I was thinking we might go to that little pizza place around the corner. Is that okay?" His light brown eyes smile down into mine.

"Pizza is great," I say.

And not twenty minutes later, I'm sitting across from him at a black-and-white checkered table and shoving garlic bread in my face. I can't help but giggle.

"What?" he wants to know.

"Nothing." I can't fight the grin, but it's not nothing.

I want to tell him that I'm usually freaked out about eating spicy or garlicky things on dates, anything that's messy, anything that shows I eat like a human person (or, let's face it, the carbohydrate-scarfing monster I am). But I feel at ease.

I want to tell him, and so...I do tell him. This is unusual too.

And when I say it, he just laughs like it's adorable and I'm adorable and I'm sure our fellow pizza eaters are somewhat disgusted by how dreamily I look at him, but I can't help but melt in his general direction, much less care about what they think.

"You don't have to worry about that stuff with me," he says. "Besides, we're both having garlic. That negates it."

"Is that right?" I shovel more in and just bask in awe because he's like a goddamn food genius. I beam at him over our pepperoni, sausage, and mushroom masterpiece.

When we get back to my place, my nerves begin to Irish line dance, as now it's time to pick something to watch. I hand him the remote and excuse myself to the bathroom—hopefully he'll have chosen something by the time I return and—*poof*—the pressure will be off me. Way to deal with things!

I look at myself in the mirror, and this is how I know I'm sliiiiightly tipsy, because whenever I'm a scooch inebriated, I make faces at myself in the bathroom mirror. Like every upstanding American.

But this time, while I do stick out my tongue, I also say a pseudo prayer.

If this guy is not a waste of my time, then please don't have him try to sleep with me tonight.

I scrunch my face at myself a moment. Purse my lips.

Not that sleeping with him wouldn't probably be fun and not that I'm not attracted to him, but please. If that's all he's after, then let me know now.

I ball both my fists to seal the deal—that's how one prays, right?—and venture back out into the wild.

When I return to the living room, James is still flipping channels. Dammit. Billie has her head on his knee, and she's holding a stuffed hedgehog that's seen better days.

"Billie." I laugh and snatch it from her unsuspecting jaws. Toss it down the hall.

"Come by me." James grins and pats the cushion next to him.

After a surprisingly painless few minutes, he suggests *The Bachelor*, and it's perfect. We can snark at it (and we do); it's got cheesy romance (and we totes seem to be headed toward that stage); and, most important, we cuddle and it doesn't feel weird (which, in turn, feels very weird). Billie has made herself at home next to us too, and she's peacefully snoring by our feet.

I relish in this idyllic scene, beer making me comfortably bubbly. James has got an arm around me and the fingers of his free hand are threaded through mine, his thumb absently making slow circles on my skin.

Somehow I'm not stiff or sweaty. The conversation comes easily, and the only time it's awkward at all—and it's probably just awkward for me—is when one of the *Bachelor* girls is trying to get the rose on the one-on-one date, and she starts talking about falling in love right away and if that's possible. Neither of us says a word or makes fun of her the way I normally would have, and so I wonder what he's thinking and I simultaneously hate myself for wondering what he's thinking. It makes me wish someone could eject-button me out of his arms and away from the couch entirely—but I realize that's just because I'm feeling ooey-gooey about him and I didn't expect it.

And the last time I felt ooey-gooey about someone—

James kisses me. He does it right then as if he knows he's shutting up my internal turmoil, and it's much appreciated on my end.

He kisses me during commercials and every once in a while, but he never takes it any further than that. A hand to my face. Fingers sifting through my hair. But he's never reaching for the button on my jeans. And while I know I'd asked in my tipsy-pseudo-mirror prayer for him not to do so if he's worth it, this disappoints some stupid part of me.

Is he rejecting me?

While Bachelor Ben, or whatever his dumb name is, looks at the portraits of his sixteen beloveds and decides their fates, I internally yell at myself for even thinking some dude not trying to bed me right away is a rejection. I hate the world.

When James is gone, the sense of peace that has blanketed me all evening remains. I clear away the beer bottles, and it's kinda therapeutic.

James is kinda therapeutic.

And he's from Spark and everything! #ugh

I didn't want Quinn and Valerie to be right, but doesn't it feel good that they might be?

As I finish straightening up, I rack my brain for the last time I felt anything like this. It stops me cold when I come upon it, my chest splits in two, and a chasm of memory consumes me.

*   *   *

We're the last two patrons and the last two of our group. All the others have early sessions tomorrow, early flights, and so it's just Jesse and me left telling our tales against the neon back-lighting of the hotel bar.

"I guess the rest of these so-called writers can't hold their liquor like we can." Jesse toasts me with his Jack and Coke.

I take a demure swig of mine, a demure smile curling its way across my lips. "I'm not so sure we should be proud of that."

He laughs. One loud guffaw that makes me wonder at an instant just how strong he is. If I can get him to make that sound again. What exactly is happening here?

Sure, I can hold a decent amount of alcohol, but that's not why I'm still at the bar.

And that's not why he is either.

Most of the rest of the party filed out a good forty-five minutes ago, and we barely noticed as we exchanged stories of our writing processes. Oxford comma or no Oxford comma? (Oxford comma, obviously.) Things that Normal People wouldn't find interesting at all, but things that make me smolder at him at the mere suggestion that he even knows what they are. That he even thinks about them at all.

"I'm glad we ran into each other today," he says. "I was hoping I'd get another chance to serenade you after last night." A flick of his dark brow.

"Oh gawd." I snort. "Unless you promise never to sing to me again, let's consider this the last time we run into each other."

"Booooo. That would be a shame." He finishes his drink and puts an index finger up to the bartender for another. Wipes his lips. Swivels toward me. Scoots closer. "So how is it that your husband lets you out of his sight for one second? If you were mine..."

The four words hang there, electrifying.

He lets the thought trail off in a way that's knowing. He knows of the fireworks he's set off beneath my rib cage. I can tell. His stare is like a goddamn x-ray. And he's loving every minute of it. But he cloaks it in the trailing off since he doesn't know my situation and probably isn't sure if I'm about to throw my drink in his face or what.

My gaze drops to my ring. "I guess this is a little misleading," I say, still looking at it sparkling back up at me. "But I'm separated. Like the divorce-isn't-quite-final-but-it's-

getting-there separated. Separated for almost a year. Separated by more than a thousand miles. Separated." I shrug. "He isn't a bad guy; he just isn't the guy for me."

I feel raw at the spewing of all this detail, so I take another sip of my drink. It's such a matter-of-fact way to account for five years of your life. For a marriage.

And a way to sound like a crazy person!

But something that looks like amusement rounds out his chiseled jaw. The corners of his eyes crinkle.

"Why are you still wearing this, then?" He takes the white gold circle between his fingers, and his hands are warm against mine, ever frozen.

"I don't know." I look up at him. And I contemplate that for a second because I haven't really thought about it. My throat goes dry and the words scrape as they come out. "I'm just so used to it, I guess. I haven't been without it in years and it seems like I'd feel naked. Empty."

He's still holding my ring finger in his grasp, the heat still emanating from him to me. Connecting us.

"We have more in common than you know," he says, and he drops my finger. Takes my face in his hands. Glances from one eye to the other in just a hitch of a moment, and then . . . he dives forth.

Jesse kisses me like he's under water and I'm his one source of oxygen. His tongue searches mine like he's searching for answers to all the world's questions and I'm the only one who holds them.

I'm all at once overwhelmed with a longing for him unlike any longing I've ever known.

Somehow, we've settled our bill—I think?—and he's crushing me against the wall just outside his room, his strength I'd wondered about earlier greater than I imagined. The way he lifts me onto the bed like I'm an itty-bitty thing. It's magic.

We miss the morning sessions the next day and the panel just before lunch. But I've never felt calmer, more relaxed, more at ease, than I do in his smooth, inked arms. Listening to him breathing. Feeling his chest rise and fall against my back.

Wishing the moment never had to end.

*   *   *

CHAPTER 16

Where is Hot Sub Guy? And what's going on with that?" Sarah asks during her afternoon visit. She sits atop one of the desks at the front of the classroom and swings her long legs.

"I don't know—all our coworkers are in suspiciously good health." I snort. "And nothing is going on with that." I give her a glare.

But I'm relieved I've somehow managed to eke by with another Nickless day at school. No one's in need of a sub, apparently, and so I take this as a sign that the moons are aligning just as they should be: *No Nick. James.*

"Right." She hooks a perfectly penciled brow my way.

"I woke up to a *When can I see you again?* message from James. Yanno, I'm really digging his total disregard for subtlety. It matches my inability to be subtle."

"That it does."

I smack her in the gut with a stack of worksheets.

"Ow! And where are Valerie and Quinn? I haven't seen them at all this week yet and they're usually attached to your hips."

"I don't know that either." I put the papers in the color-coded homework tray and don't meet Sarah's eye.

I haven't told her about the weekend and I don't intend to, but I'm keeping so many damn secrets—Nick the Stripper, Valerie's Stripper Sex, Quinn's Stolen Car, Nick Driving Us Home—that I'm likely to have an aneurism by three.

"Oh, you're holding out on me." Her eyes sparkle, and she starts grabbing at my arm. "Tell me something. Tell me one little thing."

I chew the inside of my cheek. "I think I might actually like James."

"Who's James?"

#headdesk

"You know, if you had the attention span of even a gnat or a squirrel, our conversations might go better."

"Oh, right—the house flipper. Has he flipped you yet?"

I laugh. "Not yet."

"Hey, I like this one." Her tone more serious: "He's not a Halloween costume. Usually you go for Halloween costumes. Firefighter, dentist—"

"Ax murderer. Hey, I think you're right!"

She just smiles and shakes her head. "So are you going to see James tonight? Flip, flip!" She raises her eyebrows on each *flip*.

"Naw, I think I'll opt to take the night off. Everything in moderation, right? I want to savor this positive feeling and stave off the inevitable disappointment that comes with getting to know each other better. I'm happy right now, so I'm sure it will end horribly."

"Aw, be positive," she says, a pout to her bottom lip.

"Okay, I'm positive it'll end horribly."

We both laugh until the bell rings and ruins everything because #work.

*   *   *

Once Thursday rolls around, I have nearly forgotten Nick exists,
except for the fact that we have rehearsal again, and I'm pretty
sure he'll be there.

I still haven't responded to his messages and it still twists my
insides—he did do us a solid by driving us home in the midst of
a crisis, after all.

So I can't wait to see how awkward this will be...

I'm just glad all this Jamesing is keeping me occupied and
Eyes on the Prize because, if not for him, I'd definitely be writing
Nick back and probably getting myself into a world of trouble.
Or at least a compromising work situation.

#dramaqueen

James and I spent another dreamy, yet sex-free, evening
together—this time at his place—and we made plans for Friday
before I even left, so I have basically been floating around my
classroom all day.

Valerie peeks her head into my room while the kids are at
music and catches me humming to myself. HUMMING TO
MYSELF.

"Are you..." She pauses at the threshold.

"Sick? Dying? I know, right? No! I'm just basking in the glow
of—" I reel it in and remember Saturday. Sunday. Eek. Tone it
down, freak. "How have you been?" I try to recover.

"Fine." She seems unaffected by the saccharine oozing from
my pores. "But I can't drive Quinn home after the fitting and
everything tonight. Can you take her?"

"She's been getting rides to work? How come you guys... of course I can take her. No pr—"

But before I can even finish my sentence, Valerie is gone. And in her wake, I feel a *whoosh* of cold air as the door shuts.

*   *   *

At rehearsal, things are too hectic among the kids to allow for much awkwardness between Nick and me. Although he's sweet with the kids and he sends me a smile early on, he spends most of the time backstage, nailing things, as evidenced by the very loud banging occurring every few seconds and rattling my brain. But I'm thankful he's back there doing it and not out here working up some sort of sweat that would render me incapable of fulfilling my directorial responsibilities.

Yeah, that's it.

When we get to the dress shop, formfitting lace clings to Quinn's curves and drapes at her tiny feet. The dress is not white this time; it's an ethereal silvery sheen that's luminous in the fluorescent lights. It drips down into a beautiful mermaid-style bottom, the back of which flows into a glittery sea of a train.

My throat tightens at the sight of her. She's stunning.

After the proper squealing and eye wiping, Val and I each take one of Quinn's hands and help her step up on the block in front of the wall o' mirrors so the seamstress can teach us how to bustle the dress.

Once we've got the hang of it and she's all pinned and adjusted, it's our turn to try on our bridesmaid gowns—hot pink, tea-length little numbers. Very busty, very Quinn. I'm thankful I don't look straight-up hag in it, and luckily, none of us will require major alterations before the big day.

By the time we're at dinner and we're each a few sips into our respective wine choices, things feel back to normal. The stick up Valerie's ass seems halfway out and Quinn's not evading my stare anymore. I almost mention it—*Hey! Glad to see we've all recovered from the weekend*—but something holds me back. I never can leave well enough alone and it always backfires, so I decide to shut my trap this time.

Everyone's in such good spirits (#nopunintended) that I catch them up on my coupla dates with James. Val's all girly claps and Quinn's all pokes and prods with her freshly painted claws. It's a wonder I don't have more bruises on a daily basis, really.

"Have you asked him to the wedding?" Val wants to know. She beams brighter than she did on the mechanical bull the other night, so I know she's legit excited.

"This weekend," I say. "But I have a pretty good feeling about it." And I can't help the woo-girl glee that's slipped its way into my whole existence. Gag, I know. "So what's left for us to do?" I ask.

"Not much, really," says Quinn, back to being enamored with her phone. "Writing out the place cards, really, if that's something you're able to help with. But no big deal."

"I'd love to." I even surprise myself in saying it. "Tonight?"

Quinn's mouth hangs open. "Well, sure, if you want to. Is that okay?"

"Of course."

She yanks back. "Wow, this James must have a magic wand because I don't even know who you are right now."

"I wouldn't know anything about his magic wand," I say, palm to sternum, feigning a *How Dare You?* look.

"So are you ready to admit we were right about this? About love?" Valerie asks, and I cut my stare her way.

"Not yet—are you nuts? But from what I've seen so far, this James seems promising, sure."

"Very diplomatic." She gives me an eye roll.

"That's me. Miss Diplomacy!"

We spend a very comfortable, very regular evening, but on the way to Quinn's apartment, she gets quiet and tense.

"What's the matter?" I ask, taking the turns like a Formula One racer.

When she says nothing in response, that itchy feeling under my skin acts up again, so I continue. "Where have you been this week? Have you been avoiding me?"

She takes a few paranoia-inducing seconds, breathes deep, and then she deadpans, "Does it always have to be all about you?" But she doesn't laugh or even smile afterward, and I get the feeling it is all about me.

"What's going on, Q?"

As if the silence isn't bad enough, she bursts into tears.

"It's Phil." She's gone ultrasonic. "He's just—super not enthused about the weekend. I told him everything, and—"

"Everything?"

She snaps her head toward me. "Yes, everything, Rae." Like I'm some moron.

But she's used my name, so I know this is serious.

She continues in a huff and wipes her eyes on a crumbly tissue she's discovered in the depths of her Michael Kors purse. "You, of all people, ought to know how important honesty is in a relationship. In a marriage."

"Whoa, whoa." Like she's a horse. I take one palm off the steering wheel and hold it out in front of me.

"I'm just saying." She softens. "He's pissed about the car and that's why he's been driving mine this week—"

"Like a punishment?" I scoff. I can't help it. "What are you? A child?"

"I insisted." She drags out the last word and then lets out an audible exhale like I'm the most ridiculous person in the world.

"I thought you said the other day that this wasn't my fault—which it wasn't, by the way. Other than us being parked at the wrong place at the wrong time, how am I involved in this? You're getting married. We've been friends for years. So we went on a bachelorette weekend. I looked out for you guys and kept us safe. And regardless. We are grown-ass women. I didn't force anybody to do anything they didn't want to do. I didn't leave anybody behind." I think of Valerie's little romp, and my stomach gurgles.

Still—I shake it off—*not my fault.*

I jerk into her driveway and throw the car into park, my blood threatening to burst its way through my skin.

"I know," she coos. "But Phil kind of blames you—"

"For what? Am I the mastermind behind the fucking car-theft ring that stole his precious Porsche?"

"Of course not. No." She presses her fingers to both temples and starts to rock back and forth like I've broken her brain. "I can't—"

"You can't what?" My tone, expectant.

"I don't know," she says, still avoiding my gaze.

"Have you even defended me at all?"

"Well, no, but—"

The admission all but knocks the wind out of me. My mouth is hanging open like even my jaw muscles have given up, and it takes seconds—minutes?—to recover. I have to control my breathing.

Steady. Don't say anything you're going to regret.

But then the words shove their way out without filter, without shame, without any way to save face—or friendship. Her betrayal by mere reticence is far too much for me to deal with.

"All we've been through, Quinn. Everything. And this?" My demeanor is one of pure defeat.

There's an ear-piercing silence—an almost...hum—that washes over the front seat while we just sit there. Letting it happen.

And then: "He's my husband."

I snort. "Not yet, he's not. And besides"—I stare straight at her—"I'm your friend. Since forever. How many guys have we been through? Boyfriends, fiancés, husbands. How many jerks?"

"Phil is not a jerk."

"Fine. I'm not saying he is. But just because you're marrying him doesn't mean he knows you better than I do. It doesn't mean everything he freaking says is right. And it doesn't mean everything I do is wrong. Right?"

She doesn't answer. Her bottom lip quivers a bit as she holds it shut.

"Right?" I repeat, but she's gone. She opens the door, slams it, and she's nearly inside before I can even ask *What about the place cards?*

*   *   *

CHAPTER 17

Friday is still tense and awkward during our first-grade team meeting since the first-grade team consists of just Quinn, Val, and me. It's clear to me the two of them have had a conversation about last night, and I'm just #overit. So I shrug my way through their ideas, offer no opinions, and I try to avoid eye contact with both of them as much as possible.

When my phone buzzes with a text, I'm all too happy to check it, and it's Sarah.

You're welcome is all she says, and suddenly I realize why, when I see Nick traipsing across the courtyard, brown leather satchel across those fine, broad shoulders.

Quinn shakes her head.

"What?" I blurt.

It's the first time I've spoken directly to her all day.

"Nothing. I just...can't believe we've got some stripper working here with kids. That's all."

Valerie laughs a bit unnaturally—a bit like a crazy person—and her face turns the color of my raspberry iced tea.

"He's not—" But I clamp my mouth shut. No point in continuing to argue with the Almighty Quinn who's always right, even when she's wrong.

"What?"

Her stare all but burns my skin, and I look down at my plan book. I definitely didn't want to get into this today.

"Nothing. It's just—you don't know him, is all," I say to the calendar section.

"And you do, is that it? Is that why you took us to that place? Because you knew he'd be there?"

"Are we still on this?" I slam my hands to the table a tad harder than I meant to. "No. God—I was just saying. You don't know why he—"

"I don't care why," she barks. "Just because you have a thing for him doesn't absolve him from anything, nor does it make him a good person."

Valerie chuckles.

"Oh, you're gonna weigh in on this, Val?" I stand. My chair scrapes across the linoleum with a cringe-worthy grate, and her gaze snaps back to the table, her giggles instantly squelched.

"I'm sure she's just laughing at the irony," Quinn keeps on.

"What irony?" My tone says *I dare you.*

"Just that if you have a thing for him, then it probably actually means he's not a good person."

Well, I mean, I did dare her...

I start tossing my pen, my legal pad, my phone into my bag. "I don't know what I did to deserve any of this, but fuck you. Fuck you, Quinn. And Val"—I catch her gaze—"you should know better."

And I storm out.

When lunchtime rolls around, I eat in my room, door

closed, shades drawn. No Sarah means I'm officially out of friends at work, and I don't want to risk running into Nick on this particular afternoon since he's Sarah's replacement. No way.

I'm halfway through the macaroni salad when my phone buzzes. It's Nick anyway, like he goddamn knows.

Nick: Are you avoiding me?

The accusation—him calling me on it—sends a buzz through me. I stare at the message, a shot right to my already heavy heart.

So he noticed. Dammit.

What's the breeziest way for me to fix this?

Me: Oh, gosh, no! I've just been super busy! You know how it is …

Blasé. Brilliant.

I brace myself for some kind of pithy response; but after a few minutes of silence, I breathe easy and decide I got away with it.

Excellent lie, Rae.

#nofollowupneeded

*   *   *

After I've got the kids busy with their literature circles, I take the argument out on my keyboard, my fingers *tap, tap, tapping* away at my poor laptop, which is an innocent bystander in all this. But I knock out a solid six hundred words before it's time to go on to social studies, and my manuscript has this angsty vibe I'm sure any literary agent will be dying to sign.

Right.

While the writing gets some of it out, when I get to James's place in the evening, I'm about a sneeze away from slitting my own wrists. But he's so sweet and so thoughtful—he's got everything taken care of for this meal we're cooking together tonight—*We're cooking a meal together*—that I just about cry. The chicken is thawed and cubed, the stoplight peppers (red, yellow, and green) are washed and waiting for my nimble fingers to slice the hell out of them, the water is a-boiling, and the brown rice is sitting out and already measured.

Still, I can't really take pleasure in any of it.

"What's wrong?" He lifts my chin with a finger.

"Girl drama," I respond, not able to meet his eye. My vision blurs over, and I don't want him to see me cry. Not this soon. Not like this.

Ew—emotion!

But he just lays a soft kiss on me and it makes me forget for a second. He scoops me in for a long hug that not only cracks my back but also squeezes some of the tension out of my torso.

"That's the worst kind of drama," he says. "But remember, your friend is getting married in two weeks. She's probably stressed out. Not that I'm defending her. I'm on your side, of course." He offers a smirk, and I kiss him again.

"Thank you" is all I say because it's all I can say. I want to enjoy this evening with him and, dagnabbit, I will.

And before I can even ask, he's opened a bottle of red and poured me a glass the size of my head like a goddamn wine angel.

"Where have you been all my life?" I snort and ease back the oaky wine. Curl up in its full body, like a recliner.

Not only is the company divine, the stir-fry is heavenly. And that's only in part because it's the only thing I can make so I've learned to make it well. Baby corns add just the right oomph; water chestnuts give it an authentic feel. I'm three merlots in, and I'm nailing this whole domestic thing—as far as James can probably tell, anyway. For all he knows, I can make our smart and attractive children ravioli and brownies and quiches from scratch.

Poor James, I think as I empty the rest of the bottle into my wineglass. *I'd better ask him to be my date to the wedding before he discovers the truth.*

He's washing the dishes in the sink, and I get behind him. Attach myself to his thick, delicious middle.

"What are you doing?" He chuckles and rinses off the cutting board. Places it in the soapy water and gives me a peck on the top of my head as he maneuvers his way around me.

"Speaking of the wedding…" I've detached myself from James now, and I'm walking two fingers around the counter like they're a tiny little soldier standing guard of this conversation.

"Were we?" He grins, and I playfully frown.

"Earlier, yes. Well, so—I know it's not even been a week, but do you think maybe—"

He does an about-face, his light eyes full of what looks like hope. "I'd love to," he blurts.

I pull back. "Love to what?"

"Be your date, if that's what you're asking. I assume that's what you're asking, right?"

And all I can do is beam up at him. This guy knows me.

He's not afraid to be vulnerable. To be real. Not afraid to speak his mind, and in turn, it makes me feel good about speaking mine.

"So that's a yes?" I walk my fingers up his biceps now. I mean, at least I think it's cute.

And he lifts me up onto the kitchen island. Pulls me to him.

"Yes." And he covers me in kisses that leave me weak, so thank God I'm sitting on a counter and not, like, standing, or I'd be on the floor by now.

*   *   *

The next morning, I'm up and at 'em bright and early, putting the finishing touches on a love scene I've been having trouble with for weeks. But this sudden bout of good fortune from the Spark gods seems to be doing me some good. I'm able to write happy things without feeling sad about it because it's reminiscent of a happy memory from something that ended in a soul-scathing sort of way.

So it's nice.

Thanks, James. Thanks, Spark. Thanks, Valerie and Quinn.

Valerie and Quinn.

The thought of arguing with my two best friends levels me, and James was right. Quinn's in the middle of wedding preparations. I'd probably be somewhat on the tense side were I about to get married again. Hell, I had a panic attack at the last ceremony I even went to, so she's got to be terrified, the poor thing. What if it doesn't work out again? What if she's making another huge mistake?

So I take to my phone and decide to send a peace offering. I can swallow my pride on this one. Lord knows I've done it before. And hopefully they'll both return the favor when I need them to do so some time in the future.

I load up the group text.

Me: Asked and answered...

After a few moments of anxiety—will they respond?—Quinn comes through.

Quinn: And?

I send back the thumbs-up emoji, and Val is back to gushing about love.

We haven't addressed our blowup, but we've been friends since high school. #bygones In no time, we're all systems go with the wedding and the planning, and I'm filling them in on last night with all the fervor of a tween at a One Direction concert. I'm aware that this doesn't seem like me, that all this Happiness, all this Excitement, would ordinarily be vomit inducing.

But maybe I really have been the problem.

Maybe I should continue doing the opposite of what I've trained myself to do and I'll feel the opposite of how I inevitably feel every time.

I've already started, in that I bought into this Spark thing at all—albeit on a mission to prove my friends wrong, but still. Look at me now.

I'm so pleased with myself that I didn't sleep with James last night (we just watched more episodes of *The Bachelor* and enjoyed each other's company with our clothes on—who knew?) that I felt—it feels—way, way different. We even discussed it because I can Talk About Things with James. I asked if we could wait a little while until we got to know each other better, and James was great about it. Said he knew the attraction was there, knew the want was there, and that was good enough for him.

So maybe my friends are right and I've been an idiot this whole time. Maybe I've been in the way of my own happiness.

But as I chip away at my word count, an icy feeling creeps back in because I don't want my sudden positivity to be about a guy. I don't want to be one of those women who can't do anything—who can't truly succeed—if she's not in a relationship. I'm not a man-hating feminist, but I'm a Raeist nonetheless. And that's crap. It's weak. I've come too far on my own to allow some endorphins from a fantastic set of lips to take my accomplishments away from me.

I'm torn.

So I opt to keep my feelings in check and not let them go flying off like a Chinese kite without my brain right there to hold the string and tether them to the ground.

This takes the form of me deciding not to text James, no matter how many syrupy kissy-face emojis I'd love to be sending him right now.

But we haven't been apart for even twelve hours yet. #getagrip

I find myself checking my phone every hundred words or so, but I'm convinced this is the result of habit and nothing more.

And I resolve to be less hung up on my phone too. I'm killing this whole be-a-better-person thing today!

The result is that I get a lot of writing done—good for me. And I'm almost ready to venture back out into the querying world again, try to snag an agent and get started on that whole, yanno, lifelong dream of mine thing.

But after the bulk of Saturday goes by and I've had about

three cups of coffee too many and James still hasn't made a textual move, panic sets in and I take a small step back for all womankind.

I pace the length of my kitchen and think about his kitchen. Where we cooked not twenty-four hours ago. Where he said nice things and soothed me about my friend problems, stroked my hair. Where he did the dishes, where he agreed to be my date to the wedding.

I go to my phone, which stares blankly back at me with no notifications, no indications of any network problems, nothing. I turn it off and back on—I'm an electronics wizard—and yet nothing.

My fingers are getting twitchy—and if we're being honest, so is my face. Rather than text him, however, I think: *What's the opposite of what I want to do?*

Change out of my pajamas?

Progress!

Put my phone away?

Yes!

And so I get into some workout gear and decide to take Billie for a jaunt.

"The fresh air will do us both good," I tell her.

She just stretches and scampers to the door, tail high and waggy.

But as we walk—my hair sticking to my temples, my neck—the warmth of the breeze only fans the flame of crazy inside me. I go back over the evening with James. Everything we did, everything we said.

Was there something I missed? Something I took the wrong way?

But there's nothing.

When we return and he still hasn't said boo, I decide this is stupid. There was nothing to indicate any issue, and there's probably a perfectly logical and innocent explanation for James's silence today. Worrying about when to text and when not to text is like playing a game, and I'm not about that.

So I just do it.

It doesn't mean I'm weak. It doesn't mean I'm giving up my power. It just means I'm a goddamn adult and I'm sending him a message.

I settle on: Hope you had a good day!

Brilliant.

But when no answer comes for the remainder of the night, I change back into my pj's. Switch from coffee to wine. It calms the crazy and lulls me back to sanity. Back to what I know, anyway.

Back to the only things I can count on.

*   *   *

CHAPTER 18

Characters are supposed to have motivations. They need to be well rounded. Three-dimensional. "A villain is always the hero of his own story." You hear that at writing conferences a lot, and whenever someone says it, there are appreciative nods—eyes close in reverence—because it sounds smart. And every time it's like the first time anyone's ever said it. And the concept is true.

But it's also complete bullshit.

I repeated that sentiment over and over to myself as I edited the night before. As I added depth to my characters, atmosphere to my scenes.

But one of the things authors never say, one of the things editors don't tend to touch on, is that sometimes you never learn someone's motivations. In life, sometimes a DB is just a DB. Sure, he may have his reasons for doing whatever his DB thing is and he may have justified it to himself and that might make him three-dimensional or a richer character—it might humanize him—but the thing we don't like to say is that sometimes we never learn his side of things.

So we make up a narrative for him. We say he's a liar or maladjusted or a jerk, to make ourselves feel better. We say he's immature, afraid of commitment, selfish—you name it— because we don't know the reason he ghosts, as the kids call it nowadays.

Something you said or something you did or some way you are scares him off. Turns him off. Cools his affections toward you.

Or, really, maybe it has nothing to do with you at all— maybe his dick just points in someone else's direction and he forgets to be a decent human being, but what does it matter? You just met.

So move on.

Forget.

Swipe, swipe, swipe.

I think all this Sunday morning when James still hasn't answered me, and now my memories of last Sunday, of Tuesday, of Friday, our bantery messages from the week, are too painful, too annoying, to stomach thinking about or looking at anymore.

I don't want it to take anything from me. It shouldn't— I'm not sixteen years old. But self-loathing swirls in my veins because it does. It does because I gave a shit for, like, four seconds.

And when you've let your guard down over and over, when you've had hope, when you've had hope squashed, when you've loved with abandon, trusted without question, and been wrong—time and time again? Allowing yourself to go back there—even for four lousy seconds—only to be wrong again? It's torture. It's an eternity.

"So what are you going to do?" Sarah asks on the other

end of the line when I finally break down and decide to call someone.

I pick at the remnants of the touch-up manicure I gave myself before James came over Friday night.

"A year ago, I would have sent as many scathing texts as I could, just to tell him what a prick he was. But now?" I chuckle. "I'm too exhausted."

"Are you going to tell Valerie and Quinn?"

I let out a deep exhale. The question of the hour.

"I don't want to tell the girls yet because the one thing that's been holding us together since last weekend has been my pink cloud of optimism about that stupid guy. And now that it's gone? I'm not sure how they're going to react to my Rae despair. Plus, I can't very well be gloomy right before Wedding Week, can I?"

"Hmm—probably not. Well, let me know if you want to go out tonight. A bunch of us are heading up to Blake's Tavern."

My overactive mind is already picking out which skirt to wear, and so I know what my answer has to be.

"Thanks, but no thanks. I have more work to do."

*   *   *

Come nine p.m., I'm regretting that decision, but I suppose drinking alone is safer than the alternative. How much trouble can I get into at home? *Too much*, I realize, as I'm checking Spark and can see that James unmatched me because his profile is gone and all our messages we sent before we exchanged numbers and started texting are also gone. Kaput.

This gets my proverbial goat in that I didn't even get the satisfaction of unmatching him first. One more little jab he was able to get in before I could. I delete his texts and block his number, but what good does that do? He's not going to message me anymore anyway and doesn't even know I've done it.

shakes a fist at the sky

And then some doofy guy's profile pops up and he grins up at me, like some roly-poly clown—

Swipe Left or Swipe Right?

I laugh. Like I'm really going to subject myself to this torture again. The wedding's almost here. I'll go alone.

But before I toss my phone aside for the night, Nick texts. His first reply since I lied to him the other night.

Nick: I figured you were busy, but I just thought I'd check.

I chew my bottom lip as guilt kneads my insides.

It's time to let all that avoiding business go.

The Spark experiment didn't work—my life experiment didn't work—and I decide I'm done looking for love. It sure as hell isn't looking for me.

Beagles are way better snugglers than boys anyway.

But maybe it would be good to have a guy's perspective on all this.

So I start to type back.

Me: Real talk? You were right—I was avoiding you a little. The new guy didn't work out, and so dodging all those of the male persuasion seemed like a good idea.
Nick: It's true enough.
Me: But that's stupid. And I'm sorry. Friends?

Friends.

The cursor blinks at me after the word. Hangs there for a second like Am I Actually Capable of This, but I decide I am. I have to be, for my sanity.

So I hit SEND.

Apparently Nick didn't need much to warm up to me again because we message the rest of the night, and I feel that same calm I felt in the car. A burden lifted.

He has all sorts of Opinions on why James ghosted, the number one being because I didn't sleep with him.

> Me: Then why'd he act like he was fine with it? Why'd he agree to go to the wedding with me?
> Nick: My guess is because he probably thought he could get you to change your mind with his sweetness. But when you didn't...Dun, dun, DUNNN.
> Me: Ugh. Are all of you like this?
> Nick: Ouch. No. *rubs at the sting*

"Yeah, right," I say to my screen but write back a simple Haha.

*   *   *

Monday Nick subs for third grade, and I first learn this when an adorably oblivious student runs into and subsequently knocks down one of my bookshelves with his ginormous backpack.

My phone buzzes a nanosecond after the crash.

> Nick: Everything all right in there?
> Me: ?

Nick: Yanno, you're not supposed to be drinking on the
job.
Me: Har har.
Nick: But seriously—you need me to come over? I'm in
Jenkins's room.

I hear two bangs on the other side of the cinder block, like
he's beat his elbow against the wall, and my heart leaps into my
throat. I don't know why.

Or, rather, I do. I allow myself to get lost in inappropriate
memories of what he looked like shirtless—and, just as quickly,
shake it off. *Why am I like this?*

We're fine, I write back, and I feel the trace of a smile. Just a
lesson in awareness that Robbie learned the hard way.

I push it down to the best of my ability, but there's something sort of thrilling about knowing Nick's right there, so close,
the rest of the day. Every time my phone vibrates in my pocket
as I'm reviewing murmur diphthongs (which he, too, thought
was hilarious), as I'm starting the unit on solids, liquids, and
gases, a piece of me is over there. Through the wall. And a piece
of him is over here. In my pocket.

I know I'm not alone.

*   *   *

Lunch is another story.

I'm sitting in the lounge between Sarah and Quinn. Valerie
is more interested in her Caesar salad than the conversation—
or, lack thereof, really. Nick is on the other side of Sarah and
chomping away on a highly illegal peanut butter and jelly.

I can hear the wet, squirgly sounds of everyone around me

chewing and my misophonia sets my nerves into a tizzy. Quinn's banana, *splergh*, *splergh*, *splergh*. Each muffled crunch of Val's pear.

And the room is warm. Too warm. Blanketed in tension. Everyone is somewhat on edge, it seems, except for Sarah; and I suppose that's because she's the only one of us here who doesn't know about Nick's other part-time job.

My head starts to pound at the gross noises I'm trying not to hear and as I think of all the webs of secrecy and deception running through the five of us. Connecting us all in some ways but also keeping us at a distance. I wonder what secrets Val and Quinn have kept from me, and this is the first time I've thought this, in all these years. How naïve—oblivious—am I?

The poison of self-doubt, of loyalty and where theirs lies, leaks its way through my system, and I'm just about to burst when Sarah breaks the silence.

"You're not supposed to have that here, you know," she says to Nick, amusement tickling her tone and wrinkling her nose.

"This?" He considers the half a sandwich in his hand. "Why not?"

"Because we're a peanut-free school," Valerie answers. "Tons of the kids have peanut allergies, and so that's a thing now, after the last incident we had a few years ago. No one's told you?"

He grimaces with what looks like genuine concern. "Yikes. Think I'm going to be in trouble? I honestly didn't know."

"Something tells me you don't mind walking on the wild side," I offer and ensnare him with an eyebrow.

"Guilty." He meets my gaze like I'm the only one in the room, and heat blooms in my cheeks, beneath my blouse, every-where.

"So when are you seeing James again?" Quinn cuts right

through our stare with her pointed comment, and guilt pricks in my chest like I'm Billie and I peed on the rug or something.

"You still haven't told them?" Sarah scoffs, her mouth forming a perfect O of what looks like astonishment.

"Told us what?" Quinn wants to know. But just then Ida struts her way in, mail and folders and chocolate in tow.

"Well, if it isn't my favorite coworkers," she says with a wide, red grin. "I just wanted to come by and give you all kisses. One for you." She drops a Hershey's Kiss in front of me. "One for you, you, and you." She follows suit with Valerie, Quinn, and Sarah. "And an extra one for you," she says with a wink, plopping two in front of Nick, who flashes a grin at the candy.

"How's that girlfriend of yours?" Ida asks, and he nearly chokes on the last bite of sandwich he's shoveled in.

She claps a hand on his back and he stands, still clearing his throat. Gives his chest a little beating with a strong fist.

"Oh, she's—good." His voice is scratchy. He reaches for his soda.

I stifle a laugh.

"Don't hurt yourself, kid," she says to him, a hand on his shoulder. "And don't worry about me. I'm only playing."

"Right." He gives her half a frown.

"So what am I interrupting?" she asks and pops a squat next to him.

No one says anything.

"Oh, come on." She *tsks*.

"Actually," Sarah offers, "Rae was just about to tell her be-fris that her latest squeeze was more of a squish."

"Huh?" Ida scrunches her face, contour makeup obscuring most of her natural features.

"Damn." Nick shields his crotch area like Sarah's comment has something to do with hitting him in the crown jewels, and I just shake my head at all of them.

"What do you mean?" Valerie asks.

"You slept with him," Quinn says.

I exhale in disgust. "No." And I proceed to tell them how the exact opposite is probably why he disappeared. "In fact, I'm done with all men. Period."

"Yeah, right." Quinn laughs.

"I'm serious," I say. "I'm too old, and I'm too tired. I'm good with it."

Val: "But what if Mister Right comes a—"

"There's no such thing. And, honestly, this realization has given me peace. It's time for me to focus on me. Better myself. Not better myself for someone else."

When I'm done, Ida clicks her tongue. "I'm so sorry, love." Then she turns her attention to Nick. "It was so great to finally meet your little woman," she says. "I ran into the two of them at Starbucks the other night. Such a cute couple."

His features take on a deep red. He doesn't even look at her—he looks at me. "It was just coffee," he says, talking with his hands. "And anyway—"

A laugh bubbles its way from the depths of my gut, because of course. Of course he was lying about the girlfriend.

I shrug. "No skin off anything of mine, hombre."

But I don't want to hear any more. It's not my business, and even though we've established we're just friends and I've talked to him about my dating situations, the thought of him out in the world with a girlfriend I thought he was done with twists like a sword.

He's saying words and I'm nodding along with the rest, but

I can't help it: The rage monsoon descends upon me. And I'm trying not to laser off his face with my stare.

How? How can he discuss this all so freely in front of me? The way he flirts? The amount we've talked?

Yes, we're friends, but it pisses me right the fuck off because how dare this dude make me Feel Things when he isn't available. How dare he lie?

And how could I allow myself to be so trusting and so stupid?

Again?

I've reduced the saltines that accompanied my chili to dust in their packaging by the time the conversation is over. When there are about five minutes left before the end of lunch, Sarah, Ida, and Nick leave before the girls and I do.

"Hey—I'm sorry about James," Quinn says with a tentative touch to my forearm.

"I am too. What an idiot. Why didn't you tell us?" Valerie's right there with the comfort too, and it feels like we've been transported back in time a few weeks before things were so weird between us. Before the secrets. Before the resentment.

I meet their gazes. "I don't know. But do you believe me now?"

They both just press their lips into firm lines like *Poor Rae* and offer sad headshakes.

"And to top it off . . ." I continue, still stewing over learning the truth about Nick's little girlfriend.

I brandish my phone, but for a fraction of a second I hesitate.

Do I show them my conversation with Nick, how much we've been talking, and make him look bad just because I'm hurt and harboring some stupid feelings for him? Would an adult do that?

I think of our conversation on the way home from South Beach. The connection we seem to have.

But then I replay how he told me he wasn't attached. And now the discovery that he was, in fact, with someone just the other day.

So is he with her or not?

Really.

And it's decided.

I shove my phone toward them and scroll through two days of jokes, sexual tension, and innuendo.

Jokes, sexual tension, and innuendo I've thoroughly enjoyed, but still.

"What are you saying?" Quinn grasps the device and her copper eyes mist as if she's Nick's fricking girlfriend being shown the messages.

"I'm just saying, he told me he didn't have a girlfriend—that things had ended—and here I come to find out he was with her just the other day. I tried. I played by your rules. I went out with some guys. I gave James a chance—even felt something for him. But at the end of the day? I was right. Nothing is sacred. You can't really trust anyone with your heart. You think Nick's poor girlfriend would be okay with this?"

Quinn stands, her hands out in front of her, and she closes her eyes like she Can't Even with anything I'm saying. Like this evidence right in front of her is scorching her corneas.

I can't take her reaction. It's kindling to the fury that's been swirling inside me the last twenty minutes.

"What?" I bark.

She twists her face, arms crossed, in what registers as judgment to me. Like it's my fault. Like I knew.

"You think I messed with an attached guy on purpose?"

"I have no idea," she says. "But I wish you'd stop acting like this is everyone. This is not everyone."

I realize this is coming from a place of sheer terror on her part—terror from being hurt before. Terror that I might be right. But I can't help but snort. And before I can stop them, the words erupt from my throat.

"Why are you acting like you know so much better about how guys are because you've hooked one? Why do attached women do this? Being in a relationship doesn't mean you know more than a single person does. It might just mean you got tired and gave up—and when you rolled over one morning, that was who was next to you. That doesn't make Phil man of the fucking year. Just like getting married doesn't necessarily mean you're happy or successful. Or that it's a happy or successful marriage. You of all people should know that. I could have stayed married too. So why are you acting like this, Quinn? This is me."

She steadies herself on the edge of the table like my words have knocked the wind out of her. It was too far, I know, but I couldn't help it. Had to be said.

She clears her throat, gaze misting even more—the calm before the storm anyone who's ever argued with Quinn before would recognize. But instead of launching into a tirade, her voice is low. Her tone is even.

And that's even scarier.

"I can't believe I'm saying this, but I think Phil is right."

"Right about what? Look, I wasn't saying Phil's a bad guy or that your marriage isn't going to be good. I didn't mean it like that. I'm sorry. I just don't understand why—"

"That you're toxic." Moisture drips down her face, but her voice remains steady.

Her words are like a club to the chest, and each new one

all but topples me, but somehow I remain standing, albeit bent. Letting the words I've feared run me through, if that's how she wants it.

"I'll never be able to be happy with him as long as I'm friends with you. Because you're miserable. And you want everyone else to be miserable too. We wanted to help you." She looks to Val. "To get you out of this man-hating funk. And it seems as though all that did was make it worse. Look, I'm sorry things didn't work out with the first guy you've actually tried to give a chance to since—"

"Don't you say it—don't you dare say his name—"

"Since Jesse," she shouts. "But that doesn't mean I'm stupid for wanting to marry Phil or for wanting to try again. For trusting someone else. I've been hurt too, but I've moved on. And I'm not going to allow myself to be dragged down by you anymore. Not this week. Not this marriage. Not anymore."

"What are you saying?" is all I can eke out of my throat.

"I'm saying—" Her hands are shaking. She wipes at her face, her jaw tight, but she doesn't break eye contact with me. "I don't think you should come to the wedding. You happy? You were right. But I don't want to be reminded of how right you are about guys anymore. I want to believe Phil is an exception to that. I want to be happy. You're not in it anymore. It's done. You got your way."

"You think this is my way? You think any of it—" My knees feel like they've each taken two shots of tequila. I steady myself and look over at Valerie. "Anything you'd like to say?"

She averts her stare to her ballerina flats.

"What have I—" My tone is injected with so much venom, it poisons the very air between us. And then I'm shaking my head. Looking at the wall, the floor, the coffeemaker. Anywhere

but at these two human beings who don't know or understand
me at all.

Or maybe they do.

It's a whisper of a thought that hits me right in the gut, and
I can't stay in this room another minute.

"You should know better," I direct toward Valerie. Quiet.
"You both should. But fine. Have a beautiful wedding. Have a
beautiful life."

I finally look Quinn in the face again, and all the color has
drained from it. She looks like a shadow of the Quinn I know
her to be. Or maybe that's just who she is now. Maybe it's who
she always was and I was too self-absorbed to notice.

Either way, I say, "Count me out," toss my tray, and slam the
door behind me.

*   *   *

CHAPTER 19

I get home, and I try being productive. I take to my laptop to hammer out more of the query letter I pored over a few nights ago only to find that the file was corrupted and I lost everything. Two hours of work to get the words just right, gone. I try balancing my checkbook. Try cuddling Billie. Try walking her. Try running it all away.

I try all the healthy and responsible ways of dealing with my emotions, but this is too big. Too intense. Too much.

So I stop trying to make everyone happy, being what I'm not, and embrace what everybody apparently thinks I am.

There is not enough alcohol in the world, it seems, but there is a decent amount in my pantry, and so I forgo food for dinner and opt to drink it all away.

Even as I'm rifling through my choices, I know it's stupid and that it won't fix anything. I know it. I know. But it's too much to think through right now. Too much to deal with.

I pour myself a liter or two of wine and sink into my bathtub. Inhale the steam and feel it seep into my lungs, warming me from the inside out. Hot water pools around my feet and makes islands of my knees and arms. Lulls me into a delicious haze.

I keep hearing Quinn's voice. *I think Phil is right. That you're toxic.*

Mike's. *She was married, buddy. You kinda had that before and didn't want it. And now you don't really seem to go out with the same guy more than a few times.*

Valerie's laughs.

Before I know it, the glass is empty, but never fear! I brought the bottle with me! I bite down on the cork and yank it free with my teeth. Spit it across the room, and it's bottoms up in record time.

And then my phone rings. It jolts me into a more upright position, heart jackhammering, water sloshing onto the bathroom tile.

Nick, it says, flashing across my screen, which is foggy from the thick air. The mirror has fogged over too.

He's calling.

He's calling?

I lean halfway out of my tub to get to the phone and answer it. "Hel—"

"I wanted to talk to you about today. I know what Ida thinks she saw, but it wasn't—"

"So you weren't out to coffee with your girlfriend, then?"

"No. Well, yes. Well—"

I let the silence steep.

"I was with her," he continues. "But we aren't together. I actually met with her that night to talk things through because we had been in limbo for a while—she had wanted to try again, and I wanted to make sure she knew that, definitively, it was over."

It takes me a few minutes to catch up to his words. #alcohol

"I don't know why you're telling me this," I say.

He's quiet a moment. I hear him breathe, and then: "I don't know—I just wanted you to know."

"Okay. Well—"

"Look, do you think maybe we could get a drink? Something happened and I need to talk to a friend about it. I need to figure out what to do, and—"

He keeps talking, but I've stopped listening.

Maybe I've misinterpreted him all this time. Maybe he really does see me as a friend and I'm just a pathetic loser who thought there was a connection between us when there wasn't one. Not in the way I thought.

Or maybe I'm just drunk.

For whatever reason, he's turning to me during whatever this upsetting time is—and, according to my dearest friends in the world, I push things too far anyway, so why not give in to my impulse to be near him and just go for it? What's the harm now? I don't want to be alone right now either, and that's exactly what I am. Alone.

"Okay," I say, "but do you mind coming here? I've had the worst of all days and I've already gotten into some wine."

His laugh electrifies me through the receiver. It's a light, happy sound that I didn't even know I'd been craving all day.

"Sounds like it! Where are you, the tub? It's all echoey."

"Right. I'm going to tell you to come over and then tell you I'm naked. If you want to get together you're going to have to be on your best behavior." My words are scolding, but there's a hair flip at the end of them that I just can't fight.

"Scout's honor." He chuckles. "Now, what's your address?"

*   *   *

I manage to make myself presentable again before Nick arrives. I pull on some yoga pants, a tee shirt; tie my hair back in a ponytail; apply minimal makeup. Nothing about my appearance says I've tried too hard or that this is a date. Something I'd wear to Valerie's on a Tuesday night to watch E! and bitch about work in.

Well, maybe with a trace more eyeliner than that. #trufax

The good news is, when he gets here, I'm still tipsy enough not to be nervous, and so I greet him with a hug, which I think surprises both of us.

His body is solid. Unwavering. It ignites me from my toes and slithers like it's following a line of gunpowder up my legs as I throw my arms around him, his free hand gripping my waist almost as though he's holding me at a distance. Careful. But I think maybe it's just that my sudden burst of affection caught him off guard.

"Well, helloooo," I say.

I had forgotten about the whole me-always-touching-him thing, but I can see it's in full effect already. I break away once the flush in my cheeks registers, because this might be a problem.

"I'm sorry!" I clap a palm over my mouth and quake with laughter.

"It's okay." He flashes those teeth at me. "I guess I just underestimated the shittiness of your day and how much wine you'd gotten into. Do tell. Got a corkscrew?" He indicates the bottle of white in his hand and then slaps a palm to his forehead. "What am I thinking? You probably have one in every room."

I give him a playful shove into the kitchen and it barely

fazes him. Something about the way my non-muscles have no effect makes me want to try again. Harder. Pick a fight just to ruffle his feathers. Make him set that perfect jaw at me. Punish me for it.

I'm leaning against the doorjamb, steady, watching him rifle through my drawers—the shift of powerful shoulders visible through a delectably snug tee shirt. All at once, a mere flick of the wrist, his big back still to me, he produces the gadget— *Ta-da*! The sleek metal glints off the light above the sink.

"Well, don't you just know your way around..." I say, playing footsie with my tone.

"So I'm told," he throws over his shoulder, playing right back, and his voice fills the room. Fills the void. Fills me.

We're silent at the joke. The insinuation. But it stirs a kind of ache beneath my skin.

Once we've made it to the couch, he stretches out. Long. Like he's sat there a thousand times, like he belongs nestled among the soft pillows. Like he owns them. He takes one in his hand. Palms it. And my heart pounds as he launches into his story.

"So Deborah called me into her office after school today. I thought she was offering me the long-term sub position in fifth grade, since I heard the science teacher is going on maternity leave, but instead, she fired me."

I struggle to a seated position. "What in holy hell—"

I'm not sure if the throb in my chest is from him or the words I can't believe he's saying, but I can barely hear him over my own pulse.

"What did she say?"

"Not much. She just said that she doesn't think Wesson will be needing me anymore—that they're oversaturated with subs as it is, which I know is garbage. And that after today I should look for sub jobs elsewhere but she's happy to act as a reference for me. What the hell is that about?"

"Can she just do that? With no real reason?"

"It's an independent school; they can pretty much do whatever they want. And technically she did provide me a reason—I just know it's a bullshit one. You didn't say anything about the stripping thing to anybody, did you?"

My mouth goes dry. "Of course not."

"I didn't actually think so. I'm just so…" His gaze drifts, tigerlike in intensity. "Can we talk about something else now?" Forces a smile. "Why was your day so bad?"

I relay my story to him in between sips of wine, careful to leave out the Nick-specific parts that had me cranky. Just the lost friends and the lost query letter and the lost dreams. Yanno, run-of-the-mill Tuesday night stuff.

I watch his lips, the way they curve gently upward when I tell my tale. Slide slightly downward during the particularly rough parts, just when they should.

"I'm sorry you lost all that work. What's your manuscript about?" he asks. "I'd love to read it."

A guffaw booms from me, and I have to clap a palm over my mouth to silence it. "I've never let anyone read my stuff," I say.

"Well, maybe that's your problem. You've got to let people in a little bit to get the most out of something. To get it to its best. No?"

I grin through a narrowed gaze. "All right over there, Dr. Phil. It's erotica, not Shakespeare."

"So what? You want this to be the Shakespeare of erotica, don't you? The Chaucer of chiseled abs!"

"The Beethoven of bondage!" I raise my glass.

"That's music…"

"Yeah, that's what I said!"

We're both cracking up.

He continues. "But you want it to be the best it can be, which I'm sure is already pretty great because you're pretty great. That play you wrote for the kids was fantastic." His mouth quirks downward a bit at the realization. "I guess I won't get to see the finished product."

I shake my head. "Such bullshit. I'm sorry. Well, *Indigenous People of Florida* is a tad different from *Playing Doctor*, but I like to think I'm a versatile writer."

He laughs. "Tell me what it's about."

After I've sufficiently discussed my manuscript and we're a bottle of wine down, I go back into the kitchen to get another. I try to hurry—fumble with the cork this time—because I don't want the bubble of intimacy to burst. And the longer I'm in here…

At once, I feel the warmth of his body radiate mere centimeters from mine. Close enough that the space between us buzzes, the energy desperate to reach out.

He slides his hands over mine, and I gasp. My head rolls to the side in response, the curve of my neck cold without his lips on it. Tingling. Imagining just what it would feel like if he clamped that mouth upon it and claimed it as his.

But he doesn't.

Bastard.

I chuckle. He's toying with me now. I can toy with him too.

And as his hands swallow mine, together gliding the corkscrew up and down slowly, I graze my ass against his front and he's rigid against me. He sucks away the air from right behind my ear with a sharp intake of breath at my lightest of touches.

I wasn't expecting it, but: #Winning!

Then *pop* goes the cork and we both jump at the noise, and immediately start laughing.

"I'm really sorry about Wesson," I say, flipping around to face him. Letting him suffer the absence of my body, no longer touching his but still experiencing the knot through his jeans like muscle memory. Like he branded me with the feeling.

"Does this mean you're going to be..."

"Stripping more? Ha-ha. No." He takes a step back, one side of his mouth bowed in a grin. He runs his tongue over those perfect teeth and scratches at the back of his head like he's trying to regain his composure. Starts pouring the wine like none of it ever even happened.

His faux nonchalance makes me want to torture him even more.

I have no doubt he knows exactly what he's doing. I'm not misreading this.

"What then?" I play along, leaning my elbows on the cool granite, the chill of the slick rock sending a shiver all down my arms. "I know you need the money right now..."

Faintly, my nipple pokes out from the chill and I brush it against his biceps. In an instant, a lightning strike of nerve endings electrifies my whole breast as if he's reached out for it.

His breath catches again, and our gazes magnetize.

"Hey." He leans close, hot air from his lungs tickling the end of my nose, swirling on my lips. They tingle with longing, my pulse rapid with want.

He's farther away than he was when—hello—we were on-stage and he was throwing me all around, but somehow it feels like he's closer. Already inside. He lassos me with his stare, my breast still warm against him, and there's a grasp that's taken hold. He binds me without touch. I'm a prisoner to these eyes of his and he can see straight through me to the wine rack on the counter.

And, somehow, I'm more naked, more alive, than if I stripped off every last stitch of clothing and surrendered right here, right now.

"I've been wanting to talk to you about something," he says, not moving a muscle.

His eyes are two pendulums. Two hypnotist's watches. Drawing me out of consciousness with a power I can't explain. They're onyx. The unknown. Inviting as a skinny dip in a forbidden forest. But they shine bright like moonlight reflecting off dark water. Sincere. They look straight into mine, and I don't need him to say anything else.

I don't care.

I haven't been imagining whatever this is. It's there. He tells me with that hint of smolder behind the darkness. That tinge of a smirk. I felt it moments ago through the thin fabric of my yoga pants. That longing. His body betrays him, and so I don't care what's right or what's wrong. I'm not interested in propriety; I'm interested in the truth. And the truth is staring me right in the face. Radiating with a torment matched only by my own, which pulses—writhes—through my every liquefied cell.

His mouth opens, those lips I've craved all night, and whatever he's about to say, that's nice, but I just don't want to hear it. Not now. Maybe not ever.

Gracelessly, I grasp a fistful of his tee shirt at the collar. Yank him to me. Those lips on my lips, and he gives an almost imperceptible whimper as the two meet. Firm. A little rough even as I hear the *clink* of him trying to wrap his mind around it all— clumsily setting his glass on the granite without looking, without parting our kiss, all the while pressing me into the counter with his full weight.

I imagine the bruise blossoming down the ridges of my spine like clusters of verbena as he arches me back, and I all but cry out, the warmth of his body spreading a wildfire throughout mine.

I drink in his scent, deep into my lungs. He smells like clean linen. Like perfection.

Like wine, as the glasses topple against the backsplash and sauvignon blanc soaks its way into my hair and trickles down my neck.

"Let me get that." He laughs, a ruthless quaver against the delicate skin behind my ear, as he buries his face in the flesh of my neck. It's slick with wine, and now with the flicker of his tongue, and my senses elude me.

He's sucked them into the vortex of his mouth along with my breath. I clutch at his every contour, fingernails scratching against the fabric, the ripples in his back pleading not to be contained.

My breath catching, I throw my head back with each new undulation of biting winter. My vision blurs with fire and ice. Crimson and silver.

I'm falling, falling, sinking into the abyss, my hands at the base of his neck, and I pull him down. Pull him to me. Pull him closer. Devour him the way I've wanted to but couldn't.

But when he lowers me to the floor and the small of my back brushes the unforgiving surface of the hard wood, I snap back. My wits about me. I can't go down yet. Not without a fight. Not without a struggle.

In a desperate tussle, I pin him to the floor and anchor him there. Hover over my kill, so still, so unsuspecting. I dangle my breasts like forbidden apples ripe for the picking and run my hands underneath his shirt. Feel the smooth, hot skin of his pecs as he trembles at my touch. His heart thuds beneath my fingertips. And it's too much. It's a crime against everything good and holy that his form is restricted by cloth and thread, so I tear the shirt off him and he ensnares me with a look.

I linger over him, a few strands of hair framing my face skimming either side of his. I slide out my ponytail holder and my hair flows free, soft. He sifts his fingers through it and then tangles them tight. Crushes me to him.

We move like a live wire together. Sparking. Burning. Endangering everything in our wake. We roll, bang arms, shins, elbows, heads against the pitiless wood without caring what's at stake besides this moment.

With one sweep, he rips my shirt right off me—and then *snap* goes the bra, like it's nothing. The power, the control in his fingers, sends waves of frantic desire coursing through me. His chest, every swell glistening and tattooing itself into my memory.

This time, it's all just for me to see.

"Should I make stripper jokes now?" He takes my shirt and swings it overhead, half a sexy smile, half a snarl looming over me.

"No jokes," I say and curl my fingers through two of his belt loops. Tight.

He grunts in response, deep in my ear, and his voice is low. The bass timbre sending goose bumps all down my left side as he makes his way back to my mouth by way of my neck. My throat, still sticky with the sweet remnants of wine I can taste on his tongue.

I grapple for breath as his scruffiness—this five o'clock

shadow I've not seen before tonight—scrapes its way across my jawline, my chin. He seizes handfuls of my hair. Yanks. Then he's back at my mouth, taking all he can from it, taking everything I'm giving. My bare skin burning against his, flesh on flesh. Nipples stinging against teeth.

I'm overcome with the need to satiate this starvation, this torture.

At long last, he tugs my yoga pants down, gently at first, trying to give off the illusion that he's composed, I suppose, but his cock gives him away. He's trying to play it so cool—a smirk here, an exhale there—but his erection betrays him; it's too hard, too desperate, pressing into my hip, and I know it won't be long before he'll have to stop playing the sexual martyr and vanquish what it is he really wants.

When he twists the lace waistband of my tanga panties—nothing gentle about that!—and twirls the fabric at my hip, the tension builds between my legs. He pulls it tighter, tighter, until there's not a measurement small enough to describe the distance between it and me—there isn't any. I've soaked it through, and the sensitive skin beneath it pulses. Stings. Yearns for more, for something, anything, to relieve the pressure sure to break me apart.

He teases me with kisses along the curve of my abdomen, a thumb pressed firmly against the outside of my underwear, against my clit.

And then I reach for his belt buckle. Enough is enough.

He gives a soft chuckle and leads my hands away, above my head. Holds both of them there by my wrists in the grip of one of his.

"Not yet," he says.

Dick.

"Oh, you think you're running the show?"

With his free hand, he reaches down, beneath the lace this time, and kind of growls when he feels how wet I am. It breaks his gaze, which has been so disciplined up until this point. His eyes take on a wild look, and a thrill skates down my legs at what he's doing.

"This—" he starts to speak, but the fire in his stare has completely taken over, and he squeezes his eyes shut as he slips a finger inside. Slow. His breaths catching. Ever increasing. Still steady and hot against my chest as his weight bears down.

I move against him. I can't help it. Beckon him. I need more than this.

And all at once he lifts me up—flips us—so now he's the one on his back.

My body shivers, pangs of raw hunger emanate from the void of where his fingers just were. I tear into his jeans like a ravenous forager, and he's just as I felt against my ass, against my hip—rigid against gray boxers, hard and hot and helpless.

My turn to drive him crazy.

I position myself between his supple legs, and with each whirl my tongue gives, each slide of my hand down his cock, his whole body spasms. I glance up at him, powerless, and an evil laugh bubbles from the depths of me. Such control never gets old. I toss my side bangs with a flick and decide it's time.

He must sense it too because he eases me back toward his mouth, cradles my head in his hands, and takes command once again. Sucking in every breath he can, sucking me breathless. Before I can even take off my underwear, he's slipped on the condom like a goddamn sex magician, and I glance down at the wrapper.

Magnums.

"Wow, you certainly think a lot of yourself." I pull back playfully and beckon him through my eyelashes, a grin tugging its way up my face.

"Shut up." He laughs. And, just as quickly, the joke is gone. He's slid the seeping fabric to the side, a shiver zapping me when my wet skin hits the cool air. He holds me there a second, hands coiled around my hip bones. The urgency throttling me, throttling him. I can feel the restraint pulsing in his very fingertips. They shake with desire.

And then, finally, mercifully, with trembling hands, he eases me down onto him in excruciating, exhilarating slow motion.

I'm helpless to stifle a gasp—good God, he is steel. And suddenly his giant hands have taken hold of my ass—squeeze. The friction setting my abs, my thighs, ablaze.

"I have wanted this since—" He bites down on his bottom lip, his voice strains just above a whisper, and it compels me forward, the two of us struggling against each other, our bodies lapping at each other like two angry waves on the sea.

This is nothing like I've ever written. I take notes with my body, with my hands, the rubber band of tightness that stretches down my calves as I rest them upon stalwart shoulders. Memorizing every bend of his torso, each dip of an ab. Each eager touch is mouthwatering research I beg will go on forever.

My eyes threaten to roll back in my head, to sink into the darkness, but there's no stopping now. He wears a snarl of hunger, of beautiful pain. Sweat drips from his forehead to mine in one splash, and it startles me. I tighten against him, and he groans, not far off from his own oblivion; but before I can slow down, relinquish control, I'm done for.

I lose myself, every muscle constricting against him without limit without recourse

without mercy.

"Jesus," he exerts, and a fireworks display is contained between the two of our bodies, the aftereffects swelling, undulat-
ing, shocking their way through my limbs and sparking down
to my toes.

*   *   *

By the time three a.m. rolls around, we've repeated the task on
just about every surface I've got.

After the last round, he gathers all our clothes into a ball and
sticks them under one arm, lifts me over his shoulder like a goddamn caveman, and carries me up the stairs to the only place we
haven't done it—my actual bed.

And then he body slams me onto the pillow-top mattress.

"My body cannot have any more sex with your body," I say,
swathing myself in Egyptian cotton, all my parts tender and sore
from overuse.

"Yeah, I know—mine either." He laughs and does an exaggerated hobble to the other side of the bed, slips under the
covers next to me. "Well, I'd give that an A plus for sure. How
about you, teach?"

I melt into his arms, every ache in every muscle, every even-
tual bruise, scrape, and burn totally #worthit.

A delicate sheen of sweat settles over us as moonlight spills in
through the window sheers, and he wraps me up in a bear hug.
I lie there on his arm, outstretched, not facing him, wondering
if it's getting all prickly, falling asleep, and he's just being polite.

But neither of us says a thing.

Our breathing slows, my eyelids start to get heavy, and eventually I can tell he's asleep. At least it sounds like he is, as a gentle snore crackles on the air.

I want to turn around and see what he looks like while he sleeps, but I don't want to wake him. We've been through the sex equivalent of war tonight, and boy's gonna need his rest.

Besides, it's been a long while since I've been held this way, and I don't want it to end.

I tell myself that the longer I can remain motionless, barely breathing, the longer I can stretch the hours of this night into spools of silk and weave them into a tapestry of infinite time and space. Into eternity.

I wish I could tell my girlfriends about it.

Quinn and Valerie.

Just the thought of them makes my heart twinge. While I'm able to stifle a cry, traitorous tears leak across the bridge of my nose and drip onto my pillow, and I'm really thankful Nick's asleep.

But also that he's here.

I pull his arms tighter around me. Nuzzle closer.

Sad as it may be, I'm going to savor this moment. No matter the ramifications tomorrow. Whatever happens, happens.

But it sure as hell feels incredible tonight.

*   *   *

When I awaken, however, the morning sun beams directly into my eyes like it's trying to give me Lasik surgery and casts a new light on—everything.

I karate-chop my way out of the arms that no longer comfort me but *confine* me, and all at once, my vision does a sort of *a-wooooo-guh* with its focus, first panning way back, then zooming way in, again and again, in a fashion that makes me both startled and seasick.

Nick.

Naked Nick.

The sun.

Way too high in the sky.

My alarm clock.

Seven fifty-three.

"Shit."

I leap from the bed, rip off the sheet and hold it around me in a makeshift toga. It leaves him completely bare against the morning, his dark skin illuminated by the sun pouring in, but there's no time to admire his body right now.

Nick rubs at his eyes. "What time is it?" His voice is thick. Sleepy. It'd be cute if I weren't freaking the fuck out.

"You've got to go. I'm late!" I'm flapping around like a headless chicken on shrooms, bumping into the bedpost, my dresser, the bathroom door.

He laughs. "What are you doing?"

My fingers flail against the keyboard on my phone as I text Ida to tell her I'm having car trouble and ask if she can get one of the aides to cover me for, like, an hour.

Just then, a muffled *ding!*

I retrieve his jeans from the floor, and his phone falls out of one of the pockets and into my hand.

A message lights the screen.

Stephanie: I need you.

And my stomach feels like it's dropped out from under me.
Nick is the type of guy who someone feels she needs. And

I've had a taste of that, of him. So I get that. More now than in all the weeks we've chatted, flirted, connected. More now that he's lying here in my bed, that I laid in his arms all night and felt safe, felt protected. Felt understood.

The text message scares the bejesus out of me.

Because I don't want to need him.

I don't want to need anybody.

I have wanted and needed enough in my life, and all it's ever gotten me is nothing.

Is this, right here.

Is a night or two—or maybe a few months—but never a lifetime. Never love for real.

I look down at this girl's words. This girl who's also had a taste of what it's like to be with this man. And what's it gotten her, being with him? Nothing.

I can't do it again.

And suddenly, I feel angry for her. Why can't he love her? Why can't he need her like she needs him?

Why can't it ever work for chicks like us?

And, just like that, the decision's made.

I need to cut this Whatever It Is off #effectiveimmediately before history repeats itself, or worse.

Whatever that could be.

"Nick." I shove his jeans, his phone, everything, at him as a barrier. Shield my eyes from his glorious, mesmerizing body before it entices me again.

"Yeeeees?" He grins at me, arms out, hands now folded behind his head. He's got one leg crossed lazily over the other, even though he's naked as the day is long. He's confident AF, and it's both distracting—and infuriating.

"Stop it."

"Stop what?"

"You've got to get your shit and go."

He sits up. Tone still even. "But don't you want to—"

"No—we shouldn't have. Dammit, Rae." I bang the heel of my palm into my forehead and feel the effects of All the Wine.

"And now you're talking to yourself? I've been with some crazy chicks, but—"

His nonchalance stirs a tidal wave of anger that crawls from the depths of my soul, unfair as it is—he can't hear my thoughts. I try to keep my voice calm, but if he doesn't GET OUT OF HERE or at least stop being so goddamn effing cocky, I won't be able to hold it back. Release the kraken!

"I can't do this."

He utters one incredulous guffaw that ricochets off the headboard and hits me right in the face as I'm ransacking my drawers for any remnants of clean clothes I can possibly wear to work—or, yanno, hide all the shame I'm about to feel.

"You were pretty capable of doing this last night." An eyebrow climbs its way up his forehead, a dimple popping with his half frown.

"Stop it," I say again and defend myself from those features of his with a hand. "Last night was a mistake."

He shakes the pants out and starts putting his clothes on, his eyes taking on a more serious, worried look now. "You're not playing?"

"Of course not. I don't know what I was thinking." I start flinging skirts, tops, dress pants, pairs of socks, everywhere. "Well, of course I know what I was thinking. I'm extremely attracted to you. Yes."

It's almost like he's not in the room, and I'm just spewing a Shakespearean soliloquy at a horrified audience.

Actually, it's exactly like that, except it's an audience of one.

"I know things are messed up with my friends right now. I said some things I wish I hadn't, even though I think they were being unfair and I don't think I deserved what I got. But, you know, I probably did, because look. Look." I throw my hands up. "Look at what I do the very first chance I get. Get all drunk and have sex with you. Against my better judgment. Against all judgment."

"Rae, you—" He's still smiling.

"No, I'm talking." Thumb to sternum. "You've done enough talking." I jab my finger through the air at his perfect, arrogant face. "I can't do this. The last time I felt like this, the last time...No." I shake my head. "I'm not doing this again. All these weeks with the banter and the messaging. It was fun, sure. But at the end of the day, it's all just going to end, just like it always does. At the end of the day, I'm just going to be that girl sitting in a coffee shop, hearing why all the things we've promised each other, all the things we want, you don't want anymore. I've done it a hundred times."

"A hundred, really?" He frowns at me, his tone sarcastic.

"Whatever. I don't want to be *Stephanie* all *needing you* and you're done with me."

He kind of flinches at the sound of her name and glances at his phone, his eyes grave.

"I've experienced it one more time than I care to have, and I'm done. You can't be coming here all—whatever— with...that." I gesture wildly toward his entire body because Damn He Fine. "It's too distracting. I thought I could handle it, I thought we could be friends, but I obviously have no self-control. My friends are right. What kind of a person am I?"

"It's not like that. You don't under—"

I take a step closer. "I am so sick of people telling me I don't understand things. This isn't really about you. It's about me. And that's not a line; that's the truth. I'm sorry. That's just the way it has to be. If anything proves that, it's this."

He's quiet a moment, gaze set on me in what looks like pity. I don't like it. It lights my insides on fire and I glare back, walls flying up all around me.

"Who hurt you?" he asks. "Tell me—"

"It doesn't matter," I say. "I decided a long time ago that I'd never allow myself to care that much again."

"Yeah? Well, you can't plan everything."

"You may not be able to plan it, but you can prevent it."

Nick opens his mouth and then fastens it shut. Seems to dismiss his rebuttal with the mere shake of his head. He averts his stare and scratches the back of his neck, those lips that made me feel so good last night now frozen into a thin line, his jaw set in a way I've never seen before. It pricks at my heart, but just for a second, and I keep up my tough-girl front.

If I can keep it up for just a few seconds longer, he won't see me cry.

"I'm sorry it came to this," I say. "I shouldn't have been with you last night—shouldn't have allowed you to come over. It's my fault." My gaze drops to the floor and rests on his belt, still where I'd discarded it in a fit of *Oh hell yes* when we'd woken up for round four. Or fourteen?

The sight of it, the memory, makes my eyes well.

"Valerie and Quinn were right about me, I guess." My voice cracks, but I retrieve the belt and, with it, my composure.

I slap the accessory into Nick's hand. "We're both grown-ups, Nick, so let's be grown-ups. Last night...was what it was. And now—"

"And now?" He sits all the way up, the betrayal in his eyes tearing out my guts, but I can't let him bewitch me anymore, so I look away.

"And now you need to get the hell out so I don't get fired too."

*   *   *

CHAPTER 20

Despite my best efforts, I don't roll up into school until eight forty-five. It's like everyone and everything has received a memo: *Rae had inappropriate sex last night—make things difficult.* Between the way my fingers can't be bothered to remember how to do hair or makeup, how my keys don't care to be found and then magically decide to show up in a spot I've looked six times, the extra awesome traffic on the side streets, the manner in which Carol and her legion of besmocked little art students clog up the hallway ("Good to see you this morning, Rae!"—kill me, please), and the relentless pounding in my head, I'm ready to burst into tears of surrender at this day. Already.

I give up, world. You win.

I slide past Ida without somehow inciting a conversation about my mascara smudges, the not-at-all-conspicuous body to my hair, without any quips—and then fear clamps down on my heart.

Who's covering for me in my hour of need?

I don't even stop by the lounge for a caffeine injection because the curiosity has the better of me. Something's cray.

Well, I know it's not Nick...

My mind betrays me and I drift to thoughts of him, all
lounging in my bed this morning before I shut him up and
threw him out. His calm demeanor to my, well, insanity. His
yang to my yin.

But then I think better about letting myself remember his
yang, because that's in part how I got myself into this mess to
begin with!

When I reach my classroom, I grip the doorknob and brace
myself for the inundation of joy, the deluge of loud, the cascade
of love that my kids will blindly bestow upon me, even though
I don't deserve it.

I take a deep breath. Twist.

And I see Deborah, in all her pantsuit glory, perched at the
front of the room with a Dr. Seuss book in hand.

She cuts her stare to me above the tome, the tiny chain on
her glasses giving a slight rustle, and I think I might actually be
bleeding right there on the industrial carpet.

"Miss Wallace!" My class delights in my presence just like
I knew they would, and I have to chew at the inside of my
cheek to keep from crying—either because I don't deserve this
adoration...or because the sight of my principal stepping in
for me makes me pee my pencil skirt.

"Now, class..." It's all Deborah has to say in her boom of a
voice to calm them down. "Good morning, Miss Wallace," she
says, and the kids echo. "Everything all right?"

My eyes itch and begin to blur over. "I—"

It's all I can muster.

"Why don't you get yourself some coffee. We've got a few

more pages to go here, and you look like you could use a couple of minutes to get yourself situated."

"A—are you sure?"

"It's no problem at all, Miss Wallace." Her expression softens, and I realize the terrifying thing her mouth is doing to warm her visage is actually just...her smile.

Poor Deborah.

When I come back a few minutes later—spontaneous urination situation no longer a threat—she's got the kids working quietly in partners, drawing their own Dr. Seuss characters.

"You're like a miracle worker. Thank you," I say to her, hanging my cardigan around the back of my rolling chair.

"My pleasure, Rae. We've all been there." She offers me a squeeze of the shoulder and I watch her slip away like a mob boss in the night.

I'm a little in awe of all she's done here. And how effortlessly. Did that really just happen? #NBD

In her absence, I contemplate what she said when she was leaving as the class finishes their assignment: *We've all been there.* We have? She's been here? And then, before I know it, the caffeine is doing its thing and it's All Systems Go for the rest of the morning.

During specials time, Sarah looks in on me since I've decided to keep a low profile today—and maybe for the rest of my life.

"What happened?" she asks as soon as she steps through the door. "Someone said you had car trouble, but unless you spent the night hanging on to the underside of a semi-truck—"

Something about seeing her, about the worry on her face, makes all the Scotch tape I've used, all the rubber bands, all the paper clips holding me together, break away. Come undone. I can't pretend anymore. Can't hold my tears back for one more second.

She must sense the tsunami that's about to take over my face because she drops all her papers on a nearby desk and rushes over.

"Tell me," she says.

And I do. Every last detail.

She listens with starry-eyed attention, her downturned mouth popping open when I get to the worst (or best) parts, depending on how you're looking at it. Once I finish my tale of woe or whoa—it's really a toss-up at this point—we sit in contemplative silence on the top of the back table. Her absently rubbing at my arm, me staring at the fringe on my ankle boots until my eyes cross.

"So what are you going to do?"

I clear my throat. "I don't know," I say. "Change schools? Move to Mumbai and start that beagle farm?"

She titters into her dainty hands.

Still got it in the sarcasm department, I guess.

But it's all I can say because that's all I've got. I don't really know what I'm going to do.

"And you think the friendship is—"

"Irreparable." I shrug. "Without repair."

"Yes, I know what the word means," she snaps, nose crinkling like Billie does when I try to take more blanket. "But you guys have been friends forever. I just can't see—"

"Maybe I'll give it a few days. I don't know. Right now, the only thing I do know is I've got a wide-open schedule because I've offended just about everyone—and the kids are coming back here in a few minutes."

head in hands

She resets her lips from frown to smirk and glances up at me through wispy bangs. "Well, if it's any consolation, I still think you're fabulous."

"Thanks, love." I scoff. It's comforting, but it's not Everything Is Fine Now comforting. Everything is still all kinds of messed up.

She rises from the edge of the table and begins to gather her things by the doorway. "Not to mention—you're my fricking hero. I mean, Hot Sub Guy?" She puffs out her cheeks and explodes her hands by her temples like she can't even deal.

I muster a half chuckle and I appreciate the sentiment behind what she's saying, but it only stings my already stung insides. So I force a small smile, thank her for listening, and ready myself for the afternoon block.

*   *   *

For the rest of the day, the rest of the week, everything haunts me.

I've alienated pretty much everyone I care about, I'm out of the wedding...Mumbai is looking better and better.

Billie's sick of walking around the damn apartment complex in record time, so I start dramatically looking up airfares as a way to silence my thoughts—and I realize that the only way I can really get away from them, get away from *me*, is to rewrite my query. Finish the manuscript. I can't know if this one is going to fail unless I put it out there, as Nick said, and I can't know that until I actually query.

Also, writing will shift my focus to someone else's story, so I *tap, tap, tap* at the keys some more until my fingers are numb, and I hammer out something that's as close to what I came up with in my query before as it possibly can be:

First-year resident Eden Summers always ends up on top. She was the valedictorian of her high school class, she graduated magna cum laude in her premed program, and she landed herself a spot in one of the most prestigious medical schools in the country.

Travis Oakley likes being on top too. That's why he and the rest of his male nurse pals have a contest at The Angels of LA to see who can bang as many hot, young doctors that grace the halls of their hospital—and, so far, he's been at the forefront.

But when the two cross paths during a simple procedure gone wrong, the cocky Travis bails Eden out and he forgets all about the bet. With the recent death of her father and an increasingly impossible schedule, Eden's off her game, and Travis is all too willing to be of service to her. He knows just the way for her to blow off some steam...

A hot night out becomes a steamy night in, but will this evening of passion get the pair closer to their goals—or barred from their jobs at the hospital?

Complete at 80,000 words, *Playing Doctor* is about one woman's quest to swallow her pride in order to have it all: sanity, success, and multiple orgasms. It will appeal to fans of Mitsy Gardner's *Prescription for Love* and Ava Leon's *Between the Sheets*.

*   *   *

For the next few evenings, I stick my nose in books about craft. Scrawl chicken scratches on legal pad upon legal pad until I know just where I'm going with the plot. Until it all makes sense. Until my characters all have justifiable reasons for their actions, right and wrong. Until the atmosphere is rich, until all the plot holes are filled. The cracks smoothed over. The rough patches sanded.

And it helps.

Whenever I emerge from my laptop Wednesday, Thursday, Friday, Saturday, I can feel all my holes are starting to fill too.

Stop. #YKWIM

I've done such a good job of just avoiding other humans that there are fewer and fewer chinks in my armor. The imperfections are being polished, one by one. All but the chasm in my chest that I've avoided because I'm not even sure how to fix it.

Or if I even can.

And then I allow myself to wonder how my two best friends are doing. How Nick is.

I remember his words. The look on his face when he said: *Who hurt you? Tell me.*

Quinn and Valerie are probably slightly more affected, as my absence in the wedding is likely causing some undue stress—at least part of me selfishly likes to think so—in terms of printing programs, rearranging some of the seating, at the very least, right?

But I also know how Valerie lives for the swoop-in-and-save. She probably made up a binder called "What to Do in the Event Quinn Kicks Rae Out of Her Wedding" years ago and is thanking her lucky stars that I stayed a disappointment so she can finally put it to good use.

But rather than wallow in my self-pity anymore, I decide, now that my manuscript is as ready as it can be, I need to research literary agents to query, so I throw myself into that next step.

As I scour the Internet, scroll through agency websites, I ask myself, *Who will take a chance on me?* and the thought tastes bitter in the back of my throat.

People have given me a lot of chances already, haven't they? And what have I done with them?

So I vow to be different.

Think differently. See differently. Act differently.

React differently.

And stop blaming everyone else.

I keep typing. Face it all. Head-on.

*   *   *

I'm stretched out in the booth, sloshing around the remnants of my coffee, now cold, in my mug.

Jesse's been quiet. Distant. Since we sat down. He avoids eye contact and gazes at his omelet like it's his last friend in the world.

"What is it?" I finally ask, my chest tight with worry.

And he looks up.

What I see is a shield in front of his dark stare. His eyes are no longer a warm chocolate, no longer inviting, no longer blazing into mine like they were last night. They're a black hole. A void. A chilling unknown.

Ingrid flits over, as if on cue.

"Can I get a warm-up?" I ask her.

"Aaaabzuhlootly," she says, and the aroma of the French roast takes over as she fills my cup.

I attempt to crack a smile at Jesse, to bring him back to a place of intimacy. Familiarity. Our inside joke. But his face remains stone.

"No more for me." He clamps his palm over his mug and

doesn't even look up at her, the ring on his third finger clink-
ing against the porcelain.

I grip my own mug, steaming. But it does nothing to
warm my cold, naked fingers. I take a sip, but still it doesn't
warm me; it only burns my tongue.

"What's the matter?" I blurt when she's gone.

A deep exhale.

That's it.

I can tell in a gust of air, a breath. It's over.

The silence buzzes in my ears, reaches every possible recess
of my brain before I can make sense of what he's saying, with-
out a word.

I open my mouth to say What Exactly I Don't Know, but
he steals the words from me and speaks now, his voice low.

"My dad left for some woman when I was little, and I
never saw him again. I'm not going to do that to Jonah. I
can't."

"'Some woman?'"

"You know what I mean." He glances away, his eyes glass.

"I don't think I do, actually. Where is this coming from—
out of nowhere—over breakfast?"

He clears his throat and stares into his cottage fries.

"I wasn't under the impression I was just 'some woman' to
you. And look. I know divorce is not sunshine and lollipops,
but it doesn't have to mean abandoning your child. I never
wanted that. Of course not. I know that's not the kind of man
you are. You know how I feel about Jonah. But do you hon-
estly think he doesn't know what kind of a fucked-up marriage
you have? That staying in that kind of environment is best for
him? He's smart. Growing up like that isn't going to make his
life better. I can attest to it. My sister and I lived it."

"I know." He reaches for my hand, ever trying to squelch my emotions, his eyes now swimming. "I thought I could…" He dabs the corners of his mouth with his napkin.

He's fidgeting. He does this when he's uncomfortable. When he can't control a situation. When he can't have his way.

"It was an amazing few months—"

"An amazing few months? We made plans. What was all that, some bullshit fantasy? Lies?" My voice is raised, and he all but writhes in his seat. "Some plot you were trying to work out in your head for one of your manuscripts? This is real. Isn't it?"

A beat. Then: "Yes."

And in this moment, I feel the full impact that there is nothing worse than someone who agrees with you but still cannot be convinced.

"I know it's fucked up," he says. "And I know all we said, but—you can find someone else. I don't want you to—" He grasps at my hand with both of his, pain in his eyes. "If you could wait for me—till Jonah—" Moisture begins to fall. "But I know that's not fair. He's four years old." He closes his eyes and shakes his head. Says again: "You can find someone else."

Like a server who's just explained they're out of the salmon but I can have fish sticks instead.

I can't suppress a laugh. "This was never about that. The need to just have someone. Believe me; I know I could find someone else. This was not just me clinging to you because you were there. You live in Sacramento, for God's sake. This is about me and you. About happiness. About love. I don't want a better man, a different man, the next one who comes along. You think I'd have chosen to love you if I could have helped it? You think I wouldn't have chosen any other person? You led me to believe—you said—"

I'm stammering, and my attention darts all over the table. An uncontrollable shake makes its way through my head, my hands, and there's a stinging numbness that takes over my body.

"What about this weekend? Last night? This morning? You talked about all the same things we've always talked about. Our trip to Cancun next month. What was that? And now, boom, I'm supposed to accept this just because you're saying it here at the table? This very calculated thing that you lied to me about for—how long, Jesse? How long? Have you actually been going to that therapist like you said? Have you even spoken to a divorce lawyer? Have you talked to her about any of this? Was any of it ever even true?"

There's a ringing in my ears in the absence of my outburst.

His silence tells me everything I need to know; the look in his eyes is enough.

I have listened to him tell his pretty stories, weave his pretty tales, regale me with his pretty narratives of sacrifice and woe. Of all he was going through at home. I've been enchanted by the fairy tales he spun before my eyes—caught up in the beautiful pictures he painted of the life we'd have, the life he said he wanted.

A life with me.

But I don't see any trace of it behind those eyes now. All I see is a man I don't know.

The realization that I never did know him, never did realize it until this very moment, throttles me, hard and low.

I jump from the cushioned seat and stagger my way out of the restaurant, to the room. I hear him call after me, but I *continue. The elevator takes for-fricking-ever—nothing is fast enough to get me out of here.*

I was wrong. How could I have been so wrong? How could I have been so stupid? How could I have believed him?

At last, I'm in our room and tossing all my belongings— the silver heels I wore to dinner last night, my makeup case, my clothes—into my bag. Ripping the sheets from the bed, making sure I haven't left anything of mine—anything of me—in this cold, strange room that seemed so familiar, so comforting, so warm, not an hour ago.

I toss the leftovers from our midnight room service.

Toss everything I thought I knew about Jesse, about us.

And shut the door on what I know now will never be.

*   *   *

When I finish typing out the scene—the memory, really—I send it in an e-mail to Nick with a subject line that says: *I'm Sorry.* He may not understand, but he did ask who'd hurt me, how. So at least I'm letting him in.

A day and a half later, I'm ready to query. The first thing I do after I send off a batch of six letters is hammer out one more text—to Valerie.

Me: I need to talk to you.

*   *   *

CHAPTER 21

While Nick doesn't answer, Valerie does, and not too long after I message. I suggest we meet at our favorite brunch spot near school because, even if she can't stand the sight of me, how's she going to pass up made-to-order omelets? No one has that much resolve.

I glance at my watch and realize she's running late. If we weren't in this weird friendship purgatory, I'd send her a jokingly passive-aggressive text and start in on the bottomless mimosas; however, since I'm trying to be better, and coherent, I do neither. I just drum my fingertips on the pink linen tablecloth and watch all the brunching families. Hear the roars of laughter coming from a group of guys in pastel polo shirts and golf shoes. I don't even check any of them out, because that's not why I'm here.

And, really, I just don't care.

Valerie finally arrives, a frumptastic gardening-looking hat flopped down over her head like it's 1992. I'd giggle if the sight of her didn't instantly make me feel like two of Snow White's reject dwarves, Weepy and Pukey.

As she enters the café, she dons a small smile when she sees me. Pins prick in my chest, like the lead that's been weighing me down has turned to helium, and my heartbeat quickens as I rise to greet her.

"This is the most nervous I've ever been while waiting for a date," I say and stand there like a moron. Because I'm just not sure if we're hugging or what.

She laughs and hesitates above her chair too. "Well, if my calculations are correct, this is your first girl-on-girl date, no?"

Her continuation of my joke and the fact that her smile widens eases some of my anxieties; but we don't hug. We sit. And it's weird.

We're quiet while the server pours what smells like strong-ass coffee—a warm, bold aroma that promises to deliver the upper-cut to the jaw I need to proceed.

"Hey. I hate this," I say. I don't know where else to begin. "How did we get here?"

She gives me a kind of melted look, head cocked, her usual porcelain features a bit wilted. "I know; me too. But before you say anything, I want you to know I'm not just here because you wrote me. I mean, I am—"

She softens even more and starts talking with her hands. A good sign that she's on the road to being Val and not some pod person whose exterior I can't crack.

"I was too much of a coward to write you myself," she continues, "but I guess I would have made contact in a day or two anyway because—Rae." Her eyes go serious, and she leans in. Implores me. Almost whispers: "Quinn has gone a little nuts."

I yank back.

Valerie considers wearing skinny jeans to be "a little nuts." Yet this is the same chick who had sex with a stripper at a bachelorette party—so she's a complicated lady these days, all juxtaposition and hyperbole, and I need clarification. #obvi

"What do you mean?"

"Ever since our fight. She's practically despondent. Nothing I say helps. I tried throwing us even more into the wedding prep, but that only drove her further away. She's actually talking about calling it off."

This news is like a lap full of coffee.

"What? Why?"

"This whole thing with you—I don't know. You have to talk to her. She's not making a whole lot of sense. She's thinking about going on another trip, skipping town. I think the realization of going through something as big as this, without you there…put her in meltdown mode."

"Geezus," I say, and my mouth hangs open. "What do you think we should do?"

"Have you texted her?"

"No. I didn't know if you would even answer. I was just sort of testing the waters and, luckily, you're a lot less scary and a lot more forgiving than Quinn."

We both chuckle, and it feels good. Normal.

"I can see that. Good call," she says, wiping her eyes.

I straighten up. "I mean, not that you've forgiven me yet."

"I'm here, aren't I?" She eases on a smile and leans back in her chair. Her shoulders relax. "What exactly did you want to see me about anyway? I mean, I didn't kick you out of the wedding. I've sort of been forced to choose sides, as the one and only bridesmaid now, but I'm not really upset with you, per se." She hasn't lifted her gaze from the cream she swirls in the delicate coffee cup, but the tension we seem to be wading through has dissipated.

I set down the menu I've been using as a barrier for my shame and look full-on at Valerie. My best friend.

"I just—I'm sorry. That's really first and foremost. I guess I've had a chip on my shoulder for a while now. Just—looking around here, being around you, your family—these are all things I don't have. And, sure, that sucks. But it's not your fault. It's not anybody's fault. It's just the way things are. And I can't keep resenting you, resenting Quinn, raining on your parades because I'm still searching. I need to grow the hell up and realize that things change. Life changes relationships. It's not always going to be like when we were seventeen."

She sits with that for a moment, playing with the corner of her menu under a fingernail. Then, finally: "It doesn't have to change. It shouldn't have to." She glances up. "And I don't think you resent me."

"You don't?"

"No. I just think it's hard. We're all so different. If anything, I think I sometimes resent you."

This catches me off guard, and I just sit back. Let her talk. Yanno, like I never let her do.

And she continues, her gaze fixed back on what she's doing with her hands.

"Well, yes. You're free to do whatever you want, whenever you want. Whomever you want. It's amazing! Me, I have to ask permission to even go to the grocery store by myself. To take a shit without at least two kids there in the room. Not that I'm blaming Mike—I'm not—I'm..." Tears trickle onto her cheeks now, and she presses them away with her napkin. "He's a good man. A decent father."

I let a beat go by. I don't know whether or not I'm allowed to ask it, but I do: "A good husband?"

The question hangs between us, and my insides are edged with ice as I await her response.

Too far?

And then she meets my stare again, wet eyes pleading. "I mean, am I a good wife?"

"Yes," I say. Right away. Without pause. "Yes, you are. Look"—I lower my voice and lean closer across the table—"I know why you're saying that. That weekend. I know. But I've known you since we were kids and I know what type of a person you are. Nobody's perfect."

"I didn't see you sleeping with any strippers…"

"Well…" I glance away, a grin tugging at the corners of my mouth, and—goddamn it. I still can't even be appropriately ashamed of my night with Nick.

Maybe I've made no progress at all. Maybe I'm more deeply flawed than I realized. Maybe I'm hopeless.

She gasps and slaps a palm to the table. "You didn't!"

The dried-apricot-looking couple at the adjacent table flinches at the sound of her outburst and they make angry dried-apricot-looking faces at us.

But there's a buoyance to Valerie's tone. A sparkle in her stare. Like we're back in freshman year and I'm admitting to fooling around with Tony Valducci for the first time. She's not upset; she's happy for me.

"Yeah, it probably wasn't the best of ideas," I admit, chewing a fingernail. "But I wasn't thinking so clearly at the time. Anyway—that's not the point."

We're both smiling now, and this is starting to feel less like The End of Something and more like two best friends catching up after a long trip away from each other.

But I begin to wonder how long it's been since we've been this real, since we've connected like this. How long have we been away from each other?

I shake off the question and focus on making my way back to her.

"I just want you to know how much you mean to me. How amazing you are. Regardless of the stripper thing. You know what? Screw the stripper thing. Marriage is hard. I know. And I also know it's been harder for you than you've let on. That I never let you talk about how hard it is because…I guess, on some level, I'm afraid of what you might say."

Her eyebrows wiggle up her forehead, but she remains quiet. Seemingly interested in what I'm about to say.

"You're supposed to be the strong one. The settled one. The one who has her shit together. Who takes care of everything. You know? And that's unfair of me to put that pressure on you. I realize that. It's unfair of anybody to put that pressure on you. But I know they do. And you put that pressure on yourself too."

She lets the moisture flow openly now, but her mouth is twisted into a crooked, close-lipped smile like these words I'm saying are the words she's been dying to hear from someone, anyone, and I've just about made her whole year. Like I've freed her from some sort of mommy prison, just by validating that she's doing the goddamn best she can with what she's got.

She clutches at both of my hands and beams at me, her bottom lip taut and doing a poor job of hiding the quiver in it.

After I'm not sure how long we sit like this—silence between old friends knows no measure of time, really—she finally lets my fingers go.

Readjusting her napkin in her lap, she's out with it. "We're in counseling, Mike and me." She says it as though it's as ordinary as ordering the eggs Benedict, which she also does when the server returns. "And I think we'll take those bottomless Bloody Marys now," she adds. "Is that okay?" she asks me.

"Duh." I flash the woman the ol' two thumbs-up. "I was just trying to be respectable and rehab my perspective—I'm not cutting out booze. Don't be insane!"

"You are respectable." She's back to her usual playfulness, waving a languid hand at me like *Nonsense, girl.*

Once the server's gone, I return to the topic at hand. Cautious in tone.

"How long have you guys been going to counseling?" I squeeze a lemon wedge into my water just to have something else to do.

"We've been seeing a therapist for about six months."

She utters a soft chuckle when my mouth drops open.

"So you can see why this digression might be particularly… bothersome. But I caught Mike texting some woman from work last year, and I don't know. It doesn't justify what I did, but—"

"It doesn't have to." I hold her gaze.

"I wanted to tell you. But, at the same time, I felt like admitting that would be making it real. Admitting defeat. Failure."

"Hey—don't talk about my friend that way." I frown. "That's not failure. That's working toward something instead of just running away."

She snorts. "Well, I don't think sex with a stripper was probably all that helpful to the process, but—" She pauses. "And you didn't run away. You just realized it early enough. I didn't." She shrugs. Blows a few strands of hair out of her face. "I think that's been the source of some of the weirdness between us too, if you want to know."

"What?"

"My insane jealousy of you."

"Jealous of me? How many of these drinks have you had?" I lift her glass and pretend to inspect it.

"It's just—and no one wants to talk about this—but marriage can be really... isolating. You can lose yourself if you're not careful. And then you blink and all of a sudden you have four kids and you're not allowed to say anything. It's not okay to have a bad day."

I give a conceding nod. "Well, right. Because you're all set."

"Do you know how many times—I'm actually embarrassed to admit—I have wished I could trade places with you? Be you? That I think, if I didn't have these kids, would I even stay married to this stranger Mike sometimes is? That I'd run?"

I emit a long, relaxing sigh. Or maybe it's the alcohol that calms me.

"Probably as many times as I wonder what things would have been like if I hadn't left Daniel. But, at the same time, I don't have any regrets. I know I can't go back and I wouldn't want to. Even as hard as things have been. It doesn't change the fact that I sometimes feel a bullet in my chest when I see you coloring with Mandy and Mae. I still would like a chance at that, you know?"

She laughs. "You do have the chance. Your life is full of possibility—even every Spark date—ha-ha—yes! While mine has already been decided. I know I'm the one who decided it, but still." She takes a drink and her face takes on an *Imma level with you* look. "Even if by some magic I were offered the chance to change things, I know, deep down, I could never do it. I couldn't. Kids or no kids. I'm not brave like you. I couldn't leave Mike, no matter what. At the end of the day, I do love him. And I just don't know what I'd do on my own. I couldn't do it."

"It sounds like you're apologizing for loving him. Don't. Me surviving on my own is less *bravery* and more that I just have no shame anymore."

We both crack up, and a knowing silence spreads itself across the table as thick and creamy as the garlic butter I smooth on my croissant.

"You know what? We're both going to be okay," I declare after a time. "Marriage is hard; being single is hard. We are destined to envy the other, no matter what, and that's just how life is. But at least we're talking about it instead of letting it fester and doing dumbass things."

The server finally brings out the goods. Valerie's eggs Benedict, so gelatinous and perfect, the hollandaise sauce as yellow as a spring daffodil, not to be outdone by my choice—sweet hunks of pink shrimp swimming in mountains of cheesy grits. We inhale everything and agree that it's enough to never need a man—husband or boyfriend, Spark or otherwise—ever again.

"Speaking of doing dumbass things…" She gestures at me with a forkful of fresh melon. "I know we're making up and this might set things back"—she winces—"but I'm the reason Nick isn't at Wesson anymore."

I blink at her. It's all I can do. "You told Deborah he's a stripper?"

"No—but I may have made a false claim that he was making

some of the girls uncomfortable and suggested it would be best if he subbed elsewhere." She chews at her bottom lip and turns on the wounded puppy look she's perfected. "I'm sorry. I know you have a connection with him. But, at the time, I was doing it for me and for you—more for me, because I just couldn't handle the daily reminder of my incredibly wonderful, incredibly *stupid* night with his cohort...and, for you, in that I thought I was doing you a favor keeping him off your radar. Guess that backfired."

"Drastically." I snort.

"I'm so sorry. Are you mad?"

Over the rest of our feast, I explain to her why Nick has been stripping in the first place—not to make her feel like an ass but to clear his name and show her that he might not be all bad. When I'm done, Valerie's eyes are the size of the blueberry muffins on the pastry table.

But I assure her I'm not upset about it. It is what it is. I've tried to apologize to him and he hasn't responded, so it doesn't matter anyway.

"It's a shame you can't tell him how you feel about him, though. Why can't you?" Her tone takes on the cheerleader I've always known her to be. Team Rae! Love conquers all!

But I shake my head and glance at my empty plate. "Meh. I think I'm going to leave well enough alone."

Somehow we're still sipping cocktails, and I recline in my seat. Rub my belly like the lady ogre that I am.

"I'm glad we did this," I say, stretching my arms overhead.

Food coma in three...two...

"Me too—thanks for messaging. Sorry I was too spineless—"

"Oh gawd, we're so nauseating right now." I laugh.

"So what now?"

"Well...I guess I need to text Quinn. Maybe even call her. Crazy, I know." I do the one-finger cuckoo windup at my temple and reach for my phone. "There's just one more thing I want to ask you before I do."

"Of course," Val says, finishing off her coffee. She looks at me with hope in her eyes. "What is it?"

"What *the hell* is with that hat?"

*   *   *

CHAPTER 22

W ant me to go with you?" Val asks as we leave the café and I'm about to go to Quinn's.

I think about that a minute but ultimately decide no. "I need to do this on my own."

We stand, sunshine beating down on us, and hug the circulation out of each other's arms.

Quinn hasn't answered my phone calls or text messages from the restaurant or on the drive over to her apartment, but that doesn't stop me. I have to make her listen. Irrational Quinn stubbornness be damned.

Like that time senior year when Valerie and I had to physically pick her up and carry her out of the art room during the Homecoming dance because she was convinced her date was hooking up with some sophomore in the boys' bathroom. She had broken into Miss Rombalski's class and was ransacking the place for a pair of scissors, determined to burst into the bathroom. Catch her guy in the act. And cut his balls off.

We had to talk her down then, and that's exactly what I've got to do now.

When I get to her place, Phil answers the door all wringing hands and twitchy mouth, like he's gotten into the strong stuff. He envelops me in an unprecedented hug, his beefy man arms all but squeezing the life out of me.

"I'm so glad you're here," he says.

"You been smoking something?" I pull back, dust off a shoulder.

But he doesn't laugh. He offers a firm shake of the head and takes me by the arm into Quinn's kitchen.

"I don't have your number." He sounds winded. He's glancing all around the place, everywhere but at me. "I should get it. Will you write it down? I just never thought—"

"What's going on, Phil? Where's Quinn?"

"That's what I'm trying to tell you: I don't know. We had breakfast. Everything seemed normal. Then I jump in the shower, and when I get out, she's gone. Her car's still here, but she's not answering her phone, she didn't leave a note. I'm just freaked out. Do you think she could have been kidnapped?"

I try not to cock my head like some bewildered spaniel, but I can't help it. It's Quinn. Does he really not know this?

"How long's it been?" I ask instead.

"Just over an hour. Should I call the cops?"

His eyes are edged with red, deep with distress, so I try to sound soothing. "It's way too soon."

"Right, right. I just…don't know what to do." He plunks himself down at the breakfast bar, head in hands.

Something about his concern, even if dramatic concern, warms my cold, dead heart.

"I do," I say, and I give his arm a pat. "Don't worry. I think I know where she is. I'll bring her home."

And, well, it's only a *teensy* lie, but it makes his ginger features go from ashen to pink in two seconds flat, so I'm determined to find Quinn and see what the hell she's thinking.

Return her to her senses before I ruin her wedding too.

I drive all over Plantation—past our old haunts, most of which aren't open right now anyway, the dance club, the marina—and she's nowhere. I rack my brain for something, anything, any whisper of a memory from our special time together that might trigger where she would have fled. What her next move would be.

But I come up with nothing.

I briefly consider that maybe she's gone to burn down her ex's place in the woods, but even that's going too far for Quinn.

I think.

After a quiiiiiick detour just to have a look-see, I find the house still standing, palm trees flanking the fountain out front.

No smoke, no visible trip wires across any expanse of the driveway.

And I'm mostly not disappointed.

Dickface.

I give the place a flipperoo of the ol' bird, just for old times' sake, but Phil's texting and calling since he has my number now and it ruins the moment, so it's time to go let Billie out and think some more.

Where could Quinn be?

The mystery is solved, however, when I pull up to my place, and there's our girl, perched on the sidewalk. Her knees make a tent of her maxi dress; her back is straight against my front door.

She dangles a can of wine from one noodle arm, sways it to and fro like the afternoon breeze.

Or, yanno. Like she's a panhandler.

#potatopotahto

"Where've you been?" She squints up at me, her lips dry and in full pout.

I snort. "Where've *you* been?" I grab her hands, and she staggers upright. Clings to my middle like a baby koala to center herself, and sloshes some wine onto my peep-toe wedges.

"Good thing those are old," I say.

We struggle inside and navigate our way through the labyrinth that is getting past Billie, Froggering our way through my living room furniture and out the sliding glass doors to the patio.

"How'd you get here?" I ask, once she's properly plopped herself into a papasan chair, her legs pretzeled on the red cushion.

"Uber," she says, and I roar.

"You're nuts. You know that?"

I disappear inside to scrounge for some reinforcements, which ends up being Gatorade, a bottle of water, and a box of Cheez-Its. When I come back out, she's asleep, sunlight dazzling down her dark hair—so I go back in for my laptop and opt to do some work until she wakes up.

Phil is relieved when I text him to say she's here, safe and sound and sleeping, but I know we're not out of the woods yet—not any of us—so I tell him to just give me some time with her and *Try not to panic.*

I decide to bite the bullet and send off a batch of six query letters, to six literary agents I carefully researched and feel might be a decent fit for my work. I've already received a rejection from one of them when Quinn awakens from her nap, but I'm out there. Chance taken. Rejection is part of the process.

Quinn curls her arms out in front of her in a stretch. She nearly falls out of the chair when she notices me.

"Holy shit—how—" Her face is pure horror. "Oh yeah." And then her countenance goes sheepish, worry lines tugging at her mouth.

"Morning, sunshine. Drink this." I slide on a smile as I scoot the bottle of water across the table.

"Thanks" is all she says and we sit without a word, nothing but the sound of some nearby hawks cawing away and the occasional car driving by as our soundtrack. We're quiet until she finishes the snacks and looks a tad more human.

"So," I singsong, "how's your day?"

"Shut up!" She laughs and lobs the empty water bottle at me and thankfully misses.

I miss catching it too. Yay sports!

"Look, I was way out of line. I should never have said those things to you. I just—"

"Quinn. Have you lost your damn mind?"

The question seems to have thrown her. Her mouth opens, but nothing spills out of it except a stray cracker crumb.

"What are you doing?"

She fixes her stare upon her fingers. "I don't know." She takes a long breath and eases her way back. "I was sitting there on the couch with Phil last night. We were watching HGTV. And I was just like *Are you kidding me with this? This is life? This is it?*"

I laugh. "Dude, HGTV is legit—"

"I know!" She rises and starts what, at first, is a wobbly pace of the length of the patio, but then she balances as her wheels keep spinning. Billie follows her zigzag with big eyes but never lifts her head from her paws, and I wonder how she's not getting dizzy.

Quinn continues. "One of those Kennedy-looking Property Brothers was wearing something so insanely douchey and I turned to Phil and I'm like 'Check that out,' and he all lazes his attention over to me and goes 'Huh.' Can you believe it, Rae? *Huh.* Like this is the guy I'm supposed to be marrying in six days?"

She opens and closes her hands all jazzy, like she's performing a Fosse routine. Like *pop—pow.* But when I say nothing, she presses on.

"Once I explained to him what I had said and what I meant, he just...laughed. As though he really didn't get it and I was being ridiculous and..."

She's doing *the vapors* now, fanning herself with stiff wrists, and I'm just smiling and shaking my head because #Quinn.

"He's a guy." I shrug. "He's not concerned about what the Property Brothers are wearing; he's probably trying to absorb techniques on how to, I dunno, open up a bathroom. Knock down some wall in his place. Or whatever goes through dudes' minds when they're watching HGTV." I dismiss it with a swat. "It's going to be okay. Trust me."

"How do you know?" Her gaze, intense.

When I don't have an answer right away, she groans and starts pacing again.

"I just think, it's not too late, right? I can call this off." She grabs my hands in a frenzy. "We can go somewhere. Like we did before. Get away."

I search her face, and there's a hopefulness there, a desperation.

She's saying all the words I've wanted to hear her say since she and Phil got together: She chooses me! She's just as terrified as everyone else! And yet I don't feel any amount of satisfaction at all.

Her words tether me to my seat.

"You mean run away," I correct, and snap my hands back. "Listen, I will respect whatever your decision is here, but taking some girls trip isn't going to solve anything. Unless we're moving to Ibiza this time, we still have to, yanno, come back. Do you not love Phil? Is that what this is about?"

She gives an exhale fit for a Greek tragedy. Sophocles himself couldn't make this thing up. It reaches me from three feet away.

"I do love him," she says. "I just—"

"Because he loves you. He's been blowing up my phone all day because he's worried about you. He thought you were kidnapped."

She scrunches her nose.

"I know, I know." I wave it off. "But he's been sick to death about where you are. He wanted to come with me to search for you. It must have taken a lot for him to rely on me, your screwup friend, to find you and bring you back without him. But he did it. And that says a lot about his feelings for you."

She cuts her copper stare to mine. "You're not a screwup. I shouldn't have said any of that. It's not true. I don't even think he really thinks that. He barely knows you. I just think he feels threatened by you. You know more about me than any other person, and that's intimidating."

"It's probably better that way..." I squish my face and widen my grin.

"Truth!" She laughs. "But I shouldn't let him say all that stuff about you, because he doesn't know what he's talking about and it's not true and—"

"Calm down." I stir some aloe into my tone. "He's just trying to be on your team. Have your back. You know, because of that whole love thing I keep talking about?"

She presses her lips together. "I know, and really, I've allowed it because I'm a petrified idiot."

"How so?"

"I just...what we went through before. What you're going through now. It's not that I pity you—I don't. But I don't want to go through any of that again. Ever. And you, your stories, the memories that flood my brain whenever I think of you, whenever we're together, are a constant reminder of all that. That's why I've pushed you away, I guess."

I let a beat go by. It's weird to hear her admit what I've suspected for so long.

"It's why I've resented you," I say. "Why I've been defensive. I don't want this marriage to be the death of our friendship. You think I want to be the last one out here, floating along on this stupid raft? It's lighter without you. Unsteady. So I've been a little tough on you lately because of how easy it seems to have been for you to sail away without me. Dismiss my life as silly now because that isn't your life anymore. Believe me; I get it. But I also think it's crap. You think I don't understand why? Think I don't get that you're scared? Of course I do. It's scary every time I start to like someone. It's hard to put yourself out there. But we're in different spots now. And you can't do what I've been doing and just not try. You can't give up what you've got."

She's nodding over and over, tears dripping down her flushed cheeks, but she says nothing.

"Quinn. I don't want to ever hold you back. Here you are, days away from marrying a good and decent man who loves you enough to fight for you, and if you're thinking about skipping town with me to have some stupid adventure—all because he didn't answer you 'the right way' about HGTV? Well, then I must be holding you back. And I'm sorry for that. If what you're telling me means the sight of me brings up too much for you, then fine. I'll go away. I'm not going to be happy about it, but I'll do it for you because I don't want you to throw away what you have. I'm not saying it won't be hard. You're my best friend, and we work together. But I want you to be happy. And if this is what you need, then this is what we'll do. That'll be my wedding present to you because I refuse to drag you down.

"I'm sorry my existence reminds you of all the bad times. That kind of...stings. Because, to me, so many good things came out of us dealing with all that together. But if all you see in me is a reflection of what you don't want to be anymore, then— guess what—I don't think that's on me; it's on you. Because we have twenty years of memories together. And I choose to re-member those."

We're silent a long time. Until the mosquitoes start a-feasting on us, the hawks have flown away, and the sun has begun its de-scent toward the west.

The tang of the citronella candle burns in my nose, and I'm starting to get buggy. Twitchy. We've reached that point in a breakup conversation when there's nothing left to say, unless you start talking in circles.

An impasse. A stalemate.

Time to go.

It's that point when you know, if you walk out that door, this is it. And while you want to leave, you don't want to too. Be-cause then that will mean it's really over.

"So is this what you want?" I finally ask, reaching for the goddamn cheese crackers because apparently I'm insatiable, even at a time like this. "Look, I get that you have your life preserver. But what can I say? We're different people. For you, getting married again is your life preserver. For me? It might not be. And that shouldn't make you sad, or sad for me. I don't think I've ever realized it more than today that it doesn't make me sad. I don't consider myself down. I consider myself…full of possibility."

Something in me brightens at my paraphrase of Val's words.

When she said them at brunch, they didn't quite hit me, but coming out of my mouth now, they kind of light me from within. Even in the face of losing Quinn. Because Valerie is right. And I've never really thought about my life like this before. I've conditioned myself to see the negative, to dwell on the failures, instead of recognizing all the opportunity—excitement—that's yet to come.

"You don't hold me down," she says, voice hoarse. "It's my stuff. You're right. And I'm sorry." Her face twists with emotion.

"Hey, if I had a guy who loved me like that, I'd be freaked out too. I wouldn't be sure whether to run or to hold on for dear life either."

I think of Nick.

Force a smile, but a C-clamp tightens around my chest. I rub at my sternum as if that will make it go away, but it doesn't. Something squeezes, crushes my rib cage at what a coward I've been.

There's something real between Nick and me, and I've basically messed it all up.

How stupid.

Without even realizing it, moisture has leaked its way onto my face and I'm telling Quinn all about what happened with him, our night together, all the things I've held back the last few weeks.

When I'm done, she's seated, legs tucked up under her, and she reaches for my hand. "You really care about him."

"What?" I *psh* air right out of my mouth.

"I'm serious. I've seen it before in you, but this is different. You've sabotaged it because you're scared. Well, guess what. Take hold of all that 'opportunity' you're telling me about and go tell him."

I crack up. "This isn't about me. Look. Can I promise you I know what's going to happen with your marriage? Of course not. But I know what I see. And Phil loves you. It's taking a leap of faith, but that's what love is. And when you do it, and it's right . . . it's worth all the pain and all the loss from before." And then: "He's not going to do what that asshole did to you."

"How do you know?"

"I don't!" I snort. "But he's not. Because if he were, you would know. You're different from that girl I went to Ibiza with. I'm different too. In a good way. We know better. We appreciate more. That's why we're so frickin' nuts."

We laugh and laugh and laugh.

"It's always a leap of faith—life is a leap of faith. And I know I go through my spurts of pushing people away and being so cynical, but why do you think I keep trying? Why do I keep making these stupid mistakes? Because somewhere, deep down in my chestal area, I must have hope. And you do too." I jab a finger toward her. "So don't throw it away over something as dumb as fear, or the Property Brothers. Life is scary. Be scarier."

"That's part of what I'm afraid of. What if I'm too Lifetime Movie Network to his HGTV?"

"Another reason he wants to be with you. What can I say? Dudes be cray."

By the time we've blown out the candle and polished off a frozen pizza, I know Quinn and I are good. We're messed up as all hell, but we're good.

When I pull up to her apartment, I have one question left.

"So are you doing this or what, Q?"

A smile blooms on her lips. "Yes. But not without you there. Saturday, and always. I'm so sorry."

"I'm sorry too."

We share a tight smile—no need to start the waterworks again—and then she turns to go. Flips back around, hand to door handle.

"Do you really think Phil loves me? That he's good enough?" Her eyes sparkle with all the hopefulness in the world.

"As far as I'm concerned, no man will ever be good enough for Valerie or you. These poor schmucks never had a prayer."

We laugh and hug until Phil appears outside and asks us if Quinn is leaving him for me.

*   *   *

CHAPTER 23

On my drive home, for the rest of the evening, during my walk with Billie, as I sit out back and watch the fireflies dance against a dark sky, it's like a weight has lifted. Draining day, but what I've learned about my friends—and about myself—fills me with what feels like enough fuel to keep me awake until the wedding. It's like I've been asleep for I don't know how long and now I've emerged energized. Without the curtain of grogginess I've grown so accustomed to hanging over my eyes.

And I'm not a complete moron; I realize I need to take my own advice in terms of going for things. Believe the things I told Quinn, for myself.

My phone buzzes.

Quinn: Have you called him yet?

I grin at the phone.

Me: Not yet.

Just talking about Nick, saying his name, telling my friends about him, about us, has kicked up a current of pixie dust beneath my skin. But I don't know quite how to broach that subject with him. How to make things right. I tried, but he didn't answer my e-mail.

But then I think about how weird that probably was, sending him a scene with no context. My *I'm Sorry* in the subject line. *I'm sorry* can be ambiguous, really. I'm sorry for what? I'm sorry things have to be this way? I'm sorry I let you put your penis in me?

None of these are what I had meant by the message, of course, but how's Nick supposed to know that from two little words and some break-up scene?

So as I turn out the light on my nightstand and set my alarm for work, I hammer out another quick message.

I meant I'm sorry about how I treated you. I'm sorry about the things I said. You didn't deserve that, and I'd like the chance to make things right.

I don't expect an answer, which is good because one doesn't come. But I replay our night together. The way Nick makes me feel—and not just when he's sexing me into oblivion. I exhaust all the possibilities. How I can make things right.

And just before I drift off completely, I've got it. I fall asleep, at peace and feeling optimistic, with a smile on my face and a beagle at my feet.

*   *   *

I tap my thumb against the steering wheel, the scrape of the windshield wipers grating on my ears.

I left the house early for once and this is the thanks I get? Do I have to hit every frickin' red light?

But I finally reach Wesson, and it's nearly deserted on the grounds. The rush doesn't really begin until much closer to eight, I guess. I hop my way around the puddles, and once I step into the main building, I wipe my boots. Give my umbrella a shake, droplets stippling the hardwood floor.

When I stride up to Ida's desk, she stops mid nail-file sesh and looks me up and down, over the rims of her glasses.

"What are you all dressed up for?" She gestures at my getup with her emery board.

"What do you mean?" I chuckle and smooth the excess moisture from my trench coat. "Is Deborah here yet?"

"She is . . . Why?" She narrows her gaze, all but shining a light in my face.

"I have something I want to talk to her about; that's all."

"Are you quitting or something? Trying to get a promotion?"

"Geez, woman. Would you just ask her if she's got a minute?" I give an eye roll.

"Okay . . . but I don't like people keeping things from me."

I laugh and sneak a piece of courage chocolate from her candy dish—here's hoping it will give me just the boost I need.

Deborah's office is a lot bigger than I remember, cushy parlor chairs and a settee situated in one corner, her oppressive-looking cherry desk catty-corner to them.

"Rae." Deborah's tone is poised. Graceful. Like the grand sweep of a ballerina's arm.

And all the nerve I've mustered since the parking lot threatens to fade, but I focus on Nick. His brother.

I gulp back a gag. "Deborah, hi, yes. Thank you for meeting with me. And thanks again for bailing me out last week—"

"No problem at all." She dismisses it with a wave of a hand. "And how is your car doing?"

"It was my tire. Flat," I lie. "It's all better now." My heartbeat quickens, and I'm pretty sure she can hear it across the room. "Much."

Words, Rae. You need words.

"Wonderful to hear. Shall we?" She stands and motions toward the seating area.

"Well, I have sort of an unusual request, but I hope you'll hear me out."

She just stares, stony expression on her square-jawed face.

I clear my throat and continue. "This is about a former employee. Nick Greene?"

"Ah yes." She gives a curt nod. A frown. "I really liked him, but it turned out there had been some incidents or something. Are you one of the ones he made feel uncomfortable?"

"No—" I almost shout it. Straighten my coat. "No. My apologies. That's what I wanted to talk to you about. I know my friend Valerie came to you, but it turns out she made that story up. And I'm not trying to get Val in trouble—she was just trying to protect me—but she didn't have her facts straight. And, anyway, I would really appreciate it if you could maybe…give him a second chance. He's a friend and a really good guy—he's trying to pay for his kid brother's medical bills, and I know we've got that long-term sub gig coming up with Carrie leaving, and…"

Something like amusement? incredulity? cracks half her face. "You just have it all worked out, now don't you?"

"Oh no, no." I wave my hands out in front of me like I'm an umpire. "That's not—I mean—I just—"

Very articulate.

"Well, I appreciate the sentiment and I'm awfully sorry to hear about his brother, but the long-term science position has already been filled. I sent the paperwork to HR this morning. I'm sorry." She frowns again, the sides of her mouth deflated like my imaginary tire. "And while I feel for you—I really do—and I think it's sweet you're trying to help out your friend, Valerie seemed quite upset when she approached me. I just don't think having Mr. Greene around would be good. I realize it's he said, she said at this point, but I'm sure he will find other opportunities. He's a good teacher and a likable guy. A real find."

Bullet to the heart.

"Yes, he is," I say. And I thank her for her time.

To make matters worse, Nick writes back just before lunch, and it's just about as Final as things can be:

That can't have been easy to share, so thank you for opening up about it. And thanks for the apology. I hope you're able to move past all that someday, and I wish you all the luck in the world.

I tell all the girls about our meeting when they get in, about the e-mail, and although their support provides me some solace, Nick and his absence—and the fact that I can't do anything about any of it—haunts me all day. All evening. At the play performance, where I'm forced to stare at the set pieces he built and remember him joking around with the kids as he did it. Where I'm forced to put on a happy face for the students, for the parents, for Deborah, as they all rejoice in an adorable job well done.

"I'm so sorry," Valerie says, her blue eyes shining.

"I know. Can't win 'em all."

*　　　*　　　*

The rest of the Wedding Week flies by in a whirlwind of nail appointments, bridal luncheons, and trips to the airport to pick up various relatives. By the time the rehearsal dinner's over, I'm ready to welcome Phil into the family with open arms, because if he's able to put up with Quinn this week, he'll be able to put up with her forever. #sickness #health

The morning of, Valerie, the blushing bride, and I huddle around the mirror in the bride's room at Saint Gregory's with tissues, various hair spray choices, and the whole MAC section at Sephora strewn across the counter.

"This is it, Q. You ready?" I meet her gaze in the reflection while Valerie fools with Quinn's cathedral veil for the ninety-seventh time.

"Oh, don't try to freak her out," she says, securing it with the last of the bobby pins.

"She's not." Quinn floats to a stance like an angel. "I'm ready," she says to me. "But are you? After all, you're the one we have to worry about having a panic attack. How's your chest doing?"

"Fantastic," I say, cupping my boobs and giving them a yank. "Haven't had any complaints so far."

"You know what I mean."

"I do, and I'm fine. Now let's get you out there and get you hitched. What's His Name is waiting."

She smiles through a glare.

"Kidding." I make a crisscross over my heart. "I'm very happy you're marrying What's His Name."

And it's true. I'm fine. I'm better than fine.

"Mrs. What's His Name!" I get in one last joke before the show.

As I walk down the aisle, I don't feel pins and needles in my arms, don't feel as though my heart is about to explode from my chest, and the only reason my vision blurs, the only reason my throat goes raw, is because I'm overwhelmed with happiness for my friend.

Colored light from the stained-glass windows beams brilliant onto the polished stone floor behind Quinn as she makes her way toward Valerie and me, toward the altar. Prisms backlight her in blues, reds, greens, violets. She's a goddess in silver, her gown giving off celestial winks with every step, with every movement.

I glance at Phil. Tears glint in his eyes, his lips slightly parted in what looks like what I imagine we're all feeling: awe.

Aww!

He's a good dude. He loves her.

And then I find Mike in the congregation, a twin on each hip, Jakey fastened to one leg. His expression is soft, patient, as he helps Amanda work the camera on his phone. And then he steals a peek at Valerie—they share a smile—and my heart swells three sizes with contentment.

They're going to be okay.

I'm just about to turn my attention back to Quinn when a sudden feeling floods me—

I'm being watched. I scan the crowd, uncles and cousins, people I've seen over the years, faces familiar and not so much, for whoever is breaking with wedding etiquette and noticing a bridesmaid while the bride makes her procession.

Nothing.

No one.

And then: *lightning strike.*

One set of eyes snags my attention, and our connection is instant. Unwavering.

My pulse quickens at the recognition of that hypnotic stare that had me so rapt in every room, on every surface, until we were both unable to move any longer.

My cheeks burn white-hot. Intense. I'm certain I'm flushed from head to toe. That every person in attendance can see every last one of my thoughts, exposed. Projected onto the back wall of the chapel, playing out in scenes as plain as the crucifix that hangs there.

My mouth twitches into what I hope resembles a smile, but Nick gives me little to go on with his expression.

But he's here.

Somehow.

How?

Why?

I nearly forget to take Quinn's bouquet when I'm supposed to, so distracted am I by his presence. His relentless eye contact. It reaches into my core and pulls out everything I am. He won't let me get away with anything, not even this. And that's probably why there's no use in denying my feelings for him any longer.

It's also why it's all I can do to keep myself from abandoning my post and running into his arms.

After the ceremony, I lose track of him. The photographer arranges all of us in the wedding party in various poses of fabricated candidness, and just like that, Nick's disappeared. My chest aches in his absence. Calls out.

"Look at the camera, sweetie." I can hear the eye roll in the photographer's drone.

And as the flash blinds me, crops of purple dots obscuring my vision, I begin to think maybe I imagined Nick's presence.

I whisper, "Did you guys invite—"

"Stop talking, baby girl. They don't want a picture of your tonsils, now do they?"

Flash, flash. Flash, flash, flash.

"How about one of my nostrils flared?" I say between gritted teeth.

But I slather on a smile. Gaze in the direction of the camera and Satan—I mean, the photographer—and hold my tongue until we're sequestered in the limo, a bottle of bubbly making its way through the groomsmen.

"Which one of you invited him?" I'm practically foaming at the mouth.

"Invited who? Is one of your exes one of our guests? Hard to keep track of them all," Quinn teases, a smirk tugging at her lips.

"It was bound to happen," Valerie agrees with a shrug, and she clinks her champagne flute against Quinn's.

"You know who," I say.

"Whatever do you mean?" Quinn lays her fingertips to her chest, her brand-new wedding band glittering my way.

I round on Valerie. "Were you in on this too?"

She blinks, her eyes big with faux sincerity. "I have absolutely no idea what you're talking about."

When I remember to check my phone, there's an e-mail.

Yes!

But it's not from him. It's from one of the literary agents from my first batch of queries sent off.

I clench my stomach and think.

Should I wait until later to read it? Do I really need to ruin the day with a rejection?

But I take a deep breath. Toss back the champagne left in my flute.

And tap the screen.

Dear Rae,
I really enjoyed your pitch for PLAYING DOCTOR, and I would love for you to send me the first fifty pages. Looking forward to reading!
Best,
Whitney White

Two of the best sentences I've ever read.

"What is it?" Phil's voice booms from the other side of the limo bus.

There's hooting and hollering as I explain, even though none of these people has any idea what I'm talking about, but I'm lit from within and happy to have folks around to celebrate this first big step with me.

It's not a guarantee; it's not a rejection.

But it's a chance.

And it's actually mine.

*   *   *

When we arrive at the country club, clusters of wedding peeps are nothing but obstacles to me. I give each group the once-over—the buttoned-up-looking guys already halfway through their beers, who I gather Phil must work with based on their *Great Gatsby* haircuts and the volume of their laughter; Mama Morales, draped in an aggressive floral pattern, and her group of plump sisters, each of whom looks more like her than the rest;

Quinn's statuesque cousins and their husbands cleaning house at the hors d'oeuvres table, mini eggrolls and bacon-wrapped water chestnuts piled high on their plates.

But no Nick.

And I'm starting to think I hallucinated it. Hallucinated him. Like my mind manifested him as a sign that I've finally gone mad once and for all. I don't see him during cocktail hour, during my speech. I don't catch a glimpse of him while I mainline the poached salmon like a pro. Nothing.

Once I've made myself comfortably numb—the young bartender and I have an understanding: *Keep bringing martinis and President Grant is all yours*—I settle in at the head table like the used plates that have yet to be cleared. Even though Quinn and Phil opted not to have a bridal party dance, they're knee-deep in this one.

"All married couples, come out on the dance floor," the DJ calls.

The lights are low as hundreds of collective years of marital bliss sway in slow circles to "Unchained Melody"—and I decide maybe it's time for me to stop by the ladies' room. But my phone buzzes and scares the bejesus out of me, so I stay in my linen-covered seat and bring it to life.

Another e-mail.

I gasp when I see it. Just the sight of his name takes my breath away.

First of all, you don't need to be cleaning up my messes for me. Deborah called me the other day and told me what you said, but it wasn't your fault. You didn't need to go and do that, but, anyway, thank you.

   Because she also told me about a job that hasn't even

been posted yet. A principal pal of hers over at Saint
Robert's is about to let someone go midyear. Sounds like
the teacher's on the sauce or something. I don't know.
Anyway, Deborah is setting me up with an interview there
for that long-term position. And get this—it's in their history
department. She said it could very well turn into a full-time
gig at the end of this year.

Second, I realize you've been burned a time or two,
but who hasn't? We've all got our stuff, but that doesn't
mean every damn person from here to eternity is now bad.
It doesn't mean you should never try again. Because you
know what believing the worst in people gets you? A lifetime of being alone. And forgive me, but I don't think that's
how things are supposed to go for you.

My lips slide apart. I drink in a cool breath.

It sucks, getting hurt. It sucks that things got messed
up between us because you're afraid of that happening
again. But guess what? Your trying to avoid it hurt me too.

And that's the end of the message.

I read it again and again, each time flummoxed—flattened—
by his words.

God, I'm an idiot. I mean, I knew this, but wow.

An itch spreads behind my eyes, through my chest, down my
arms. I'm trying to pull myself out of the spiral that's about to
swallow me whole, but I'm helpless. Hopeless. He's right. And I
need to go splash some cold water on my face—get some air—
before the panic attack that's brewing actually strikes.

I leap from the table, knocking over a half-empty water glass or two, and bustle through the people dancing ("Now, only couples who have been married ten years or more!"). *Oomph* my way to the one portal of escape. Light from the hallway pours in through the outline of the door like a beacon, like a miracle, and I'm just passing the cake table when—

Clamp.

An arm catches about my middle, electricity sparking out everywhere it touches me.

I gulp when I come face-to-face with him. Rotate into his solid frame, suit clad and daunting in its beauty.

My mouth agape, throat suddenly parched, every nerve ending doing pirouettes beneath my skin.

I shake my head. "I'm sorry, Nick. I—"

"It's my turn to talk."

His eyes are menacing. Intense. He still has me in his rough hands, both of them now, fingers coiled tight around either side of my waist. He ensnares me with his stare, with his tone, and I'm entranced. I couldn't speak now even if I tried. My chest thunders beneath the satin bodice of my gown, and I struggle to push down a swallow.

"I said you hurt me—but that's because you're under my skin," he says. His jaw is set. Hard.

"Like a disease?"

I can't help it. Why do I talk, ever?

He clasps me firm, and I close my mouth.

He has to be able to feel my pulse. Hear it. Even over the sumptuous croon of the slow song.

He lets his fingers slip free, and he runs his hands up my torso, sending upsurges of sensation through me as he finds the slope of my neck, the curve of a cheek. Traces a thumb over my bottom lip. He stares at it.

"Like a tattoo," he says. And, finally, his face warms with the hint of a smile.

He moves closer, my face still cradled in his hands. His breath warm upon my skin.

"You can't get rid of me. Not that easily. I know it's hard for you to accept, hard for you to believe because of the past, but you're going to have to."

His gaze ignites mine, unadulterated fire swirling behind his dark eyes like savage storms. I'm teetering on the edge of losing all sensibility when, at once, he shows mercy and closes the space between us.

His lips, my lips, demanding to be heard. Tongues fighting to tell their stories. Each yearning to have the last word. Each wrestling with frantic desire.

He steals my breath—snatches it right from me. I beg, plead for it. My lungs threaten to burst as he buries his face in my neck, the delicate skin at the nape tingling against his kisses.

We remain enraptured in this world, where no others are permitted, where no one else dares step foot no matter their physical proximity. We remain for a time that transcends all earthly measure. We—Nick and I—are somewhere else entirely. On my kitchen floor. On the moon. Occupying everywhere and nowhere all at once. And when we finally do break, it's not for want of stopping; it's for need.

"I'm stubborn too," he says, resting his forehead against mine.

We both laugh and it's in this laugh that we return to earth. Return to the wedding. And Quinn materializes as if from nowhere. How long she's been standing there, I've no idea.

"I see you found him." The tweenage giggle she's been unable to suppress all day bubbles out of her.

"I have," I say, sliding a hand into Nick's suit jacket. And I too am unable to withhold fizzy laughter.

"Thanks for the invite," he says to her with a wink.

"Well, we did have that last-minute cancellation…" She scrunches her face and sets her stare on me. "You know, because of Rae's poor choice in wedding dates."

"Yeah—what's with that?" he teases, glancing down, and shakes his head.

"I guess it's back to the drawing board," I say, pretending to fumble through my phone.

I lay my head against him now and scroll through my apps, making dramatic gestures with my thumbs, ensuring he can see the screen.

"Let's see…Where's that trusty old Spark app hiding?"

"I have a better idea." His voice vibrates against my cheek. And then he snatches the phone from my fingertips. "How about you forget this thing for one damn night?"

I twist in his embrace. Wrap his arms about the front of me and lean into him, into the music.

"Deal. And now on to the next phase of dating politics…" My tone is playful. Blithe. It waltzes right along with the rest of the guests. Reaching up behind me for the back of his neck, I gently tug his face near mine, my mouth grazing his cheek as I speak. "I'll delete my account—when you delete yours," I whisper, softly, and then I laugh.

Compel his lips to mine.

I take the offending device from him and slip it into his pants pocket with a *thunk*.

And I lead him out onto the dance floor.

ACKNOWLEDGMENTS

Just like love, writing is a matter of persistence. Of learning humility. Being tenacious. In order to find "the one," you have to become smitten with projects, to make bad decisions in order to realize what good ones look like, to fall in love with ideas, to put yourself out there. You have to get your heart broken, and then you have to bounce back. To learn. To grow. To evolve.

None of that would have been possible for me to do without a slew of wonderful people whom I'm incredibly lucky to have in my life. People who listen, who offer advice, and—most importantly—who believe in me.

At the top of that list would be my badass agent, Barbara Poelle. When I think of your unwavering support all these years, it's actually staggering. I couldn't have done this without it—or you—so thank you from the bottom of my heart, B. I'm incredibly fortunate to have you in my corner.

Likewise, this book could not have become a reality without my amazing editor, Lindsey Rose. Your unending enthusiasm for all things Rae as well as your keen eye have given me the tools to shape this thing into the best book it can be, and I'm proud to have it out in the world.

Additionally, I am honored to be with Grand Central and so lucky to have such an insanely talented team of folks helping me make *MR-S* really shine! Thank you to Jordan Rubinstein,

Tiffany Sanchez, Emily Chen, Nancy Wiese, Nicole Bond, Brigid Pearson, Beth deGuzman, Tom Whatley, Abby Reilly, Dianna Stirpe, and Yasmin Mathew. I owe you all a coupla thousand rounds of drinks!

To my writing besties, Renée Ahdieh, Sarah Nicole Lemon, and Sarah Henning, I am eternally grateful for your friendship and guidance. I could not have stayed (relatively?) sane without all the phone dates, writing conferences, Snapchats, or old-fashioneds.

To those special folks who took the time early on to show me the ropes of publishing or to be another set of eyeballs on one of my first manuscripts, including Wendy Toliver, Copil Yanez, Chuck Sambuchino, Alison Miller, and Marice Kraal, thank you for giving me advice and for supporting my creative endeavors such as The Write-Brained Network.

And lastly, to my parents, thank you for putting up with me and thank you for a lifetime of love and encouragement. I can't even begin to articulate how much you mean to me.

ABOUT THE AUTHOR

Although she's originally from Cleveland, Ohio, and has spent the most time there, Ricki has also lived in Georgia and Virginia. (She promises she's not a drifter, though.) In addition to writing, she has molded the minds of tweens and teens as a middle school and high school teacher in both the CLE and the ATL—and she also spent a year teaching writing and communications at the college level. She's back in Atlanta now, and she owns the cutest beagle ever (Molly).